I0746364

WETLAND
COLIN KING

First published by Accidental Publishing 2018

Cataloguing-in-Publication entry is available from the National Library of Australia
http://catalogue.nla.gov.au

ISBN 978-1-925900-05-7 (paperback)
Fiction A823.4

Typeset in 11 pt Baskerville
Printed and bound by Ingram
Cover photography by Kate Monotti

Accidental Publishing
An imprint of Of The World Books
PO Box 8070 Bendigo South LPO VIC 3550
Australia

www.oftheworldbooks.com

Accidental Publishing

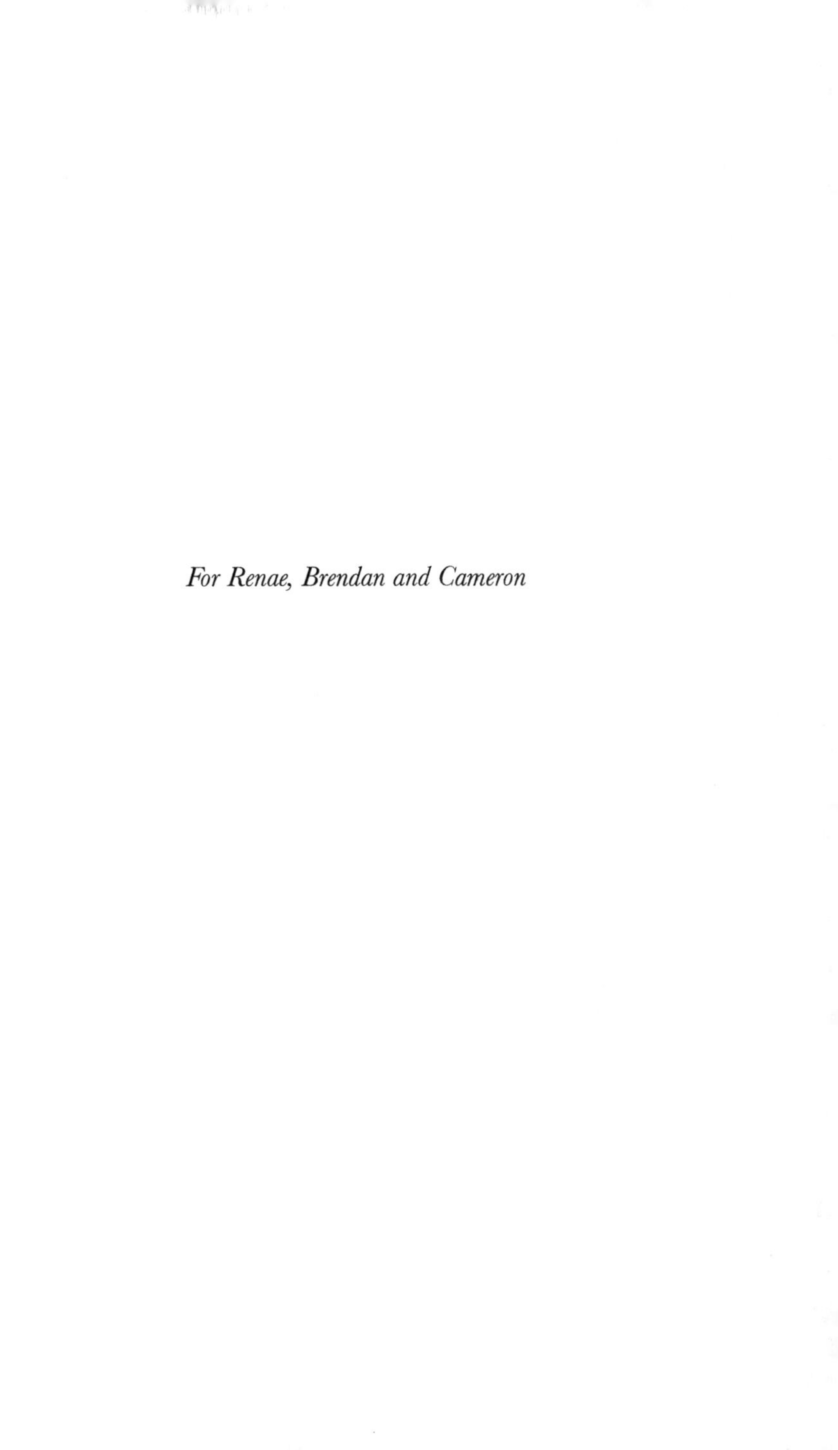

For Renae, Brendan and Cameron

1

He had already settled into the khaki hammock-chair slung midway up an ancient sprawling red-gum. The vantage point was perfectly positioned along the marshy shoreline and safe from on-ground movements likely to spook his amphibian research subjects — the Pobblebonks, Spadefoots and Eastern Banjos. If he was lucky, he may even hear a Maniacal Cackler, the kookaburra of the frog world.

Everything was strategically arranged at his fingertips. His backpack hung within reach on a twig to his left. Snack bars and a banana were zipped in the main compartment, along with his long-lens camera — superfluous for a sortie ending after dark. The pack's smaller outer compartment was left open for easy access to notepad and pen, but not the mobile phone. It would be switched off, of course. He donned his head torch in readiness and gave a self-congratulatory smile at a peculiarly formed fork in the branch. It held his drink bottle as snugly as the dashboard holder in his battered Corolla.

The first summer after the drought broke guaranteed an instant population explosion of every species known at the La Trobe University wildlife sanctuary. Week one of the breeding season had already provided a sporadic assortment of mating call recitals. Now it was time for the headline act — a frogophile's equivalent of Brahms Ein Deutsches Requiem sung by a massed philharmonic choir. Warmups were well underway for the evening performance, and, was that the sound of a Growling

Grass frog? Was a resurgence of the endangered species really on the cards for outer-urban Melbourne?

The chance of a positive ID vanished as quickly as it came when the wetland-wide prelude snapped to silence — a shift so sharp it might have been cued by a conductor's baton tapping the podium. Annoyance overrode alarm when the lull caused his body to stiffen. *Fuck! Fuck, fuck, fuck,* he said in his head, still not able to commit the cardinal sin of sound. *What's someone doing stamping around here at this hour? The sanctuary closes at three o'clock.*

The interloper was closer than he thought. A red dot of tobacco ember appeared in and out of shadowy gaps between the leaves until the shuffling shape came to a standstill directly below the hammock-chair. The gap had shrunk to mere metres of vertical air space.

Shit, he's stopped. *Keep going you prick, there's still time. If you go now there's a chance they'll get back into the swing of things before the evening is totally lost.*

He didn't know how long he'd been holding his breath. He forced himself to inhale again — slowly and soundlessly. Soundlessly enough to lean slightly and peer down at the trespasser. A toad of a man with a toad head, toad lips, toad arms and white toad legs in drooping baggy white toad shorts, topped off with a short frizz of thinning red hair. Could be fifties, even older with that shape. *Rhinella hominis.* Toad Man, he decided.

Toad Man looked back along the bush path he had walked, then peered ahead around the wetland shore. The treetop bystander knew Toad Man wouldn't look up. In his experience, only ornithologists looked up when they walked in the bush.

Toad Man dropped his cigarette butt to the ground and ground it out with a rubber thong. His left hand was clad in a blue surgical glove and holding an A4 envelope. He placed the envelope on the log of a giant limb that the red-gum had shed at its feet, then peeled the single surgical glove off and placed it in his pocket.

What the fuck is that about?

From his other pocket, Toad Man removed a handgun. He appeared to check the safety setting, then jammed it into the waistband of his shorts with the muzzle wedged into the crack of his plumber's-hairy-bum-cleavage. Toad Man's loose shirt fell to screen both the weapon and the eyesore from view. The image nonetheless lingered until he sat on the log beside the envelope. He extracted another cigarette. A sugar glider barked faintly in a nearby wattle.

Alarm at the sight of a lethal weapon overrode the frog researcher's initial resentment of the intrusion into such a significant breeding event. He wanted to sink back into the hammock-chair from his awkward leaning position but was afraid it might creak.

Why don't I just ask him to move on, he wondered. I'm authorised to be here after all and no other visitor would be sanctioned at this time. Who knows how many years before all these frog planets align again? It's a crime against science to interrupt such a rare phenomenon, especially while it's under study. Even if he has got a gun, he's not here to hunt and kill aspiring zoologists. I'll simply explain to him why he should take his business elsewhere. Whatever that business may be, there's absolutely no way it depends on this one-off set of frog-breeding conditions. He's got the whole rest of the world to do whatever he's up to.

Oh no.

He abandoned his internalised argument as another evil-induced silence fell. This time the malefactor emerged from the opposite direction. He cast fear to the wind to let his head drop back into the hammock-chair with an eye roll of exasperation. It gave no creak. *This is beyond a joke. The place is turning into Bourke Street.*

A taller slimmer shape came into view. Unshaven, black hair, black shirt, black jeans, black boots. *Acanthophis antarcticus* perhaps — a black death adder. Not the Rowan Atkinson Black Adder, he decided — although he was a fan — but the deadly reality. A species not known around these parts.

Another smoker. Black Adder stopped his saunter a few metres short of Toad Man. He took a pensive look at his cigarette, flicked it to the ground and ground it out in a careful and restrained way with the toe of his boot. The theatre of the inconsequential act was evident from the hammock-chair.

'So, you came in person?'

Toad Man rose from the log without responding and made a shorthand gesture that Black Adder knew to mean *hands up and spread 'em*.

'Against the tree okay?' Black Adder asked and complied casually as if passing through airport security. He raised his palms onto the broad trunk. Toad Man was thorough.

'Okay,' he finally announced with an abrasively thin voice that surprised their unseen audience of one.

Toad Man handed back the packet of cigarettes he had taken from Black Adder's shirt pocket. Black Adder lit up. The glow of the lighter's flame illuminated his face and a neck tattoo below his shirt collar. A poker hand. A club, a spade, a diamond …. The vision died with the flame, too quick to discern the card combination, even when viewed from above.

'To answer your question, I'm *not* actually here in person,' Toad Man said, setting an adversarial tone. 'I'm attending a live-in training session as we speak. Witnesses from inside and outside of the Force. My presence formally recorded in the minutes.'

'Then you'd better make sure it's *your* handwriting chalking up KPI's on the butchers' paper.'

Toad Man cocked his head and gave a quizzical open-mouthed glare.

'Are you being a smartarse?'

The menacing ice-blue eyes dared Black Adder to respond. The still-unsighted researcher felt every ounce of inherent threat. *Toad Man didn't need the gun*, he concluded. By contrast, Black Adder nonchalantly peered at his cigarette again rather than lift it to his lips. He decided to forego the rest of the pissing competition.

'I've come to this over-rated mosquito-ridden puddle. Are we on or not?'

He parked the cigarette in his mouth to swat a mosquito on his arm.

'It's the best tadpoling spot you'll ever have the pleasure of gracing,' Toad Man said defensively.

'Not if I had a choice, Harry Butler, and I don't reckon I'd be on me pat. Fuckin' waste of money locking this place up like Pentridge. Speaking of which, did you bring it?'

Toad Man glowered at Black Adder's jibe about the outdated TV-naturalist before he deigned to answer.

'There's seventy-five grand.' He tilted his head to the envelope without shifting his gaze from Black Adder.

'And the rest?'

'Upon delivery, of course.'

'How?'

'You'll get it. Don't worry.'

'I mean the job. Where and when?'

Despite the isolated setting, Toad Man went through the motion of casting conspiratorial looks around before answering.

'Nineteen Scott Street, Balwyn, two in the morning, Tuesday week. There'll be an unplanned ten-minute gap when the surveillance teams change shift. That's as long as I can manage without anyone getting suss.'

'Is that written down in the envelope?'

'Only the money's in the envelope.'

'Then how the fuck do you expect me to remember that? Have you got a pen?'

'Just remember that Bon Scott drank himself to death on the nineteenth of February. Scott … nineteen … oh-two. Get it?'

'I wouldn't've picked you for a head banger … and that makes two things I have to remember.'

'I'm not saying it again. Google it if you need to and while you're at it, Google the address. The house was on the market last year and the real estate advertisement still comes up on line — complete with a room-layout plan and pics.'

'Okay then …' he thought aloud. 'Why so quick? A week and a bit gives me fuck all time for research and planning?'

'You get plans for the house. That's a pretty good head start that you don't want to waste. Besides, it'll be useless in two weeks because he's being moved on. We can't be too careful, you know.'

Black Adder watched Toad Man smirk at his own insidious logic.

The moment was broken by what the young researcher recognised as the beginning of the ring tone on his phone. Panic filled the next nanosecond. *It can't be. I turned it off. It's not even on Silent. How did I manage to leave it on? Get the phone out of the pack without making other noise. Keep it upright so it doesn't beam light downwards.*

The ringtone's short cycle sounded twice before he could extract the phone from the pack's open outer pouch, kill the incoming call and hold his hand over the light-giving display.

The abrupt burst of sound caused Toad Man to draw the handgun on Black Adder and begin swivelling his head in every direction except directly above his head. Black Adder grabbed the muzzle to direct it out of his face.

'It's a frog, you dickhead,' he yelled at Toad Man.

They froze and listened for it to sound again — but it didn't. In any case, neither man was equipped to recognise the difference between Nokia's electronic version and a real frog-call, let alone an endemic species.

'… and what the fuck's this?'

Black Adder shook the muzzle of the handgun they were both holding before casting his end loose with disdain.

'You think I'm going to hand over seventy-five grand to someone I've never met, in the middle of nowhere, without taking precautions?'

'Then I suggest you don't leave the safety on next time.'

Toad Man turned the handgun in his hand to confirm his gaffe. It forced a nod of regard — sufficient to mollify Black

Adder. Black Adder gave a begrudging shrug to accept Toad Man's deferential appreciation. A cautious calm settled and Toad Man pocketed the handgun. Black Adder moved things on.

'What if I need to contact you?'

'You won't. I don't know you and I don't want to know you. That's the plan. If anything changes you'll hear from Graeme.'

'So why isn't Graeme here?'

'Graeme's not paying you, I am, and I don't part with money like that without seeing what I'm getting in return. But don't worry, Graeme will be in touch if it goes pear-shaped or if it doesn't happen. He'll come to yours. I made sure his passport is current.'

The words of re-assurance were loaded with threat.

'If he's so handy, why isn't he doing the job himself?'

Toad Man stepped further into Black Adder's space.

'You know fucking well that he's more than qualified. But we need a cleanskin for this. Graeme is the first place they'll look. If he doesn't have a cast-iron alibi of several thousands, they'll have him in the frame before it makes the evening news.'

Black Adder nodded at the logic, then picked up the envelope and held it towards Toad Man. 'I'll send you an invoice for the balance.'

'So you *are* a smartarse … and by the way, his girlfriend's staying with him.'

Black Adder stilled to force a calm response. 'And how do you expect me to deal with that?'

'However you like, but either way, the fee stays the same.'

The calm deserted Black Adder. '"By the way?" By the fucking way? You're engaging a professional and you think you can spring shit like that? There's no "either way" to deal with an added live complication. I think you'd better go back to the Yellow Pages and get the cut-price amateur you obviously expected.'

He thrust the envelope into Toad Man's stomach. Toad Man threw his hands back, not wanting to touch it.

'Okay, okay. Twenty more.' The thin jarring timbre of Toad Man's voice rose a notch … and rose too quickly.

'Forty grand … and I won't be putting that in writing either.'

Silence hung. Toad Man still had his hands held up as if the envelope being held to his stomach was a gun. Black Adder noticed.

'You haven't touched this envelope have you, you lame prick? Well don't think that your arse-covering protects you from me. You *and* Graeme remember that my skill-set is his skill-set. The threat you're so willing to toss around works both ways.'

Black Adder jabbed the envelope into Toad Man's stomach again. Toad Man snapped from his disconcerting lapse into intimidatee. He dropped his arms and retrieved the well-practiced glare. 'Just fuckin' do the thing. Okay?'

Resentment filled silence ended the pissing competition. Seal the deal or walk away. Black Adder did both.

'Nineteen Bon Scott Street Balwyn, Tuesday week. Got it.'

He walked away.

'It's not *Bon* Scott Street, it's just Scott Stree …' Toad Man stopped himself too late. He breathed into his cupped hands and watched Black Adder pass out of sight. Seething morphed into slightly lesser seething before he strode off in the opposite direction.

The unobserved observer exhaled a low troubling, 'Oooooooo.' It came out with a stuttering tremor that scared him even more.

He switched off his hand-held recorder.

2

Detective Sergeant Rory James stood, one slice of toast in hand, staring at the empty butter dish. 'Perfect,' he grizzled. *What better to complement a lukewarm half-strength coffee*, he continued in his head. There was only one pod left and he needed at least two to coax anything resembling flavour from the $79 ALDI espresso machine. It was a gift that his daughter Steph had spent too-much-money-for-a-student on when he moved out of the family home — the sole house-warming anything in his one-bedroom Elwood flat. Steph was also the only one still on speaking terms with him, so replacing it with a proper machine was doubly out of the question. At least the ALDI apparatus was a step up from instant.

The coffee was lukewarm because he normally heated the milk in the microwave. That died a week ago. *Why can't I drink black coffee like any other serious alcohol imbiber?* he wondered, not allowing himself to even think the word "alcoholic". *Why does it taste like brake fluid to me?*

This was the point where Rory normally surrendered and decamped to the Bean Noir Café. In a perverse way he was lucky like that. The neighbourhood cafés, and more importantly the takeaways, were a cut above. Great kebabs, pizzas, burritos, burgers and all day breakfasts. But today there was no time. He sat down and force fed himself dry toast and faux coffee.

Rory had no wish to become a persona non grata, even

though he took full advantage of his status as a persona-not-necessarily-required. For the Cold Case Unit — of which he was its sole remaining member — attendance at Homicide Branch call-outs and briefings was not compulsory. He was on all the group email and text lists but could decline everything but the routine, full staff meetings. Rory was a standing agenda item at those fortnightly events where he self-consciously presented anything that counted as a development in the cold cases. The process served to underscore his dazzling lack of progress, notwithstanding solving the Heathcote winery murders.

Today's un-declinable summons was for a mailing list of two — Rory and Senior Sergeant Gary Cockburn. On most days, the word "Cockburn" could cause panic to rise from the shallows into Rory's oesophagus. But right now, simply functioning was his sole priority. He couldn't risk driving with last night's vodka painkillers still hovering around the breathalyser threshold. Coherence might even be a problem; after all, he hadn't put up much of a show when the Metro "Customer Service Officer" asked to see his Myki train ticket. He let his badge do the talking. "Uphold the Right", its enamelled scroll told the ticket inspector. Not a sentiment he could rely on from Cockburn. His nemesis within the Force never missed a chance when it came to Rory's tribulations, and he was about to get one on a platter.

Maybe his tenure on the Cold Case Unit was about to end, he mused. Everyone else in the Unit had been dragged off to help with fresh front-page cases. His own stint in Cold Cases had served to get him off WorkCover leave less than one year after the shooting that brought on his "disorder". It probably set a world record. Now, back on deck and with one high-profile win under his belt, Force Command might reckon he was ready for the real thing — the glue had set and it was safe to apply normal pressure again. If only.

He could barely manage things in bursts. Like last night's restaurant meal to celebrate Steph's nineteenth birthday. It was the first birthday she'd spent with him since he and Lauren separated. Both he and Steph were desperately overcompensating in their effort to forge a new normal. Her younger brother didn't bother trying, apart from turning up at Steph's insistence. Nick's usual one-word teen-answers were loaded with extra resentment since Lauren upped the ante to full-on divorce. Rory hated that Steph would go home as spent as he was from what should have been a joyous occasion. He hated that he knocked back her suggestion to adjourn to his place for coffee. He hated that he didn't see that possibility coming and hadn't bothered to tidy the place up. He hated that hard liquor was no match for his truckload of guilt.

Rory looked at his watch and hoped being late would be enough to divert their attention. It was a forlorn hope. The schism between Rory and the buffed Monday morning chipper-ness of Cockburn and Inspector Richard Bourke was blinding.

Cockburn looked dumbstruck as he leant against the credenza in Bourke's office, arms folded.

Struck dumb, that was a first. Not good.

Bourke was in his familiar welded-to-the-desk pose. His lips moved silently as he read a draft email response. He clicked the Send button but the email refused to disappear from the screen. An extra furrow appeared below his tanned crown and he leant closer to urge the email along. Finally. With mission accomplished, he leant back and took off his reading glasses.

'Close the door,' he told Rory before reluctantly relinquishing his gaze from the screen.

'Holy shit …' slipped out uncontrollably with his first glimpse of Rory. Rory wished he had at least found a fresh shirt to wear and had something to unstiffen the skin on his face. He'd already experienced his own "holy shit" moment at the shaving mirror. The usual light tan had faded to the overexposed all-white face adorning Lou Reed's *Transformer* album. Long creases that framed his mouth deepened with the contrast and his struggling-to-remain-ruly black hair hung weeks beyond its cut-by date. He was always Lou Reed thin but now he was unintentionally cultivating the rock-god's head. On the up side, the coffee spill was not visible on his black trousers.

'… what happened to you?'

Where to start? At least he was here. It would have been a different story if there was anything left in the empty bottle he found in the freezer that morning. The vodka was his stopgap for episodes that snuck up on him between WorkCover-shrink visits. The visits had been cutback as part of the deal to return to work. It wasn't quite cold turkey but cool enough, even on a good day — positively arctic when a non-good day transpired.

The less frequent psychologist sessions only instilled enough mettle for him to brave one night of nightmares and flashbacks without risking the killer hangover. For the ones that followed, he left nothing to chance.

His love life — which seemed a flattering term — gained no headway from Lauren uttering the "D" word. Mere mention of it on the phone to Sigrid brought a cool response. Where did that come from? Sigrid ran the Bendigo B&B where he would come and go while investigating the nearby Heathcote case. Pretty soon, B&B was no mere acronym. Now he came and went whenever he could — usually at weekends when Sigrid became pre-occupied with guests. Maintaining the Melbourne / Bendigo relationship was hard enough without having to deal with unfathomable and unnerving courteousness from his new partner … if he could call her that.

He snapped from his misery of thought to give Bourke the short answer.

'Steph turned nineteen. We kicked on a bit last night,' he stretched the truth. The "kicking on a bit" being entirely his own solitary post-party misery-making.

It was an opening for Cockburn to kick off his tedious

needling. 'Was she having a rave party?'

The smile at his own nonsensical joke was scarier than his permanent sneer.

'Kicked on *a bit*? You reckon? You look like something the cat threw up,' Bourke said, and drew his mouth back into a repulsed grimace.

'… the cat *dragged* in,' Rory tried to correct him.

'I know what I'm looking at.' Bourke's voice rose with annoyance. 'Are you up for this, because if you're not, you can piss off now? This is World War Three,' he said, pointing a USB stick at Rory. 'I need more than just your un-fuckin'-divided attention right now.'

Bourke's words were weighted with the shock of hearing a man who doesn't swear needlessly, swear at all. Back in the day, it was a weapon Bourke drew freely from his quiver to deal with crims. But most of his current team weren't around back in the day.

'Yeah,' Rory said, sheepish and chastened. 'The Berocca's kicking in and this is a double-shot.' Rory's eyes signalled to the cardboard coffee cup in his left hand. 'I'm good. Really.'

He sounded pathetic, even to himself … and desperate. *World War Three could only be better.*

'I bloody-well hope so, because what I have here is the missing link for the Neilson Scali murders. The smoking gun … feasibly. Compelling hard evidence from someone staking a claim on the reward.'

Bourke still held the USB stick on show in his hand.

Cockburn and Rory were struck voiceless with begging questions. The questions finally gushed forth from Rory. 'Who from? A nut job? Who do they reckon did it? What evidence? Which missing link?'

'Yeah,' Cockburn managed.

Bourke leant back and savoured the arrival of their undivided attention.

'This came in on Friday. The Commissioner called me in

over the weekend. It's a bit of a long story. You two are hearing it first because you were both on the original case.'

'As was every other bugger in the meantime,' Cockburn said as he sat down in the chair beside Rory.

'This has the highest level of security in the organisation. You both need to sign this before we start. It's an NDA. A Non-Disclosure Agreement.'

'Aren't we automatically covered?' Rory asked.

'There's nothing automatic about any of this. Just sign it. I'm not even allowed to download from this stick. My computer had to be physically taken off-line this morning for me to play it to you.'

'Jesus,' Cockburn said with a cynical head shake. He was flicking through the pages of fine print to locate the signature block.

'That's not the Facebook terms and conditions you're signing up to. You're going to have to take this away and read and understand every clause.'

'Fucking hell,' Rory joined in as he flicked through his own copy.

'Don't forget that an internal leak made this the biggest corruption case in the Force in the first place. I've been around longer than both of you and I can tell you nothing comes close. Setting off an ACC investigation and a public hearing, a Commissioner-level steering committee and god-knows how many task forces and Internal Affairs probes … not to mention a commissioner losing his job and arguably the reason the Government lost the last election. You want to be the one telling the Commissioner he's overreacting?'

Rory and Cockburn sat in silence while Bourke co-signed the forms and loaded the USB stick into his desktop computer. He sat back, ready to mouse-click Play.

'It's all audio,' he told them. 'Listen to this and tell me who you reckon it is?'

'Nineteen Scott Street, Balwyn, two in the morning, Tuesday week. There'll be an unplanned ten-minute gap when the surveillance teams change

shift. That's as long as I can manage without anyone getting suss.'

'Is all that written down and in the envelope?'

'Only the money's in the envelope.'

Bourke clicked his mouse again.

'It's definitely David Dwyer, you can't mistake that voice … is that all there is?' Cockburn said.

Drug Squad detective David Dwyer had been charged with arranging the execution-style murders of Clifford Neilson and Corina Scali in a witness protection safe house. He was also the subject of an internal corruption investigation for disclosing the safe house location where Neilson and Scali were shot in bed. The murder charges were dropped before any hearings were held following the in-prison murder of Leon "Blowfly" Blofeld. Facing drugs charges at the time, Blofeld had agreed to give evidence — albeit uncorroborated hearsay evidence — against Dwyer in exchange for a lighter sentence. Thereafter the case went cold despite rewards being offered and a string of task forces, investigations, and internal probes. The reward was upped to $1,000,000 on the recent tenth anniversary of the murders.

'You reckon it's Dwyer too?' Bourke asked Rory.

Rory nodded agreement. 'I'm stunned, actually. Ten years ago, I tried to visualise how Dwyer actually disclosed that stuff. I always expected the actual disclosing would be totally evidence-proof. He was impossible to pin down, even with straight police work. I never imagined anything written on a piece of paper, just him and the hitman speaking to each other in the middle of nowhere. Two hard men, both with an eternal vested interest in never disclosing the conversation. But here it is — totally out of the blue.' He gestured to Bourke's computer. 'Someone was way ahead of him all this time.'

'I know what you mean. Things like this aren't meant to happen. Not something so vivid … and after such a long period.' Bourke agreed.

'And everything on tape stacks up perfectly. I know there's

not much there, but the facts are right — nineteen Scott Street, two AM, and it was a Tuesday. Do you reckon Dwyer knows the recording exists?'

'I'm guessing not,' Bourke answered. 'But this is only part of the recording. There's more on offer … which I'll get to in a minute. Maybe that will give us a clue about whether he knows about it. What about the other voice?'

'Not familiar,' Cockburn said.

'It's only a few words but it sounds like a pom,' Rory added.

Rory and Cockburn resumed processing what they had heard. Bourke broke their reveries.

'See what I mean? It takes a while to get your head around, doesn't it? I'll play it again for you.'

They listened with heightened focus.

'Who's it from?' Cockburn asked after the seventeen-second replay.

'Anonymous … sort of. There's only one copy of this.' Bourke lifted a sheet of paper from his desk. 'I'll read it to you.'

He donned his glasses and read aloud:

'Dear Chief Commissioner,'

'Very formal,' Cockburn said. Bourke gave him the ray.

'How about I wait till the end.'

Bourke re-struck his formal reading pose:

'Dear Chief Commissioner,

This flash-drive contains part of a six-minute conversation about the Neilson/Scali murders. You will hear enough to be convinced that the full recording is sufficient evidence to charge and convict the culprit.

I'm sure you agree that because of the nature of the murders, any witness places themselves in the same potentially fatal position that Neilson and Scali faced. For that reason, I will only identify myself by the fingerprint I have made on the attached sheet of glossy photographic paper labelled FP1. There is also a copy in the wax-sealed envelope, which is not to be opened. I will provide the full recording if you guarantee in writing that I can claim the reward of $1,000,000 without having to further reveal my identity.

You probably think it is impossible to receive the money without somehow becoming traceable. However, I am happy to take that risk because I have a plan.

If you agree, please insert an advertisement in the General Notices of the Government Gazette *with the following heading and two-sentence acceptance.*

ELIGIBILITY FOR PAYMENT OF CLAIM
The entity identifiable solely by the imprint image labelled FP1 is eligible for payment of any successful claim for reward offered by Victoria Police. The sealed copy of the FP1 image will be opened only by the Minister for Police for the purpose of personally verifying that the payment is being made in accordance with instructions that are unmistakably from FP1. Chief Commissioner.

Yours sincerely
Finger Print One.'

'Clever …' Cockburn offered.

'Succinctly written too, they might be using a lawyer,' Rory said.

'Mmm,' Bourke said, elbows on the desk, his chin resting on his clasped hands. Cockburn also held his own thoughts. Rory thought aloud.

'Are we gonna do it? Can we do it? I mean, can we involve the Chief Commissioner and the Minister in an exercise like that? How will it look if it turns out to be a dud? I know the snippet of conversation is incriminating but now that I think about it, we don't know when or where it was recorded or who Dwyer's speaking to. It could be something he said last week. It's also a safe assumption that it wasn't recorded with Dwyer's consent. It might not be admissible evidence as it stands, you know.'

Bourke had already considered the issues. 'I don't know the legalities, we haven't taken advice yet and we won't be taking advice from anyone about anything at this stage. Once we do that, the circle of people that know about this widens. We're not ready to take that risk.

'The question we have to ask ourselves is: how would it

look if the Chief Commissioner and the Minister *didn't* respond to this opportunity? The precautions this person is taking are entirely justifiable in a case where three witnesses have already been killed. If it turns out to be a dud, so what? At least we didn't ignore it and at least we find out what's on the rest of the recording. The bottom line is: the Commissioner wants to go ahead. He'll brief the Minister and draft an arse-covering qualified letter of approval for her to sign. But she's not gonna be mug enough to stand in the way either. We are, after all, dealing with a long standing unresolved attack on the criminal justice system.'

Rory and Cockburn nodded. Bourke continued.

'Right now our priority is to make sure Dwyer doesn't get wind of this before we get the full version of the recording. It might be a long time since he was in the Force, but don't underestimate how well connected he still is.

'As far as admissibility goes, we'll wait and see what we get with the full version. Who knows, that might not be something we have to deal with.'

'Are there any clues in the envelope or any of the stuff that it was sent in? What about this use of sealing wax? You don't come across that every day.' Cockburn asked.

'Prima-facie there's nothing obviously unique about the printing of the message or the packaging, and we're not checking any of that either until we're happy to bring others in on this. Everything looks pretty generic to me, though. You can pick up sealing wax in Officeworks. It's a fair assumption that whoever sent this is clever enough not to leave clues. The letter was posted at Southern Cross Station, so it could be someone travelling from anywhere in the north and west of Melbourne, or Victoria, or even New South Wales.'

'Or South Australia on the Overland,' Rory said.

'Now he's a trainspotter.'

Bourke ignored Cockburn's crack.

'Exactly. Or it might be anyone else in the world who just happened to choose Southern Cross Station to post a letter. The envelope was addressed to the Chief Commissioner and marked "Personal and Confidential", so his PA Bev opened it. The Chief Commissioner, Deputy Commissioner and us three is as far as it's gone … and Bev, of course.'

'It sounds old-school to me rather than someone young,' Rory said. 'Someone young would use a fake Facebook site, a Virtual Private Network or some other computer-savvy way of being anonymous, not a fingerprint and the *Government Gazette*. I mean, ninety-nine percent of people *my* age wouldn't even know what the *Government Gazette* is.'

Bourke answered. 'It could simply be a lawyer's doing, but it's all to our advantage in any case. Maybe they've done it that way to minimise the risk of Dwyer discovering that the recording exists. They've also been clever enough not to mention the particular crime that the reward relates to in their draft *Government Gazette* notice. They don't even give away that the *imprint* identifier is an actual fingerprint. That's all good from our point of view, right? We'll come up with a bullshit story to deflect any inquiries if some curious media person stumbles over it. Our biggest risk is Dwyer finding out about it and figuring out the source. He must have some idea who had the opportunity to record the conversation, even if he didn't know it was happening at the time. If we let him get that far ahead of us, he's likely to shut the whole thing down.'

'So, we're gonna run the notice?'

'Bloody oath we are. I've suggested to the Chief Commissioner that we run the notice without getting legal advice. If we need to make what we do legal, we'll do that after the event when we have the full recording … even if we have to pass a special act of parliament and make it retrospective.'

'But what about paying the reward? What if it ends up being an embarrassing crim? Someone inside? In jail, I mean.'

'Well that's the beauty of it. Whoever it is doesn't want to be identified … ever.' Bourke paused to emphasise what he'd said. 'Do you reckon they'd go to all this trouble if they didn't want to stay hidden. It can't come back to bite us.'

Cockburn thought about it. 'What if we don't pay at all?' he suggested. 'This fingerprint thing is all very cute but I reckon you could drive a Mack truck through it legally. If we did renege, like you say, FP1 is not going to out himself to challenge the decision.'

Cockburn smiled at his own cleverness.

'Risky,' Rory answered. 'It could just as likely not be a crim. And if we did renege and they did find a way to challenge — maybe through a lawyer, or worse still, a PR consultant — it would be an embarrassing breach of faith from an undertaking the Chief Commissioner and the Minister had given in the *Government Gazette*. Maybe that's why they've done it that way. The more I think about it, the more it smells like a lawyer.'

'Mmm,' Bourke mused. 'Fair logic, Rory. And there's no skin off our nose if plan-A does come off. We've got everything to gain and no good reason not to proceed.'

'We could just run the fingerprint through the database.' Cockburn said.

'You've got to credit them with some sense, Gary.'

Bourke had a way of saying "Gary" that sounded as grating as his surname. By dragging the "a" out in a laboured tone, he only had to utter Cockburn's Christian name to admonish the detective sergeant's persistent miscues. The exasperation-driven habit stuck.

''spose so,' Cockburn conceded and thought better of making more suggestions. Rory shrugged that he was all done too. Bourke decided to wind things up.

'Well that's the plan. Okay? And remember what you just signed. You don't talk to each other about it in this building unless you're in here with me. Don't pull any of the Neilson Scali files. In fact, don't even Google it. Definitely no pub-talk. Right?'

Rory and Cockburn cut nonplussed glances to each other.

'I'm serious. None of this goes without saying.'

'Yeah, well I think you need to read that riot act to everyone else as well — Bev, the Deputy Commissioner, the Minister. And you can't talk to the Minister without her adviser being in on it,' Cockburn said defensively.

'Just read it, Gary. Leave the politics to me.'

'Is this a cold case … is that why Rory's here?'

'It's ten years old. I don't care if you call it hot or cold. You're both here because you dealt with Dwyer before they dropped the charges first time around. You're lookin' redemption in the face here, Gary.'

'So what do you want us to do? What about Dwyer?'

'Just go about your business. We wait and see if we get the full recording. Like I said, we don't do anything to spook Dwyer.'

Bourke stroked the stubble on his chin for a time.

'What we can do without arousing suspicion is up the surveillance on him. Dwyer knows he still gets checked out from time to time and the approvals for us to do that are still current. Neither the surveillance team or Dwyer will think it's out of the ordinary. I'll get it re-activated. We don't want him slipping away at a critical moment.'

Cockburn kept prodding.

'What about the notice in the *Government Gazette*? That's not gonna go unnoticed,'

'I'll be organising that. I know people will figure it has something to do with a homicide but that's no problem, all the rewards are for homicides. They can all play guess-the-murder.'

'And we play guess the murderer.'

'We might not even have to do that Gary. It might all be on the full recording. So let's just go back to our normal routines until then, hey?' Bourke said with mock weariness.

He pushed his chair back from the desk to signal the end of the meeting.

'Can you stay back for a moment on another matter, Rory,' he said as Rory and Cockburn stood to leave.

They waited for Cockburn to close the door behind him.

'Is this about working with Gary?' Rory asked. 'Because there's no sign of him ever moving on from the Heidi Lester stuff.'

'No. You're gonna have to wear that. You and Gary are on this for the reasons I said … and because I can trust both of you. I know you're still on the nose with most of the rank and file. To be selfish, that's a good thing for keeping something this big quiet. I know it won't filter out from you.'

Rory's face tightened with conflict.

'I can't say *thanks for that*, it's not even a backhanded compliment. What about Gary though?'

'I know he can be a prick who'd win the *looks-and-acts-most-like-a-crim* award hands down, but that's an underestimated strength when you're dealing with a many tentacle-ed creature like Dwyer. Gary's an absolute weapon that I know can't, and won't, be deviated from target. Do you know how valuable it is when someone in my position can take that as a given?'

He thought about how he could drive home his point. 'If I must piss in your pockets, he's the cunning and you're the brains, … and I need both to second guess Dwyer. So, do you want to be the good cop or the bad cop?'

'As if I have a choice.'

'I know, but none of this is why I asked you to stay back.'

Bourke slowly and carefully straightened his computer keyboard as he chose his next words.

'I've arranged for you to have a coffee with Michelle Fox-Jones.'

'Huh?' Rory didn't need to feign surprise.

'Ex-Detective Sergeant Michelle Fox-Jones. She used to work here. In Homicide. You know?'

'Yeah, of course I know Michelle. She finished up while I was on sick leave. You haven't branched out into matchmaking, have you?'

'You wish. Have you seen her Facebook page?'

'I haven't seen anyone's Facebook page, and she's married, isn't she?'

'I'm not trying to set you up. She's been diagnosed with PTSD and she's gone public.'

'Post-traumatic stress disorder? I knew she went out on stress but she didn't kill anyone. How come she's claiming PTSD … and what's it got to do with me?'

'God, do I have to spell it out for you of all people? I know she didn't kill anyone but for some coppers, everything they do counts as trauma. She copped her fair share of dead bodies, some mutilated, as well as sieges that went sour. Anyway, that's what she's going public about — PTSD and how it's rearing its head in the Force. She's got a book in the pipeline and …'

Rory leapfrogged to crankiness. 'No fucking way. I'm not going to be in any fucking book. I can settle that right here and now. Can you remember one minute ago … you were reminding me how much of a pariah I already am in this organisation. Imagine how much shittier my name would be if I started playing the victim. Imagine Gary. Fucking hell … that's the last thing I need now that I'm back on the horse. Do you realise how hard it's been?'

'Well that's the point, isn't it?' Bourke said leaning forward on his forearms.

'How do you mean?

'You, this morning, just look at yourself.'

'And when else have you seen me like this. You dragged me in on my rostered day off after a night celebrating.'

'Celebrating, my arse.'

Bourke's dismissive certainty halted Rory's rant. Bourke sighed and summoned the good cop.

'Look, Rory. You didn't let me finish. The point is, Michelle is keen for management to embrace her book. She wants them to throw her a few scraps so she can portray them as being concerned about the issue. She's on a mission to change the culture. People and attitudes like Gary's.'

'Concerned? Did you see the story about Grant Savage suing them for PTSD. Even the Association aren't touching it. And what about those poor buggers in New South Wales who are trying to recover from PTSD? Did you see that report on the ABC news? The cops' sick-leave insurers were outed for their over-the-top surveillance of claimants. Maybe everyone's being too concerned.'

'Look,' Bourke tried again. 'No one's making you be in her book and no one wants you to play the victim. Management suggested your name, not Michelle. They reckon you're a success story. You're the one that came back. Like you say, you're back on the horse, nabbing bad guys ... well at least a bad guy. You're their poster boy. You're a chance for them to claim all their new workforce improvement stuff is working, and is all touchy-feely ...'

'I'm here because I made the effort, not because of the system. There were plenty of opportunities given to me to pull the plug and still live well. Those entitlements were looking good.'

Bourke leant back from his pally position.

'Bottom line, Rory, you're here because they let you be here. I know *you* wanted to come back but you still had to be deemed capable. I did that for you. I put my arse on the line and what have I got to show for it? The only cold case solved around here lately was that ponce at Heathcote. And do you think you would have got that result if he hadn't gone and bumped someone else off the day before you showed up to investigate?'

Rory was not positive the question was rhetorical. He wanted to answer with: *It was me that cracked the case nevertheless, and solved both murders in the process,* but he was stung by Bourke's perception of his value since returning from time off. He bit his tongue rather than invite another opportunity to pull the plug.

Bourke sensed the hesitation — mission accomplished. He spread his hands imploringly to change tone.

'You only have to have coffee with her.'

Bourke's concerns about his performance on the job lingered before Rory got his brain around answering. He latched on to Bourke's mollifying tenor to avoid facing the elephant let loose in the room.

'The way you describe it, they're just paying lip service to Michelle anyway. She's not going to be satisfied with that.'

'Exactly. She won't even *want* you in the book.'

'I dunno.'

'I'll take that as a "yes". I'll email her contact details to you.'

3

Josh Marshall made his way into the public gallery. A shared all-night drive from northern South Australia had brought him home a day early. He knew Martha had a court day; he would surprise her.

Josh always felt uncomfortable in Court Room One at the Bendigo Law Courts. The closeness of it conjured older-style classrooms where the teacher's table stood imperiously on a platform at the front of the room. The exposed dock, a three-hundred-and-sixty degree exhibition platform in the centre of the courtroom, made him especially uneasy. It seemed like a form of punishment in itself, or at least a means to suggest the opposite of innocent until proven guilty. The Victorian-era wrought-iron fenced podium was positioned a mere metre from the tiered public-gallery pews. Only contempt of court laws prevented those in the front row from reaching out and touching the defendant. They could smell the defendant's body odour and, if they so wished, idly ponder a pulled thread on the defendant's sock while his or her fate was being debated among learned friends. Not likely to be friends of the defendant, however. The only comfort afforded to the defendant was the plush regency-design carpet where the accused stood on display. Josh vowed to himself never to rob a bank.

The empty jury box was jammed against the right hand wall like a mini church-choir stall. It looked barely big enough to accommodate twelve summonsed citizens and was measurably lower, smaller and less splendorous than the magistrate's bench.

Microphones and mini speakers were discreetly integrated among the ornate nineteenth-century design detail that oozed from the plinth of every dark timber fitting, all the way up to the elaborately decorated Italianate ceiling. What couldn't be disguised, however, was the computer used by Magistrate, Mr Bryce Murphy. The centuries-old visual supremacy enjoyed by magistrates succumbed to the black plastic back of the computer screen that sat front and just off centre atop the bench. Magistrate Murphy's attention constantly ricocheted between the bar table occupants and his computer screen as he negotiated his way through each case. It was hard for Josh to take a magistrate seriously when he looked to be dispensing justice like a first-day check-in operator at the airport.

Most of the police and court staff checked Josh out in passing and none of what they saw caused their eye to linger suspiciously. He might not look like he belonged, but for all the right reasons. A shield of self-contained nonchalance set him apart from the array of miscreants and their friends, family and enemies. The outdoor-shop garb of cargo pants, North Face fleece, Gortex boots and his finger combed darker-than-blonde hair was all innocent shaggy charm.

The dock remained empty today. None of the defendants came from the lockup and all took their place alongside counsel at the bar table. A few hapless regulars seemed to know the drill and vainly tried to represent themselves.

Although it was a court of street-wear rather than gowns and wigs, respectable attire did not extend beyond the magistrate and counsel. Josh watched a stream of mostly head-down, hoody-wearing defendants and their folder-laden counsels shuffle in turn to the front of the queue. The *check-in* magistrate was efficient in dealing with those carrying baggage and Martha Portillo made her appearance right on time at two-thirty. She and her client had entered shortly before without noticing Josh in the public gallery.

Martha eschewed the power-dressing heel-teetering couture of the other young female lawyer who appeared two cases prior to Martha. The bloke in between was of the Rumpole school of lawyers, but older and messier. The biggest mystery was how he ended up with a hoody-ed client without having an interpreter.

Martha opted for a black top and modest skirt with her favourite fitted grey jacket. Unfussy thick, dark shoulder-length hair and a chunky coloured necklace was all the lift she needed. Her young female client's hoody was a pale blue.

The ever-dour face of the Magistrate Murphy creased into a smile as the bench clerk announced the case.

'Miss Portillo, you're representing the defendant, I see?'

Martha lifted her head from laying out papers on the newly vacated bar table and smiled back.

'Yes indeed, your honour.'

Flirty, Josh surmised as he watched the standing up, sitting down, standing up, sitting down pantomime of polite discussion until it reached the conclusion that Martha's client — who spoke only to plead not guilty — would proceed to a summary hearing on …

At this point the Magistrate Murphy created a sustained pin-dropping silence as he peered into the computer.

'Half a day?' he asked Martha and the police prosecutor.

Yes, your Honour came in unison, at which point the magistrate began a solo two-fingered computer keyboard tapping performance. Finally, he offered: 'Twenty-fourth of November then?'

Checking of diaries all round and it was locked in. All in all, slightly less animated than an airport check-in.

Martha's head swivelled sharply into a double take as she escorted her client out past the public gallery. She gave Josh a smile far too enthusiastic for a court room, mimed coffee drinking, pointed in the direction of Pall Mall, and spread her fingers to indicate five minutes.

~

Josh rose from his seat at the tiny table in the tiny second room of El Gordo café. Martha chucked her bag aside and kissed Josh hard on the lips before the glass door closed itself behind her. She pulled back to look jubilantly at his face before snatching him into a hug.

'Mmm, it's good to see you,'

Josh held her apart to grin back.

'You should have let me know you'd be a day early,' she said.

'The plan was to check into the caravan park at Hawker, but I was asleep and Anthony kept driving. We ended up driving through the night. I knew you had a court day, so here I am. Good, huh?'

Martha answered with an eye-crinkling grin.

Josh was first to let go. 'Your coffee's gone cold, I'll get you another one,' he said.

'Sorry I was late getting over here. I had to keep holding my client's hand. She's shitting herself.'

'It looked like bottom-of-the-barrel-day today. When are you gonna get something like a decent murder?'

'I'm doing all right. I'll get there one day. Besides, be careful what you wish for.'

Martha gathered her satchel off the floor and sat down. Josh leant into the servery window and ordered a fresh latte. They were the only people in the second room. Another couple were visible through the window at a table in Chancery Lane. The London court precinct namesake was a mere pedestrian walkway that El Gordo and like-minded hipster businesses had transformed into Bendigo's scaled-down version of Melbourne lane culture.

'How was life in a donga?' Martha asked him as she spooned froth from her latte.

Josh smiled at his memory of the cell-like portable building that had been home for the past five weeks. He had scored a gig with a team of young scientists doing a wildlife survey on

Warburton Creek in the South Australian outback.

'Not bad. The Eco Whisperers look after us.' he said indifferently, 'But look at this.'

Josh swiped a picture up on his phone and held it in front of Martha.

'It's a Main's frog. It wasn't meant to be there.'

'Wow … I think. Does that mean it's rare?'

'Not in Western Australia, but it's unheard of where we were. They live in the desert, although *live* is a bit of a stretch. They survive. They burrow deep underground and can endure droughts in a cocoon for more than five years. When they do surface, they metamorphose at the speed of light … they have to have *some* life before everything dries up again. The best bit is, I got them on tape. They sound like bleating sheep.'

His infectiousness was infectious.

'You gotta love a man who's passionate about his work.' Martha smiled.

'Well, it was a dream trip for us all. The Eco Whisperers usually only score mining company work. This was for the university. Their end-game is to save everything.

'With mining company work, it's always in the back of your mind that everything you uncover is doomed. The mining companies always win no matter how every minister for environment in the country tries to spin it. And not just with the environment. Remember the mining tax?'

'So the trip was good?' Martha said to restore his jubilance.

Josh took the hint. 'Yeah.' He said it slowly as the memory stretched a smile back onto his face.

Martha leant forward to talk in a quieter tone. 'Well, I have a surprise for you.'

Josh turned to check that the young female barista was not at the serving window. He put his elbows on the table and leant forward.

'Did they print it?' he whispered.

'Yeah. It only came out today. I'll show you.' Martha pulled a *Government Gazette* from her lawyer satchel. 'Page seventy-three,' she said as she handed it to him.

Ten years earlier, Josh had made the connection between his recording and the Neilson Scali murders as soon as the street address was reported in the news: *Early Tuesday morning at Nineteen Scott Street Balwyn.* He hardly had time to think about going to the Police before he recognised David Dwyer on a TV news item about the case. At that stage, Dwyer was strutting around with the supposed good guys. By the time Dwyer himself became a suspect some weeks later, Josh's caution had morphed into total aversion. He removed the recording from his computer and consigned it to life on a USB stick at the bottom of his sock drawer.

When Josh met Martha and they eventually moved in together, they agreed on a no-secrets pact. Josh won hands down. It was also a relief for him to finally tell someone else.

After her initial surprise, Martha agreed that it had been a no-brainer for Josh to avoid becoming a witness against a still-connected ex-policeman with the omnipresent wherewithal and undisguised intent to eradicate any further witnesses. As the investigation and hearings rolled on, the innate menace of David Dwyer was evident to all who saw him on the TV news. Martha and Josh were more than happy to let that sleeping dog lie, even when a reward, albeit much less, was first offered. They never regarded themselves as greedy or particularly needy.

Money talked nonetheless and when the reward recently skyrocketed to one million dollars, idle speculation crept in. Maybe they *could* have their cake, and with a legal brain on hand, maybe they could eat it too.

Josh continued to look at the brief *Government Gazette* entry after he read it.

'It's on,' Martha said.

'So you're gonna send the whole thing now?'

'It's packed ready to post as soon as I arrive in Melbourne tomorrow. We've started this now, so we just let it take its course.

If this unfolds as it should, you'll be able to set up your own eco company. "Eco Josh and Associates". How does that sound?'

Josh lifted his unsmiling gaze from the *Government Gazette*. 'Are you scared?'

Martha tilted her head in empathy with his sombreness.

'Nooo.' She drew it out. 'Not at this stage. Maybe when it gets to the pointy end … but not now. Maybe not even then. We are anonymous, remember? We've already been through all this.'

'I know,' Josh said. 'But seeing it in print, it's like the chill I felt when I was there. I had no idea what the gun and seventy-five thousand dollars was about, but I knew I'd end up as a skeleton in that tree if they spotted me. And there I was, less than three metres away. When they eventually walked away, I couldn't stop shaking.'

He stared past Martha.

'Just deal with the positives at this stage, Josh. They'll have the evidence you always felt guilty about not handing in. If we don't go ahead with the reward stuff — and I'm not suggesting we drop it — then at least you will have done everything you could. Your conscience will have a clean slate.'

'I know. I'm happy for them to have the evidence, but it still makes me nervous.' He brought his eyes back to Martha to explain. 'When I accidently recorded such a sinister-looking meeting, it was still just a random conversation. There was nothing about it to suggest why I should take it to the Police. I only put that together after the murders happened at the actual Balwyn address. And then what?

'The couple who were killed were in police protection. Who could I take the recording to without looking over my shoulder for the rest of my life? I probably would have had to go into police protection too. A safe house? Not! I knew all that, but it still didn't stop me from feeling guilty and constantly agonising over it. I remember how relieved I felt when they arrested Dwyer and it looked like he would get his comeuppance. At that point I thought it was safe to delete the recording. Get rid of any evidence that I was ever there.'

'Just as well you didn't, though.'

'Do you reckon, because I'm still not sure. The next thing I read, the key witness against Dwyer is murdered while in custody. They had to drop the charges against Dwyer. If anyone had doubts about how Dwyer could, and did, deal with threats, then none of them were left wondering after that … including me.'

Josh demonstrated with a shudder.

'All the more reason to do this, don't you think? You keep forgetting we're doing it anonymously. If there's any risk of us being exposed, then we don't have to go any further. It's not as if we're not well enough off. We both get paid enough and we get to do the things we love. I don't want to risk that any more than you do.'

Martha clasped both of Josh's hands in the centre of the tiny table.

'I know all that … we've been through this enough times,' he told her.' But there is one link that can't be undone. They will always *have* my fingerprint.'

4

Rory felt a satisfied calm as he buttoned his shirt at the mirror. A nightmare-free night, day-old haircut and a freshly ironed shirt — it was as good as he could make himself for the re-scheduled catch-up with Michelle Fox-Jones. Deeper into the mirror, the condensed panorama of his flat reflected a far less restored countenance. Stage two, he decided as he pondered mirrored glimpses of disarray. He promised himself he'd leave work early to make the bed, pick-up the clothes, visit the shared laundry, vacuum, mop, clean the debris of dishes, take all the empty pizza boxes and liquor bottles to the bin .... He sighed as the mental list grew into stage three, four, five and six.

It was that precise over-his-shoulder vista that greeted Steph at his front door. She hadn't had time to knock when he opened the door en-route to his coffee appointment. Their mutual shock was for different reasons. Rory was shocked that she was there at such an early hour. Steph was shocked at the state of the place. She had prepared a speech in her head about how upset she became after Rory truncated their evening out celebrating her birthday. The sermon evaporated as her reaction to the mess tumbled out before any greeting.

'That's disgusting. You can't even look after yourself properly. Is that why you didn't want to come back here the other night?'

Although Rory was shocked that Steph was here at an

unexpected hour, he wasn't shocked that she had come at all. She was never one to let matters fester. Differences left unresolved always had to be got off her chest sooner rather than later. Rory knew the occasion was inevitable, but Steph had usurped any chance of him making the first move. The opportunity to choose neutral territory or at least tidy the place up was lost before he'd had a chance to go there in his mind.

Now his mind was in overdrive. He expected Steph would assume a straightforward explanation for the shambles that greeted her. Guilt-driven descent into unsightly bachelordom caused by separation and the usual collateral damage. On top of all that was the meltdown of his affair with Heidi Lester — the catalyst that set off the whole catastrophe. That was the full extent of any explanation Steph would hear from Lauren.

The fact that Rory was struck down with PTSD in the same incident that exposed and ended his affair with Heidi was of no account to Lauren in her post-Rory life. Nor did Rory's pride let him reveal it as an excuse. He didn't want to be seen as a victim at work and he especially didn't want Steph to regard him as a victim. It was a no-go zone for the discussion he now faced.

'Steph …I …'

'God, it even stinks in here.'

He noticed she had a backpack and reasoned that she had caught a tram or two well out of her way from going to uni. She appeared dressed for uni: jeans and a slightly padded coat over a long sleeve tee shirt— hood down.

'Did you come here on your way to uni?'

'What?

His mind was still catching up, trying to work out how to tackle the situation. She couldn't wait.

'Of course I did. Is that all you've got to say? Well you needn't bother anyway — this says it all,' she gestured with a look over his shoulder. 'I was upset about the other night. No wonder you didn't want me near this place. It's is a pigsty. Fucking hell, Dad.'

He winced, firstly at the swearing itself, then at the depth of her anger when it dawned on him that she was not prone to profanity.

'And don't give me that look.'

'Sorry, Steph. I've been away a lot. I haven't had a chance to... How are you?'

He felt totally hapless and looked it. She noticed and sighed to let the anger fade.

'Oh Dad…'

Steph threw her arms around him and held her head to his chest. He drew breath and smelled her hair. He had to pull back to stop himself from welling up.

'Hey. I'm sorry about the other night. It didn't sit well with me either.' He thought about how badly it went downhill for him later that night. He cringed within when he noticed the Stoli bottle still on the coffee table. He could hide his condition, but not its aftermath. Or so he thought.

'It's PTSD, isn't it?'

'What? Is that what your mother told you?'

'Of course not. I don't think she wants to know. But I'm nineteen years old Dad … and I go to uni. So don't pretend. You shot someone dead. Don't the Police provide counselling when stuff like that happens?'

'I've been through all that. I'm back at work now. The support tapers off.'

'Well you don't have to be university educated to see that hasn't worked. You're wallowing in it.'

The wallowing bit stung. He tried to play things down.

'Work's been the best antidote so far. But whatever I do, there's still going to be the odd bad night.'

'More than the odd one by the look of this place.'

'It's not always like this … really. But it's something that takes a long time to get over completely.'

She'd run out of argument and stepped around him to make a protracted appraisal. He could only wait for the verdict.

'This is not you, Dad. You're better than this. I used to be so proud of the way you cooked and helped mum take care of things around the house. Not all dads were like that. At least that's what my friends told me.'

'It really is just a bad patch, Steph, but this one's over. You'll think I'm making this up but before you arrived, I resolved to knock off early today to tidy up.'

'Do you want me to stay and help? I haven't got any important lectures today.'

'Na, na, Steph,' he was quick to dismiss. 'This is not your problem. You enjoy your day.'

Her frown returned. 'Not my problem? I'm the one who's making an effort here. I can tell you Nick's a write-off. If you and I can't have an honest relationship, what hope have either of us got.'

'Sorry, Steph. I didn't mean it like that. And don't worry about Nick. I'm a male and I understand where he's at. With Nick it's gonna take time. With you, I have to work things out as we go, and out loud like this. And I want to do that. I really do. It means so much to me that you haven't shut me out.'

He thought it was a hugging moment but she stayed apart.

'You need to see someone. Even I can tell that things won't change simply because you clean the flat.'

'As a matter of fact, that's where I was heading when I opened the door.'

'Counselling?'

'No. Another cop who went out on PTSD.'

'That's good. Is he like a support group thing?'

'She, actually. She's doing a book. I guess she's interested in me as a kind of case study. Someone who survived and returned to duty.'

'Survived? Don't kid yourself, Dad. Ask her what she thinks you should do.'

'Hmm.'

'You're not gonna, are you?'

'I'll work through it. Okay?' I've got to meet her soon. I'll walk you back to the tram.'

'I'll be making sure you work through it. Don't you worry.'

He offered his arm and she held it all the way to the tram stop.

Former Detective Sergeant Michelle Fox-Jones sat in her parked car and watched Rory arrive at the Four Three Four Café. The criminally-unimaginative name was derived from its street number. He leant into the café doorway to see that Michelle was not there and turned back to wait nonchalantly on the footpath. She remembered his imperturbable un-cop-like bearing and smiled. As a policewoman, she silently envied the way he could stand apart from the boys' club but still turn on enough machismo to avoid ever being on the outer. And now, look at his place in the pecking order — further from the sun than Pluto.

With colour back in his cheeks and the fresh haircut, signs of a lapsed PTSD recoveree were no longer on display, at least not from across the street. The creases in his face might be a bit deeper and a bit more grey had crept into his black mane — still long by cop standards despite the haircut — but none of it made him less good-looking than she recalled. *It certainly is a man's world*, she sighed and wondered about his clothes. A charcoal jacket over a dark shirt with white buttons. The shirt was not tucked in but not as a means to hide unwanted weight. It was a more dapper version of Rory. He was seeing someone, the detective in her decided. She sighed again and reached for the doorhandle.

For a moment, Rory didn't recognise her with her hair down, and he told her so.

'I only ever wore it up on the job.'

'I probably never bumped into you off the job. It's like a new you. At least it is for me. You're looking well, Michelle.'

The straight dark locks spilling onto her shoulders made her face less sharp than in Rory's memory. The slimming red shirt and jeans also made her look younger than the on-duty version.

'Thanks, Rory. I didn't contract leprosy, you know, although I might as well have.'

'Sorry. I didn't mean anything by that. I just thought you're looking well. Civilian life suits you.'

Michelle dropped her head theatrically to concede her touchiness.

'Sorry, Rory. Sometimes when I say things like that I realise I still have a way to go. But I'm probably telling you how to suck eggs.'

Rory gave a what-can-I-say shrug. Michelle read it as a sign of denial — not admitting anything out loud.

'Maybe you should try civilian life too,' she added unthinkingly.

'God, do I look that bad?'

His own hurt look was not all feigned. It was supposed to be a good day for Rory — he'd made an effort and it was a rare-ish night without the nightmare. He also felt buoyed by the unplanned yet rewarding deep and meaningful with Steph.

'Now *I'm* sorry, but will you listen to us? We can't say anything normal without thinking we're stepping on toes. And that's part of all this, you know. Shall we go inside and start again?' Michelle asked.

They were still standing outside the Four Three Four Café. It was across the road and half a block down from Rory's usual — the Bean Noir Café. At Bean Noir, Andrew knew exactly how Rory liked his double-shot flat white.

Rory had never been inside the Four Three Four Café but could tell from the clientele that the coffee would be even worse than the name. Michelle had offered to come to his patch, but Bean Noir Café was a sanctuary Rory never tainted with anything to do with work. It was too precious to risk compromising. He only hoped Four Three Four Café was beyond Andrew's eyeshot.

Rory's phone rang. He turned to face the street and answered.

'*Cockburn,*' Cockburn's voice told him. '*You'd better get your fucking arse out to Thomastown. We've got a job on.*'

'I'm in a meeting and I've got a note. Cold cases, remember. I'm exempt from call outs.'

'*Forget that touchy-fucking-feely stuff with Michelle, you need to be here now. Bourke's World War Three has just broken out and you have to see it before the crime-scene guys get here. I can't hold them off for long.*'

Rory computed it all in the shortest moment.

'Where?' he said, slipping into Cockburn's short speak.

'*Eighty Sirocco Drive. There's a For Lease sign out front.*'

Cockburn hung up.

Rory's head spun. Firstly to the up side — he wouldn't have to go into the Four Three Four Café and drink their coffee. Then he realised he wouldn't have time for a coffee at all before he faced World War Three.

'Sorry, Michelle, I have to go, a call out.'

'I hope this isn't pre-planned. Richard warned me you weren't keen.'

'Once a cop …' he said to refute her suspicion. 'I'll call you to re-schedule.'

They both did the look-back across the street as Michelle opened her car door. Both returned a coy smile.

5

Rory was halfway to the suburb of Thomastown on Melbourne's northern fringe before he realised he had no idea what the start of World War Three involved, other than it probably had something to do with David Dwyer and the Neilson Scali murders. His first concerns had been that Cockburn knew about the Michelle Fox-Jones stuff. If Cockburn knew, then the whole branch knew. How much further behind the eight ball could he go?

There were plenty in the Force who still blamed him for Senior Constable Heidi Lester's disfigured arm. The fact that he and Heidi were having an affair when it happened eighteen months ago garnered even greater loathing.

A knife-wielding suicide-by-cop candidate wasn't in Rory's bailiwick, but he and Heidi were a block away when the call went out. They had been driving to her apartment in South Yarra for their regular lunchtime tryst. The scenario was only familiar to Rory as one of too many front-page stories about purportedly avoidable police shootings. Over the years he'd thought about how he would react in the same situation. How hard could it be *not* to become a killer? Wound if you do have to fire, but surely the training mantra of aiming at the torso wasn't a one-size-fits-all solution. He soon found out.

A bullet in the leg made the knife-wielder angrier. He lunged at Heidi's outstretched capsicum spray-holding arm. Rory's rage-fuelled second, third and fourth shots answered the suicide invitation. Despite being painted a hero by Force Command and the media, colleagues believed the leg shot and Heidi's mangled arm should never have happened. Months of post-shooting-trauma-induced sick leave increased pervading ill-will within the Force. The animus was no more in Rory's face than from Gary Cockburn. Heidi had sought solace from Cockburn but later dropped him. It was from a vengeful Cockburn that Rory's wife Lauren learnt every sordid detail. Post-Divorce Shock Disorder complications didn't need to be diagnosed.

His return to work in the perceived "light-duties" cold case role was just another bone to catch in the craw of colleagues. Never mind that apart from the DNA no-brainers, the cases were all cold for good reason. And never mind the steadfast neediness of unsated victims' relatives and their support groups. Every conversation with his fellow detectives was loaded with the sham notion that working cold cases was some sort of sedate Doctor Watson, Sherlock Holmes parlour game.

Having Michelle Fox-Jones champion his cause would be another sure-fire nail in the coffin.

There was no crime scene tape strung around the place when Rory arrived at eighty Sirocco Drive. The street was an avenue of two-storey-high tilt-slab concrete boxes fronted by car-parking forecourts and Cyclone-wire fences. It was a collection of businesses people never see unless they have reason to go there for something. An aluminium window manufacturer, engineering designer, leather manufacturer, an upmarket panel beater — if there's such a thing — flooring supplier, gourmet dip factory, a so-called "village" bread maker, electronic something or other, a storage provider and a coffee roaster with café seating in its car park.

Rory spotted the red and white *For Lease* sign attached to a Cyclone-wire fence:

FOR LEASE
• Warehouse/office
• Available immediately
• 1493 sq/mtrs
• High clearance
• On-site parking

The warehouse car park was obscured by an un-trimmed vine clinging to the front fence. Cockburn's unmarked car and a single marked police car were only visible through the open double gates. A constable alighted from the marked car to greet Rory and record his details.

'Where's Cockburn?' Rory asked as they skipped through the brief formalities.

'The prick's inside,' he said.

'You didn't ask him how to spell his name, did you?' Rory guessed.

'Why doesn't he change it if it's such a sore point?'

'Not your fault,' Rory said tapping him on the arm. 'They reckon he's been copping shit since primary school. That's why the sneer's rusted on. I'll go and see if he's cooled down.'

Not even Rory knew that as a young man, Gary Cockburn had pleaded to his dad to change their surname or at least pronounce it Coburn instead of "Cock-burn" — like James Coburn the actor. How dare he talk of dishonouring a name that had fought in two world wars, came the response. It was a life sentence for Gary.

Rory opened the door from the office area to the warehouse. It felt like a portal into another universe. The unlit warehouse space was vast and high enough to house a cluster of townhouses. Here and there, stars of daylight shone from less-than-flush joints where the roof met the wall. Thin shafts also crept in around the edges of a vehicle roller-door and from several well-spaced Laserlite panels in the roof. The most central of these panels cast a pool of stage-like light onto the one thing occupying the otherwise empty expanse of concrete.

The bloodied body of a man wearing only jeans was fastened with duct-tape to a cheap, steel canteen chair. His wrists were taped behind his back and each ankle was taped to a chair leg. The lifeless body was kept upright with several windings of tape holding his torso to the chair-back. Most of the blood was on the slumped head. The scene had been cleared of everything other than a single sheet of paper that lay about a metre away from the chair.

A shoe squeaking on the concrete floor brought Cockburn out of the shadow. Cockburn said nothing. He let the crime-scene speak for itself. Rory began by scanning the massive chamber from the doorway.

'So much for cold cases,' he said as he made his way into the centre of the space. 'They don't come much warmer than this.'

The echo of his own words caught him by surprise.

'Welcome back to the homicide world where we have actual bodies … with fresh blood. Take a good look … you can use this to get another dose of time off.'

Rory ignored the jibe and kept scanning the massive chamber. He took a step closer to the body and leant towards the note on the floor.

'Is that what I think it is?'

'It is if you think it's page seventy-three torn from the current issue of the *Government Gazette*.'

'So it has actually been published?'

'Yeah. For what it ended up being worth. It only came out two days ago.'

Rory slowly moved around the body.

'They seem to have given him a good hiding but it's not the worst we've seen. No obvious signs of torture,' he said as he circled at a slight distance. 'We need to be suited up for this.'

'Yeah yeah,' Cockburn said dismissively. 'I wanted you to see it before I remove that page and let everyone in here. I don't want anyone knowing about the *Government Gazette* except you and me.'

Cockburn's pocketed hands pulled his jacket off his chest. His puffed-bantam frame dared Rory to defy the conspiracy he had just put on the table.

'Have you got some gloves and a bag to do that?' Rory said. Cockburn didn't try to hide his surprise.

'You agree then?'

''course. Only one protocol applies here. Until Bourke tells us otherwise, that piece of paper is for our eyes only. What about the constable outside … and whoever found the body?'

'A real estate woman found the body. She was on her own. She came ahead of a client inspection … to open up and check that the place was in order. Her male colleague and the client were due a bit later.'

'Where is she now? What did she see?'

'I had to get her offsider to take her home. That's her spew outside. She wouldn't have got close or even noticed a piece of paper laying around.'

'What about the clients? Did they show up?'

'No. They might have had been bogus anyway. A few things about them didn't sit well with her. We'll have to chase it all down.'

'Okay.'

Cockburn watched Rory ponder the situation.

'The other thing she said: there was no break-in. The door was locked as usual.'

'And the constable? He saw the *Government Gazette*, surely.'

Rory dropped his eyes from Cockburn and noticed that they were holding their conversation across the bloodied head of the body. He moved to the same side as Cockburn.

'Don't want you being sick as well, Rory. Do you want me to get someone to come and get you too?'

'Give it a fucking rest, Gary.' Rory's own snarly way of saying "Gary" rivalled Bourke's derisive version. A ramped-up echo of his irritation ricocheted around the concrete and steel cavern. 'I haven't been here five minutes and you've already become a tired record. I know you don't get it but dealing with this doesn't equate to killing someone. If I had to, I'd have no trouble eating my lunch in front of a garden-variety homicide like this. That doesn't mean I should be able to handle *making* them dead in the first place though. I know I can't and I know I never will.'

Cockburn maintained a so-fucking-what face. Rory felt compelled to continue.

'I didn't have to face this poor bugger in that frozen moment when his eyes filled with incredulousness pleading of why I'd just ripped the life out of him. There's a world of difference that you'll never come close to having a fucking clue about — probably not even when you end up shooting someone yourself.'

Cockburn took a step closer to Rory.

'Too fucking right. If I have to stop some scumbag in his tracks I won't be feeling sorry for myself. Or him for that matter. I won't be calling him a "poor bugger".'

'Everything is just water off a duck's back with you, Gary.'

'It's the only way to be, especially if the alternative is your pathetic pool of self-misery.' Cockburn tried to draw a line under his uncomfortableness with a righteous shoulder wiggle. 'You've had your hissy fit now. What did you want to know about our constable friend?'

Rory looked down and shook his head. 'Water off a duck's back.'

'I can do this on my own if I have to.'

Rory exhaled loudly and dug his hands into his pockets.

'Okay. I presume the constable has seen the *Government Gazette*. How do you propose dealing with that?'

'I've put the wind up him already, and …'

'So I noticed,' Rory said.

'… and we get him to sign the same non-disclosure form

Bourke made us sign. It's all we can do. For all I know, the people who did this might have photographed it and it's already up on some Facebook page. I presume that was the purpose of their exercise — to send a message to someone, or leave a message for us. If it is the mob who arranged a bogus real estate inspection of the place, they did it so the body would be found. For all we know at this stage, they might have begun World War Three and ended it in one fell swoop.'

'Why? Do you know who it is?'

'It's Graeme Stanley, isn't it?'

Rory stepped to the front of the body and squatted for a closer look at the slumped head.

'Yeah. I think you're right. Remember, we never could establish a link between him and Dwyer … or him and the Neilson Scali murders?'

'Well we can now. Maybe him and Dwyer were mates after all.'

'It just proves the saying: with friends like that, who needs enemies … and don't say you know how he feels.'

Rory thought about smiling.

'So, plan A. I bag the letter. Okay?'

As far as Cockburn was concerned it was a rhetorical question. He took plastic gloves and a clear evidence bag from his pocket to collect page seventy-three torn from the *Government Gazette*.

'Just let me take a photo before you pick it up. The rest of the investigation is your call. I'll get out of your way and let you get on with it. Let me know how Bourke wants us to deal with the *Government Gazette* link.'

Cockburn wriggled his second hand into a glove while Rory took pictures. 'Okay. Tell laughing boy out the front to organise the troops,' he told Rory.

Rory went outside and gave the word for the constable to activate the full murder response and then walked back to the office door.

He gathered the twenty or so business cards that lay scattered on the ground both inside and outside the glass door. The cards were all inspection confirmation cards that had originally been jammed between the door and the jamb by a company called Northern Security Solutions. The address of the company was also in Sirocco Drive.

A date, time and initials were entered by hand onto the rear of each card to record exactly what time mobile security guards rattled the doors and checked the windows twice each night. Rory shuffled the cards into order and noted that the premises inspections were carried out as usual for the previous night. He took the cards to the constable and told him: 'You'd better give these to Cockburn. Let him know the premises were inspected twice last night. And tell him I've gone for coffee.'

'Right.'

'And it's okay to start stringing up the crime scene tape.'

Brewdom Coffee Roasters was three up from the murder warehouse and on the other side of Sirocco Drive. The glassed front of the building was fitted out as Brewdom Café. Brewdom footpath panel barriers surrounded an outside seating area that was shaded with two Brewdom umbrellas. Untypically for the street, the Cyclone-wire fence had been removed to accommodate the steady stream of office-girl and apprentice-driven business vans and utes despatched for the morning tea and lunch runs. Brewdom even had its own mini-van doing phoned-through deliveries.

The hipster barista dude and the two tattoo-shouldered counter-serving girls were transplanted right out of Ackland or Brunswick Street. So was the coffee. The march of Melbourne's coffee culture knew no bounds. From New York, to Paris, to Thomastown.

No one was dining in and Rory had the whole outdoor seating area to himself. He took his double-shot flat-white to the outermost outdoor table with full view of the passing parade of customers and the murder warehouse. The blue-collar clientele wore anything but. High-vis fluro yellow and orange joined black logo-embroidered polo shirts to round out the complete range of apparel options. Camel-coloured work boots were mandatory for blokes.

People carrying cardboard coffee-cup trays to their vehicles were stopped in their tracks by the first wave of incoming flashing emergency lights. Small groups were forming by the time more police cars, crime scene response vehicles and news teams streamed in and began setting up. Brewdom's outdoor seating began to fill. Two young high-vis shirted, shorts-wearing blokes on the adjoining table asked Rory if he knew what was going on. By this stage, even blokes in suits had materialised to check out the drama. Rory didn't feel as conspicuous.

'Someone was found murdered in there,' he told them.

'Fuck' and 'No shit,' came their replies. Then, 'How do you know? You a cop or something?'

'Yeah. I am. Detective Sergeant Rory James. Homicide Squad.'

They looked at each other for an explanation that neither could give.

The darker-haired bloke asked. 'What happened then?'

'I'm sorry. I can't tell you. Do you work around here?'

They gave each other the same quizzical looks. The darker-haired-one did the talking.

'We're doing fitout work two doors down in RiverTech. We're shop fitters from RJG Constructions in Airport West.'

Rory took a notebook from his pocket and made a note. The exchange of nonplussed looks kept happening.

'Have you seen anything happening there in the last day or so?'

'No. The woman in RiverTech told us the empty warehouse used to be a tile place. Went broke, apparently. She said it's only been back on the rental market a few weeks. When I told our boss, he said to put a card under the door in case any new tenant wants work done. We didn't get around to doing that.'

'I saw a van go in there yesterday morning,' said the lighter-haired man.

'When?' his mate said incredulously.

'I came an' got the coffees yesterday. We were running late, remember? You stayed back to unload those frames. About eleven-thirty.'

'Did you see the driver? Did he look like a murderer?' his mate asked.

'Hang on,' Rory said. 'We'll need to get a statement from you.'

He smiled smugly at his darker-haired offsider.

'So you were here at eleven-thirty and you saw a van. Was it going in or out?'

'Yeah. It was a white van. Big, like one of them commercial Mercedes. Tinted driver's window. No other windows, though. I looked to see if it had a name on it. You know. To find out who might be leasing the place. But it was just plain white. That's all I can tell you.'

His expression dropped with the disappointment of not remembering more.

'Did you see anyone get out?'

'Na. It went right inside … through the roller door.'

His face dropped again.

'Never mind. That's all helpful.' Rory said. 'I'll get your name and number and someone will come over and get a statement from you.'

He took the guy's name and number and headed back.

Bedlam had set in. Oversized police vans and television news vehicles with temporary communications dishes robbed road space. One film guy was set up on the back of a one-tonner ute in the carpark of the adjoining premises. The original on-site constable directed traffic competing to pass through the single-vehicle width of remaining road space. A lone helicopter circled.

Diagonally opposite the murder warehouse, two white-dusted and white-clad workers watched and smoked at the gate of Sloane's Village Bakery. Rory stopped to marvel at how far removed the tilt slab factory reality differed from the quaint image of the Sloane's Village Bakery depicted on its bread bags. He gave a wry smirk before he asked the ghostly figures if the bakery did night shifts. Word had already spread that it was a murder scene. They didn't doubt he was a copper and the thicker village baker told him.

'Of course. But me and Spiros only came on at eight o'clock this morning.'

He spoke with a southern European accent.

'Have you ever done the night shifts? Do you know what goes on in the street?'

'Yes of course. It's more money at night but I not been on the nightshift for six months. Maybe more. Not since my son was born. I am being new-age … at home more, you know.'

Rory smiled as the man's hands pigeon-signed every word he had said.

'And what happens in the street at night? Is anyone else open?'

'Yes some, but not that late and not all the time like the Sloane's. The food places down the other end. They sometimes do the night shift when it is near Christmas. Always there is someone coming and going from the security place … Northern Security. Sometimes Hamal from Northern Security comes in for some buns when we are having smoko. There's other security outfits too comes past. Northern Security not have everything.'

His fellow baker, Spiros, nodded agreement throughout.

'You should check the CCTV. Everyone has CCTV for the night-time,' Spiros added with the same European accent.

'Thanks. We'll be on to it.' Rory tried not to sound patronising. 'Did you see anyone come or go into the place yesterday?'

'Naa. We always do smoko out the back. Steve, our boss, thinks it not look good to smoke outside a bakery.'

'Thanks,' Rory said again and stayed beside them — all

three silently watching the comings and goings of crime scene people in blue disposable coveralls. Cockburn was still in his regular suit. A female officer with red hair and wearing blue disposable crime-scene overalls was briefing him in readiness to front the media. Rory waited for them to finish and passed a note of the shopfitter's details to Cockburn.

'I ran into this bloke in the café. He saw a white van go in yesterday. Went right inside through the roller door, he said. My guess is they were in and out before dark. There's plenty of night time security and CCTV in the street apparently … and the door rattlers left their cards as usual. I reckon this was a brazen in-broad-daylight operation.'

'Half an hour ago you were getting out of the way and letting me get on with it. Now it's all *my guess is this* and *I reckon that*. How about you stick with plan A.'

Rory straightened and held up one hand in feigned surrender.

'It's all yours. Enjoy your weekend. I'm outta here.'

He drove two blocks along Sirocco Drive and turned left into a cul-de-sac that ended at a fenced vacant allotment. He just made it out of his car in time to throw up. His hands clasped the wire netting to support himself for the long while he stood there shaking.

6

Sigrid Dobell halted her smile when she opened the door to Rory. The pause was fleeting but not unnoticed.

'You're early,' she said.

'Would you like me to come back later?' he winced.

'Sorry. I'm expecting the weekend guests. I've got a houseful coming and I thought you might be them. They should have been here an hour ago. Grrrrrrr.'

'Just me.'

The smile sprang back. Sigrid stepped off the front door step and rose on her toes to kiss him. Rory dropped his overnight bag to hug with both arms. They broke apart to look at each other and grin. Rory noticed the same silky sleeveless blouse buttoned to a high collar that she wore the first time they met. Once again, his eyes were drawn to the discreet slivers of sheer fabric among the leafy white-on-white design.

'I wish you lived in Melbourne, you look great,' Rory told her.

'Be careful what you wish for,' Sigrid told him. 'If things stay the way they are, I can be sure you'll always be pleased to see me.'

There it is he thought, *or am I imagining things?* Sigrid's remark may have been offhand but it was the most either of them had ever uttered about where their relationship might lead. Had their phone conversation about Lauren asking him for a divorce set something off? Despite being over the hump of considering themselves a couple, neither seemed interested in dissecting their new romance out loud. They both simply enjoyed whatever opportunity they found to be together. So was the spell being broken? Was Sigrid laying down her position or was this just innocent chitchat? If the status quo was in fact just dandy as far as she was concerned, how well did that suit him? Would he be content to remain a distraction she deigned could pop in and out of her agreeably independent life — not something destined to ever become a significant part of it? He knew he was way overthinking it and he knew well enough to keep things at banter level.

'I'll take that risk,' he said and backed it up with an admiring look. He savoured her glowing, tanned shoulders and breezy, blonde hair as she led him through the grand entrance of The Manse B&B.

A fine figure was not completely concealed by her stylish greeting-clients-for-the-first-time wear. Yet somehow, being noticed had brought mixed fortunes for Sigrid. Unlucky in marriage but lucky in divorce she told Rory when they first met. Her third divorce settlement covered a move to Bendigo, buying a late nineteenth century two-storey mansion called The Manse, and remodelling its interior into luxury B&B guest suites. Rory originally arrived as one of the midweek hotel-averse corporate clients, when he was investigating the Heathcote winery case.

The real B&B action happened at the weekend. Cashed-up Melburnians flocked to the former goldfields town for its newfound raison d'etre of hosting international-class exhibitions and events. Visitors would then discover the intact historic streetscapes and a transformed, buzzingly hip, food culture. "A cultural escape for Melburnians", according to an article in the *New York Times*, no less.

When it came to accommodation, The Manse B&B was the real deal. It overlooked the CBD from a dress circle of leafy streets rising in a crescent on the west side of town. The William Beebe architect pedigree was evident in a host of Edwardian features — cantilevered Queen Anne gables, wraparound verandas, balconies with elaborate timber fretwork, and Australian flora and fauna featured in the plentiful stained-glass windows. The grounds were their own miniature botanic gardens.

Rory followed Sigrid into the expansive but nonetheless homely dining room with a twelve-seater table. She had been in the throes of setting out silverware and fine china for the next day's breakfast. The nightly news flickered on a small television set at the end of a long antique sideboard.

'Help yourself to a drink while I finish this, you look like you can use it,' Sigrid offered as she used a remote to mute the sound. He had hoped he'd recovered enough from his delayed reaction to dealing with a dead body for it to go undetected. Perhaps a brave face could only hide so much, after all, the realisation that he was not over his self-denied PTSD had preoccupied his thoughts for the entire drive from Thomastown to Bendigo. He strove to shift Sigrid's focus.

'Aren't you having one?' he said with exaggerated surprise. Matching each other's drinking efforts was the thing they most had in common.

'Not until after they all get here and I settle them in.'

Sigrid said this without interrupting the over-faffing way she was putting surplus cutlery back into the drawer and topping up the glass cereal containers that had already been topped up. Rory wondered if she was annoyed because her regular evening drink had been delayed, or whether the coolness of their phone conversation lingered. Either way, he figured his best option was to have that drink.

'Who are they?'

'It's a corporate booking. Some construction giant in Melbourne is treating their Government bureaucrat clients … and their partners. I don't think you'll read about it on any pecuniary interest register though. I've had a few of these now. They've all been good.'

'You're becoming a growth industry then.'

'Nothing wrong with that.'

'I suppose …'

Cockburn's face on the television caused Rory to pause with an ice tray above his scotch glass. He reached for the remote to un-mute.

'Hey. Here's where I spent my day.'

Sigrid stepped closer to see, a Nutri-Grain packet held to her chest.

Cockburn's face was frozen on a screen behind the left shoulder of the female newsreader as she introduced the storey.

'*… it is believed that the dead man is an underworld figure who is well known to Police. Nicole Tracy reports.*'

The screen switched to Nicole Tracy holding a microphone in Sirocco Drive with the murder warehouse in the background. Beyond the blue crime scene barrier tape, officers in blue plastic coveralls were unloading cases of equipment from a van parked beside the roller door. Rory recognised the back of Cockburn's small wiry frame standing near the office door. He was in conversation with two uniform police wearing flak jackets. Nicole wore a jacket straining across her breasts to a single button.

'*The body of the dead man was discovered about ten o'clock this morning by a female real estate agent responsible for leasing the unoccupied premises. The estate agent was too distraught to speak to the media. It is believed that the dead man was bound to a chair and was brutally beaten to death. Police have not released the name of the dead man. They said he is yet to be formally identified. Police also said they will not be making the man's name known before relatives are notified. Although the police are not releasing the man's name, it is believed that he may be an underworld figure already known to them. Police have not revealed the time of death but some locals say there was activity at the premises throughout yesterday and that the murder may have been carried out during daylight.*'

The image switched to footage of the bagged body being

wheeled out on a stretcher. Nicole's voiceover continued.

'The body was removed a short while ago. Locals were shocked to learn that a man had been murdered in their midst. Perhaps, even as they went about their daily business.'

The screen switched to Spiros being interviewed in front of Sloane's Village Bakery. The quaint village logo sat atop the monster tilt-slab factory just above Spiros's right shoulder. Their cover is blown, Rory thought.

'They say there was a white van going in and out of the place yesterday. We were just doing our job you know. Just working and having a smoko and stuff like we do every day. And a man is killed right across the road.' Spiros turned and gestured to the warehouse. *'Right in there. We didn't hear nothing. We didn't see nothing. But they did it right there. How can that happen? And while we are just doing our business. This is not Sicily, you know. People here know each other. It's just bad. You know. I hope they get these pricks.'*

A quick shot to Nicole.

'Police have begun canvassing local workers who may have seen people at the building. They have also identified several CCTV sources in the street that will be reviewed. Detective Senior Sergeant Cockburn addressed the media earlier today.'

Rory noticed the barely perceptible wince as Nicole pronounced Cockburn. Cockburn's head appeared above a ruffle of microphones with a radio or TV logo attached to each.

'I can confirm that the dead body of a male person was discovered in these premises around ten o'clock this morning. It is believed that he was murdered sometime in the previous twenty-four hours. It has not been confirmed, but it appears that the person was murdered at these premises. The premises are unoccupied and are on the market for lease. A white van was seen entering the building yesterday. We would like to speak to anyone who saw the white van or saw any other vehicle or person at the building or near the building anytime during the past two days or even before. People who saw anything should contact Crime Stoppers on 1800 333 000.'

An indecipherable gaggle of questions erupted as soon as

Cockburn paused.

'*The identity of the dead male has not been confirmed at this stage.*'

Another burst of simultaneous questions came. Something about "underworld" stuck.

'*The crime may or may not have underworld connections. It is too early to tell. Police will be keeping an open mind. In the meantime, if anyone saw anything suspicious in this vicinity, or if anyone knows anything in connection with the crime, they should contact Crime Stoppers as soon as they can.*'

Nicole came on again to sum up and sign off with, '*Nicole Tracy, reporting from Thomastown.*'

Rory muted the television again.

'So *that's* Cockburn?' Sigrid said. 'I see what you mean. He hasn't even got a good head for radio. Is that what upset you?'

Rory didn't know if he was more surprised she knew he'd been upset or why she hadn't cared to ask about it before now. He decided he didn't want an answer and grinned at her dig about Cockburn.

'No. I'm well beyond being fazed by Cockburn, but now you know what I have to put up with.'

'Why do you have to put up with him? I thought your cold cases were separate. What were you doing on that job?'

Relieved that she wasn't pressing him about being upset, Rory turned his thoughts to the non-disclosure deed he had signed.

'You heard them say the body might be someone we know. He could be someone connected to an old case that Cockburn and I were on years ago. That's all. You saw … it's Cockburn's case.'

Rory felt he doth-protest-too-much. Maybe Sigrid noticed that too, but the doorbell chimed.

'Mmm. Have I been hanging out for this?' Sigrid said.

Rory handed her a tumbler of whisky and ice.

'I've ordered pizza. How does Moroccan spiced pumpkin

from Jojoes sound?' he said and sat beside her. Sigrid leant into him and threw her legs over the end on the sofa.

'I'm a traditionalist when it comes to pizza. Does it have salami?'

'Uh-oh.'

'Never mind. Spicy pumpkin should be good for me.'

Rory sought safer ground. 'Your guests seemed nice. I reckon you charmed the backside off them all.'

Sigrid sipped and savoured. 'Well that's my job. As long as I charm the backside off you too, I'm happy.'

'Mmm.'

She pulled back to look him in the face.

'That was an opening for something better than an "Mmm".'

'No. I'm glad. I mean my backside is well charmed and I'm happy for things to *stay the way they are*, as long as you like.'

He hadn't avoided using the exact words she'd said earlier.

'Are you quoting what I said when you arrived?'

'In a good way.'

'Oh yeah?' She said dubiously. 'That was just a throwaway line. You were the one wishing I lived in Melbourne.'

He didn't need to be a detective to notice that she remembered the exchange as precisely as he did.

'So your off-the-cuff response wasn't so off-the-mark?'

'Touché,' Sigrid conceded and sipped her drink.

'Is that it? Don't you want to talk about it? We've never really discussed where all this is heading you know.'

'Not unless you're *seriously* suggesting I uproot myself and move to Melbourne to live in your tiny flat … then I might have something more to say. But why spoil things?'

'That sounds like, "If it ain't broke then don't fix it".'

'That's why you're the detective, Detective.'

Sigrid held her drink away again for another kiss. Rory used his free hand to roam her body.

'Why don't you pour me another one of these and come and meet me in the bedroom?' She sculled the remaining whiskey and handed the empty tumbler to Rory.

'Do you mind if I have another one or two first?'

Sigrid was not familiar with having a sexual lead rebuffed, even slightly. Queen Victoria couldn't have struck a more un-amused look as she snapped: 'I knew something was wrong. Cockburn and a dead body in one day. You're right back to square one, aren't you?'

Square one for Sigrid happened when they began going out together. What she took as flattering old-fashioned gentlemanliness about initiating sex, or even shyness, turned out to be Rory's fear of spending a whole night with someone.

Even with regular PTSD therapy, Rory had been unable to completely shake off the nightmare and flashbacks. He eventually confided to her: "I wake up blathering all sorts of hysterical crap… and crying. I'm so lathered in sweat I have to have to have a shower there and then. It would freak you right out. It freaks me out". Sigrid took the punt without hesitation or pity. He made it through that first night without the nightmare rearing its head and, miraculously, through every subsequent night they spent together. The common ground they both seized had the power to block out all else.

Since then, the promise of a good night's sleep, as well as sex, propelled his pleasure of anticipation off the Richter scale. Nevertheless, he knew that he couldn't put *a good shag* down to being *the* magic potion. It also had a lot to do with him always being "on" when he was with Sigrid. Having a break from continually being "on" meant facing the exile of his small flat.

He was resigned to it being a respite-scarce zone. The nightmare would sense his defences dropping and could strike with a vengeance. Just as the wearer always knows where the shoe pinches, Rory could always tell when the nightmare lurked. That's when his second line of defence came into play. The vodka, benzos and the other self-medicaments he kept on hand at his bolthole. It was a life he had so far managed to keep separate. But not secret.

With so few words, Sigrid had nailed him precisely. Facing the prospect of the nightmare without a parachute of any kind was a trial too far. Rory hung his head, knowing he had to come clean. He downed the rest of his own scotch and sighed.

'It was the body in that warehouse. It had been tortured. Not the worst I've seen but bad enough. It didn't occur to me that I might not be able to handle it … and I did handle it for a good while … right up to when I was leaving the scene.' He shook his head at her to convey how hopeless that made him feel.

Her nonplussed look drew him to elaborate.

'I have to admit it shook me. I mean, what if I do get by just doing cold cases? What kind of homicide cop am I if I can't deal with a dead body?'

He might have expected her silence was intended to conveyed sensitivity but he got a straight answer instead.

'The same kind of cop that can't accept the offer of sex from an attractive woman. You decide which one you are. You know where I'll be.'

She poured her own drink and walked out of the room.

He looked at the empty doorway in a sheer muddle. Should he be angry, shocked or self-pitying at Sigrid's lack of sympathy? Or was she in denial as he'd always suspected? He followed the latter train of thought and clarity emerged from the murk: if it was denial it had worked so far. Self-absorption would have to wait. He topped up and followed her to the bedroom.

7

End of a Deadly Career
By Sylvester Strain, Staff reporter

"Graeme Stanley, rest in peace" is uttered as anything but an epitaph by the heaviest of heavyweight criminals in Melbourne's underworld. It rang out as a collective sigh of relief among Stanley's enemies and non-enemies alike when the feared gunman was brutally murdered in a Thomastown warehouse on Thursday. The notorious hardhead had non-enemies rather than friends — albeit a permanently provisional classification that any criminal with a brain knew better than to take for granted. Stanley was an enforcer among enforcers. It is they that can now "rest in peace" and close both eyes when their head hits the pillow.

Despite notoriety among the underworld as a prolific hitman, Stanley has always managed to keep a low public profile. The only time he was ever incarcerated was in his late teens in England. It is said that Stanley, a then Londoner, was convicted for his part in a Security Express heist in the suburb of Shoreditch. Upon his release in the mid-1980s, he inexplicably managed to lawfully emigrate to Australia. Those with long memories can recall a brief period he spent as a legitimate painter and decorator in Melbourne. Most only know folklore about the so-called "Football Bandits" — an alleged Stanley led gang credited with a series of violent armed robberies carried out in Melbourne during the early 1990s. The gang's name arose from its members having cloth badges of AFL football teams sewn onto their balaclavas. At one point, the police description for a robbery participant read, "Male, about 180 centimetres tall, brown eyes, St Kilda supporter".

Armed bank robberies dropped off in the ensuing decades as police introduced radical new techniques and banks increased security. Stanley responded by diversifying, and, after Christopher Dale Flannery aka "Mr Rent-A-Kill" went missing in the late eighties, Stanley recognised an opportunity to specialise. Stanley became linked to a raft of paid killings among Melbourne's underworld, including the double Neilson Scali murders. In many of those cases, Stanley's relative anonymity has been aided by a series of suppression orders forbidding the mere whispering of his name in public. Among the underworld, he is often referred to as "Michael" because of his Michael Caine-like cockney accent and his similar, but deceptively fatal, charm. Stanley was sixty-two years old.

When Inspector Richard Bourke was asked if Stanley's killing was connected to the unsolved Neilson Scali murders, he said that Police were keeping an open mind. Clifford Neilson and his partner, Corina Scali, were executed in their bed while being held in police protection ten years ago. Clifford Neilson had turned police informer to implicate serving drug squad detectives in serious drug offences. The then drug squad detective, David Dwyer, was later charged with arranging the murders, albeit on uncorroborated hearsay evidence. Those charges were later withdrawn following the murder in custody of Leon "The Fly" Blofeld. Blofeld, who was facing drugs charges at the time, agreed to give evidence against Dwyer in exchange for a lighter sentence.

Police sources revealed that at the time, Stanley was investigated as a "usual suspect" for pulling the trigger in the Neilson Scali murders. He was quickly able to be eliminated with a strong alibi supported by CCTV footage from the casino. Police nonetheless strongly suspected, but were never able to establish, a link between Stanley and Dwyer. A reward on offer for the Neilson Scali murders was increased to $1,000,000 on the tenth anniversary of the crime. Inspector Bourke confirmed that no claim has been lodged for the $1,000,000 reward.

David Dwyer, who now lives in country Victoria, said he did not want to comment.

Josh watched Martha's exhausted running style as she materialised from the box-ironbark forest and succumbed to a body-shaking halt within a couple of strides. The fat lady hadn't quite sung, however. Martha lifted a smart phone from its upper-arm pouch, gave a single tap to record the official end of the run and re-holstered the phone. Then it was time to double over, hands on knees, and regain breath. Martha felt his attention between gasps and lifted her head. Eighty metres away, Josh sat at a wicker table on the back veranda of their bush-side cottage. The already-read Sunday paper sitting under his emptied coffee cup normally initiated a reclining morning-sun-induced nap. On this occasion, he sat pensively forward with his elbows on his knees. Martha acknowledged him with a lingering look — speech required more breath than she could muster. Besides, it already looked like a conversation worth postponing.

She straightened and swiped the smart phone as she sauntered across the lawn. Distance covered, total time, average time per kilometre, comparison with average time et cetera. At the veranda edge, she lifted her left lycra-clad leg onto the deck and leant into a cool-down stretch. She sensed it was her move.

'What's up?'

'Have you seen the story in the paper?'

'No. What?'

'It's about the bloke who was bumped off in Thomastown during the week. His name is Graeme Stanley. The same

Graeme they talk about on the recording.'

'You're joking. How do you know that? Does it say?'

'He was a hitman called Graeme Stanley. It says in the article that the cops think he is connected to the Neilson Scali murders. How many hit men called "Graeme" do you know?'

Martha stood up from her stretch and looked up to Josh with hands on her hips. She finally acknowledged his annoyed tone.

'Shit,' she said. The sweat had dried to red splotches on her cheeks. 'Does it specifically mention the Neilson Scali murders? Let me see.'

Martha came up the steps for the paper.

'Page four,' Josh told her as he handed over the paper.

Martha shuffled for page four and read the article while still standing. Josh watched. She finally closed the paper and sat in the other cane chair. She knew he was leaving the ball in her court.

'They wouldn't have the full recording yet. I only posted that last Friday,' Martha thought out loud. 'My God, this has happened because of the thing in the *Government Gazette*, hasn't it?'

'Of course it fucking has, we're into this up to our eyebrows.'

Martha was startled. Josh wasn't given to histrionics, however moderate.

'Josh, it's okay. Don't panic. *We* didn't kill anyone. And no one has any way of finding out who we are. Let's just think about this.'

'I have been thinking about it. That's all I've been thinking about while you trotted around the bush. I know they're the bad guys and the recording should be given to the police, but that bloke would still be living if we hadn't mailed the recording to them. The whole bloody thing is still as corrupt as ever, isn't it? I mean, we just give one snippet to the Police and bang, a bloke we've never heard of is snuffed out. Just like that. Nothing's changed in ten years. If someone's that determined, resourceful and well connected enough to wipe out anything linking them to the crime, then how safe are we?'

'We've always known what we're dealing with. That's exactly

why we're done things the way we have. It's still a good plan. Everything is still alright,' Martha said and sat back in her chair, determined not to be panicked.

'Still alright? Doesn't it shock you or scare you, because it does me. I know I'm the one who always gets cold feet but this is way beyond cold feet. This is frost bite on every toe. Saw the buggers off.'

Martha mustered a modicum of empathy. 'Fair enough, but like I said, let's just think about this. We are safe. We haven't taken any risk with our identity. We could walk away from this now and no one will ever know where that recording came from. The whole thing will play itself out. Dwyer will eventually go down and people will write true-crime best sellers about the mystery recording. We'll read them in bed and have a laugh. So, don't panic about what has happened and what might happen because we won't ever be part of it. We will never be responsible for whatever happens. This is what we agreed to do, isn't it?

Josh crossed his arms in disinclined agreement. Martha felt safe enough to continue.

'The other thing about all this and about Graeme who-ever-he-is being killed is that that's precisely why we have to see this thing through. The police have to have that evidence. Handing that in is the right thing to do. You don't have to beat yourself up about doing nothing ever again. They have all the evidence available to them to ping Dwyer. He needs to be held accountable. This is good versus evil and you're with the good guys. You know you don't want him to get away with this. So let's just wait and see if they can convict him when they get the full recording. Don't even worry about the reward at this stage. As I keep telling you: as damning as the evidence may seem, it's no lay-down misère the way the courts work.

'The reward's the last thing I'm worried about. I'm worried about you and me.'

'Look. That recording has sat on your computer, or wherever you kept it, for ten years now. You're no less safe than any other day during those ten years. You've always known that because you know that no one knows you have it … well no one other than you and me know. If you were ever really worried you would have deleted it and you haven't. The reason you haven't deleted it is because you know what's right and wrong and what needed to be done in the end. I know it took the reward thing to bring it to fruition but I also know that's not why you didn't delete it. You're a good man who's simply doing a good thing and I wouldn't love you if you did anything differently.'

Martha breathed out with theatrical fatigue.

Josh gave a grudging half-smile. 'No wonder you're such a fucking convincing lawyer.'

8

The Graeme Stanley homicide incident meeting was late getting started. They were waiting for Inspector Richard Bourke to return from being summoned to the Chief Commissioner's office. A few detectives stood around drinking coffee and talking in the meeting space at the end of the open-plan office. Others had wandered back to their workstations to peer into computers and make phone calls. Cockburn sat at the table placed in front of two whiteboards on casters. The collection of ten-by-eight photos displayed on the whiteboard comprised an old arrest shot of an unsmiling Graeme Stanley, one of his dead body duct-taped to a chair in the warehouse, another one of the warehouse exterior, and a stock internet image of a white, high-roofed Mercedes Benz van.

Cockburn was studying a document that a young female detective with red hair had placed on the table in front of him. She was leaning over his shoulder to point to things in the document.

Cockburn sensed Rory arrive and lean against a low screen that separated the workstations from the meeting space. He held Rory's eye for an extra moment to acknowledge his arrival without interrupting the red-headed detective. A couple of other detectives gave Rory a nod or quick hello.

Hamish Lynott entered by the stairwell door near Rory and looked headed to the other end of the floor. Hamish was the civilian manager of the Commercial and Electronic Branch that occupied the whole of the next floor down, apart from Rory's office. The one-man Cold Case Unit was the sole operational presence on the Commercial and Electronic Branch floor. During his six months back on the job, Rory and Hamish had struck up an affable tea-room connection. On Rory's worst days, hearing Hamish espouse his incisive views on how modern life worked was oxygen itself.

Hamish was by far the sharpest knife in the drawer, at least as far as civilian employees at the St Kilda Road police complex went. Rory was often left wondering how long the organisation would be able to hold on to him. Hamish defied every boffin-cliché to become the IT manager in his early thirties. His fitted shirts and fitted suits without pleats in the trousers were otherwise unknown in the building. He would have succeeded on looks alone.

'What are you doing up here?' Rory asked.

'Taking Bourke's PC off-line again. You guys must have something super-hot happening.'

'I wouldn't say it too loud,' Rory said. He cast his eyes around furtively to demonstrate that the information was not common knowledge within the branch. Hamish winked and negotiated the workstation labyrinth to Bourke's office.

It sounds like Bourke has the full version of the David Dwyer recording, Rory concluded to himself.

Bourke was a further five minutes.

'Let's get this show back on the road,' he announced to the world when he emerged from the lift and made his way to the briefing end of the floor. He sat beside Cockburn and slapped a manila folder on the table, then cast an eye among the detectives making their way back from their workstations.

'Is Rory James here?' he said and at the same time spied Rory. 'I want to see you and Gary in my office after this briefing.'

Rory nodded across the room.

'Have we got everyone?' he asked Cockburn. Cockburn lifted his eyes to the assembled throng.

'Good, let's get started,' Bourke said before Cockburn could begin his assessment.

'I've seen the news reports and I've read the Sunday paper. Now tell me what's really happening.'

'Okay,' Cockburn paused for a moment as he leant on his forearms to glance at the notes laid out in front of him.

'The body's been identified, so we can officially confirm it's Graeme Stanley.'

'I read that in yesterday's paper, for God's sake. Who identified him?'

'His brother flew across from Perth. As far as we know he's a straight tradesman. He owns an established painting and decorating business,' Cockburn said. 'But what's more interesting is: Graeme Stanley died of a heart attack.'

'What?'

'We just got some preliminary post mortem stuff this morning. It appears that whoever was roughing him up didn't get far, because it brought on a heart attack.'

'Well I'll be buggered,' Bourke said, crossing his arms and sitting back in his chair. 'A heart attack. How old was he?'

Cockburn consulted his notes. 'Uhh, sixty-two. His brother says his ticker's been crook for a year or so.'

'Hmm.' Bourke looked pensive in the way that a sixty-two-year-old man does when he hears that another sixty-two-year-old man dies of a heart attack. Cockburn knew better than to interrupt the thought.

'Okay. So that gives whoever did this the opportunity to plead manslaughter, or even GBH. Kidnapping too, of course. They could argue they never intended to kill him.'

'That's if we find whoever did this,' Cockburn reminded him.

'Too true, Gary. Keep going. What else have you got?'

Cockburn dropped his eyes to his notes. 'He died around

two o'clock the previous day. That's Tuesday afternoon. So it was a pretty brazen affair. They could have been sprung by the real estate people who are dealing with leasing of the building. Maybe by the building owners or even a nosy neighbour. Or maybe they had some intel on all that because there was no break-in. Someone used a key or picked the lock and then went to the trouble of re-locking it. Nothing's come up yet but we're working on it.'

He looked down to his notes again.

'According to a couple of witnesses and at least one CCTV camera, they arrived at eleven-oh-nine. Came in a current model white, high-roofed Mercedes van, the same as the one up here.' He gestured to the picture on the white board. 'It even had personalised number plates — MYLOLA1. Stolen plates, of course. Its windows are tinted, so neither witness saw the driver. Same result on the one CCTV image we have. We're looking for other CCTV but most businesses turn it off through the day. Usually they're only worried about what happens when they're not there. They switch it on before they head home.

'The security company checked the perimeter doors that night, apparently while the body was inside. They literally left their calling cards. The van left at two-twenty-two on Tuesday afternoon.'

'What about word among his acquaintances? What's Stanley been up to lately? What about the MO? What does that tell us?' Bourke asked.

'Nothing distinctive or sophisticated about the MO,' Cockburn said. 'Julia's been working on intel. Can you give us an update?'

Cockburn looked over his shoulder to the detective with crinkled, red hair.

'It couldn't be quieter on the Graeme Stanley front. It's like he'd retired. In fact, we even found a Seniors Card in his wallet. He spends most of his time at his holiday house on Phillip Island — Ventnor. His latest partner hadn't missed him yet, He left the island that morning, on Tuesday, to do business in Melbourne. She thought he might be away for a night or two. Nothing out of the ordinary as far as she was concerned, although she was worried he hadn't phoned. She doesn't know what business he was attending to but she knows better than to know what business he attends to. We're chasing up his phone records and his car's gone missing. That's it for now.'

Julia finished with an apologetic grimace.

'So what are the chances of seeing that van again?' Bourke asked Cockburn.

'We've put out a description and asked people to call crime stoppers …'

'I'm not the bloody *Herald-Sun*, Gary, what are the chances?'

'Fuck all, to be honest. My guess is its back in service somewhere with its regular plates on. No Mercedes vans have been reported stolen and there's nothing distinctive about it … although it did leave clear tyre prints on the concrete in the warehouse. Good enough for a match if we did locate the right van.'

'The story that Sylvester Strain did in the Sunday paper. Do you reckon he knows anything? At least check the sources he normally plugs into within the Force.'

'He's just pissing in the wind. He's been trotting out Neilson Scali conspiracy theories for years. It was just a rehash.'

'Well he's gonna keep rehashing like he *does* know something we don't until we do actually know something. This underworld-on-underworld stuff is grist for the media mill and I want it to stop with this investigation.' Annoyance crept into Bourke's voice. 'They may as well have leased the place and hung up their shingle, "Murders R Us, hours of business, 9.00am to 5.00pm".'

Silence fell. Bourke slammed his folder shut and stood. The briefing was being unexpectedly truncated. Detectives looked questioningly at each other. Bourke sensed the collective curiosity for justification and snapped.

'I don't want to read any more theories in the newspapers,

okay? I want to hear what is actually happening and I want to hear it from the people in this room. I want the people in this room going down every rabbit hole there is and then going down those rabbit holes again. And when you've finished doing that I want you to find more rabbit holes to go down. You're professionally trained investigators, so let's see some professional investigation results on this.'

Bourke picked up his folder and strode through the workspace to his office.'

Cockburn and Rory entered Bourke's office at the same time and closed the door. Bourke was leaning under his workstation to install a USB memory stick into the computer case.

'What was that about?' Cockburn asked.

'I didn't want to waste their time. The full version of the recording came in this morning. We need to arrest Dwyer. Then we can put everything on the table and let the rest of the team know what's going on.'

Bourke was looking at his screen and navigating by mouse as he spoke. Rory and Cockburn's questions were stifled by Bourke's haste to play the recording. They sat down in the two seats in front of Bourke's workstation and waited.

'Okay, here it is …' Bourke clicked the mouse and sat back. It began with the unrecognised voice.

'So you came in person?'

No answer came and the same unrecognised voice said,

'Against the tree okay?'

A longer pause followed with the sound of low level activity in the background. Dwyer's voice entered the aural landscape.

'Okay.' Dwyer's voice said.

The striking of a cigarette lighter sounded before Dwyer's voice continued.

'To answer your question, I'm not actually here in person, I'm attending

a two-day live-in training session as we speak. Witnesses from inside and outside of the Force. My presence formally recorded in the minutes.'

'Then you'd better make sure it's your handwriting chalking up KPI's on the butchers' paper.'

'Are you being a smartarse?'

'I've come to this over-rated mosquito-ridden puddle. Are we on or not?'

'It's the best tadpoling spot you'll ever have the pleasure of gracing.'

'Not if I had a choice, Harry Butler, and I don't reckon I'd be on me pat. Fuckin' waste of money locking this place up like Pentridge. Speaking of which, did you bring it?'

'There's seventy-five grand.'

'And the rest?'

'Upon delivery, of course.'

'How?'

'You'll get it. Don't worry.'

'I mean the job. Where and when?'

'Nineteen Scott Street, Balwyn, two in the morning, Tuesday week. There'll be an unplanned ten-minute gap when the surveillance teams change shift. That's as long as I can manage without anyone getting suss.'

'Is all that written down and in the envelope?'

'Only the money's in the envelope.'

'Then how the fuck do you expect me to remember all that shit? Have you got a pen?'

'Just remember that Bon Scott drank himself to death on the nineteenth of February. Scott … nineteen … oh-two. Get it?'

Cockburn and Rory exchanged the same frank look of surprise.

'I wouldn't've picked you for a head banger … and that makes two things I have to remember.'

'I'm not saying it again. Google it if you need to and while you're at it, Google the house. It was on the market last year and the real estate ad still comes up — complete with a room-layout plan and pics.'

'Okay then …. 'Why so quick? You're giving me fuck-all time for research and planning.'

'You get plans for the house. That's a pretty good head start that you don't want to waste. Besides, it'll be useless in two weeks because he's being moved on. We can't be too careful, you know.'

The next bits of dialogue were punctuated with gaps and the sound of movement.

'It's a frog you dickhead … and what the fuck's this?'

'You think I'm going to hand over seventy-five grand to someone I've never met, in the middle of nowhere, without taking precautions?'

'Then I suggest you don't leave the safety on next time.'

Bourke paused the recording.

'I don't know what that was about but it sounds like Dwyer pulled a gun.'

He held up his non-mouse hand to repress any comment from Rory and Cockburn and pressed Play again. The recording continued to the final antagonistic exchange between Dwyer and the unknown other voice.

'Just fuckin' do the thing. Okay?'

'Nineteen Bon Scott Street Balwyn, Tuesday week. Got it.'

'It's not Bon Scott Street, it's just Scott Stree …'

The computer paused itself.

Bourke laced his fingers on his stomach. 'Thoughts?'

Cockburn jumped in.

'No love lost there but who gives a fuck. Dwyer delivered up on a platter. And someone's been sitting on this for ten years. Do you reckon they were hanging out for the reward?'

Bourke allowed himself a smile and swivelled slightly from side to side in his office chair, still with his fingers laced on his stomach.

'On the face of it, I reckon Jackie Gleason would agree with you, Gary. "How sweet it is!"'

'Jackie who?'

'Never mind, what do you think, Rory?'

'Funny you should mention Jackie Gleason; did you pick up on the retro references they mentioned on tape? That could help narrow down the era it was recorded in.'

'What references?

'Pentridge and Harry Butler. I mean Pentridge prison has been out of action for the best part of twenty years … and who remembers Harry Butler? Wasn't he a wildlife guru on black and white TV? The stone-age version of Steve Irwin? You'd have to go back at least ten years to find his name rolling off anybody's lips.'

'Or go to a nursing home.' Cockburn couldn't resist.

Bourke shook his head. 'You shit-stirring ignoramuses. Don't tell me you didn't see his show as kids … and on colour TV. Which by the way, had been around for yonks before Harry made Australian of the Year in … what … 1980? And it wasn't that many years ago that they named him a National Living Treasure. Jeez.'

Cockburn shook his head with a satisfied smirk and Rory continued.

'I presume the "Graeme" they are talking about is Graeme Stanley and that's why the *Government Gazette* was left at the scene. It sounds like Graeme Stanley sub-contracted the job and he's the first place Dwyer went looking when he got a whiff that this recording existed.'

'No "sounds like it" about it. Stanley or the subcontractor, or both of them, must have recorded this exchange as some form of insurance.' Cockburn said.

'But if that was the case, they'd risk incriminating themselves if they used it to claim the reward without seeking immunity or leniency — which doesn't crack a mention in the request from FP1. An even greater risk they'd face is that Dwyer would name names to take them down with him. Or that he'd simply take care of business, which is what seems to be what happened already with Graeme Stanley. My guess is the recording is in the hands of someone else. Someone who has been living with the dilemma of becoming a witness in the murder of a witness. I think you're right about one thing Gary: the reward seems to have done its job.'

Cockburn gave a smug nod. Rory continued.

'The other thing is: I don't reckon Dwyer knew about this recording until FP1 sent it in. There's no way Dwyer would have recorded it himself. It wouldn't serve him any purpose. Its mere existence would be dynamite waiting to explode.

'To me, that stuff at the beginning of the recoding sounds like Dwyer is making sure the hitman isn't wearing a wire. That means the hitman got there ahead of time to bug the place or, like I said, someone else has somehow got in on the act.'

Bourke stroked his chin for a long moment before speaking.

'All of that's right and the worst thing for us is that Dwyer is still dangerous. The fact that he found out about the recording in the first place means we probably still have an internal security problem. What he might not know is what is actually on the full version of the recording. The longer we wait, the greater the chance he'll find out and we'll have more shit to deal with.'

Bourke turned to Cockburn.

'I want you to arrange his arrest and bring him in right away, Gary.'

'My pleasure.'

Bourke switched his attention to Rory. 'I know what you're thinking, Rory, but the end is more important in this case. You can start by analysing the recording. There's umpteen leads to follow up in there. Forget about Harry Butler, the training course Dwyer says he's supposed to be attending should give us an actual date. They mention a tree and frogs, so the recording took place somewhere outdoors, and it's a secure "locked up" area. Dwyer also mentions passports and the hitman has a pommy accent. We might be looking for an overseas operator, which makes sense. Graeme Stanley wouldn't outsource to anyone local — that would mean giving a leg-up to his competition. Even the Bon Scott thing. I agree with the hitman. Dwyer doesn't seem like the AC/DC type but someone in his circle could be. Follow it all up and start getting advice about how this thing will stack up in court.'

'Okay boss, but the way I see things at this stage is: We won't have a problem proving one of the voices is Dwyer. And to my ear, the tape doesn't appear to be tampered with. I'll get that checked out. But that will still give us fuck-all to use as court evidence. No matter how compelling the full recording sounds, we still need provenance that nails where, when and who he was speaking to.

'Right now, the only person who can authenticate it is Dwyer … like that's gonna happen. If it did get to court, you'd expect his counsel to question whether it was properly obtained in accordance with the Surveillance Devices Act. He'll claim his privacy was illegally invaded under the Privacy Act. How many admissibility hurdles do you need? I'm sure the Director of Public Prosecutions could come up with a few more.'

Bourke was way ahead of him.

'All of the above. That's why I was late for the briefing this morning. We were on a conference call to the DPP's office. If the recording is destined to fall over, the Chief Commissioner wants that decision to be on the head of a judge or jury. The public would eat us alive if this didn't get tested in court and the recording later showed up on *YouTube* or a transcript in the *Herald Sun.*'

Neither Rory nor Cockburn argued.

'Well that's it. You get onto the arrest, Gary. You can tell whoever you need to involve in the paperwork and whoever you take on the arrest team. Brief the rest of the branch once he's in custody. Rory, you start looking at the evidence and find someone who can read body language. Get someone good and I don't care how much it costs.'

Rory and Cockburn's faces said: *Why?* Bourke obliged.

'My gut feeling is that when you and I play this recording to Dwyer, Gary, he'll be re-hearing the conversation for the first time since he actually spoke those words ten years ago. I also reckon that until FP1 came out of the woodwork, Dwyer had no idea that conversation was ever recorded. I would love to have sprung it on him without him having got wind of its existence but thanks to the leak, we know we've lost the element of surprise. That means Dwyer will be wearing his best poker face. I can picture it now.'

He paused to view his mental image.

'All the same, I think the reality of re-hearing it will still have an impact. The absolute un-deniability and the consequences of the recording are sure to hit home on some level. I guarantee he won't say much, so understanding his non-verbal response is vital. And it has to be done professionally. Dwyer's calculated reaction will mask anything that experienced judges of liars like you or I can pick up.

'At the very least, it will give us an additional credible strand of argument to support the genuineness of the recording. A bonus would be somehow unlocking who recorded it, who FP1 is, and why it has taken this long to surface.'

It wasn't up for discussion and Bourke wound up the meeting.

'We'll have a full team meeting first thing in the morning for a proper briefing and planning session.'

9

Rory watched travellers on Flight 200 from Sydney descend the escalator to the baggage carousels and exits at Melbourne's Tullamarine Airport. The first wave appeared to be energised rather than wearied by the one-and-a-half-hour flight. Its posse leaders took the escalators two steps at a time while speaking into surgically attached smartphone earbud/microphone sets. The devices allowed them to resume their breakneck lives without being impaired by carrying what little carry-on luggage they toted.

Those with check-in luggage to retrieve indulged in the full escalator ride, albeit so they could text with two hands while they rested cabin luggage at their feet. Rory wondered if a collective noun had yet been coined for a group of smartphone users. A *gossip* perhaps, or was that already assigned to some bird species?

It was too late when Rory noticed Tony Elmer, the head of the Property Crime Squad, among the travellers. Tony had already spotted Rory and his path was leading him through the cluster of sign-holding limousine drivers by the sliding door exit. Rory groaned inside. All he could do was keep holding the sign, "Calvin Steele", and cop it.

'Hi Rory, what are you doing being a driver? I thought you came back to the Force.'

Tony said it with genuine curiosity. Rory decided that digging his way out might sound worse than it looked.

'I did come back. This is work,' he answered and looked past Tony for Calvin Steele.

'Who's Calvin Steele then?'

He didn't want to tell Tony that Calvin Steele was a body-language expert.

'A consultant.'

'Oh …' Tony tried to digest the information. 'For a cold case?'

'Cold-ish.'

Rory's filibustering created more silence. Tony took another look at Rory's limousine-driver sign-holding pose.

'RORY?'

The loud town-crier size voice of Calvin Steele stumped both Rory and Tony. The tall Californian let go of the telescopic handle of his wheelie-case and extended his hand. Rory's hand went into automatic pilot for Calvin to pump. Rory's voice took a moment to catch up. Calvin still wore his morning television-appearance garb, a lighter-than-charcoal bespoke wool / silk blend suit. Enthusiasm radiated from what were otherwise unremarkable middle-aged features. Only slightly more handsome than not, shortish greying hair and a faint natural tan. Not so unremarkable, and not noticeable in his television appearances, was the way Calvin's incisive grey eyes locked on.

'Pleased to meet you,' Rory said. '… err, this is Detective Sergeant Tony Elmer. It appears he arrived on the same flight as you.'

'How do you do, Tony? So you've been in Sydney too?'

'I have …' Tony answered, still taking it all in.

'And are you with Homicide too?'

'No. The Property Crime Squad. Me and Rory work out of the same building, though.'

'Ohhhhh, I see. I see …' He looked at Rory and back to Tony. 'Well I suppose you want to get going, Rory.'

'Yeah. We'd better. I'm parked out the front and they don't

like the Police taking up their pick-up spaces. I'll see you back at the office, Tony.'

Tullamarine airport is on the northern outskirts of Melbourne. Rory and Calvin were quickly among thistle-dotted farm paddocks as they drove through Bulla and Diggers Rest along the back road to the Bendigo-bound freeway.

David Dwyer lived on a hobby farm between Castlemaine and Bendigo. Upon his arrest, he had been taken to Bendigo Police station for questioning. The questioning was deferred until late the following morning because Dwyer's Melbourne-based lawyer was in court for the rest of the day.

The delay was fortuitous in that Calvin Steele had flown to Sydney the day before to appear on a breakfast television talk show. Rory arranged to collect him from the airport that afternoon and take him to Bendigo. They would both stay in Bendigo that night. "Yes", he had told Calvin Steele, he did know somewhere good to stay in Bendigo. 'A friend of mine runs a historic B&B that I think you'll like.'

It was an offer he could not avoid making but as soon as Sigrid told him there were no other guests that night, he rued the lost opportunity of an undistracted evening together. It was sorely needed after the tribulations of his previous stay when he was still reeling from seeing Graeme Stanley's tortured body. After eventually having sex, Sigrid woke to find Rory had retired to the couch in fear of having his PTSD nightmare. The fact that the nightmare never happened was no consolation to either of them. Sigrid rebuffed all his efforts to explain by continually pandering to her B&B clients. The most he got from her during the rest of the weekend was: "I'm not your counsellor, you sort it out". He was still feeling unsettled by her indifference.

On the drive from Tullamarine to Bendigo, it was apparent that every stray moment would be filled with actual aural language rather than body language — Calvin Steele was a talking machine. On first encounter, a brash American, or a normal American, depending on which side of the Pacific Ocean you were born. Or perhaps it was simply the sound of a showman without a pause button. Rory had watched his performance on the morning talk show. His melodramatic demonstrations of politicians saying one thing and meaning another were both convincing and riveting.

Rory nevertheless decided that Calvin's on-screen tone was not much different to motivational speakers, performing memory artists or even illusionists. He didn't regard himself as a body-language sceptic, but he recognised a not dissimilar line of finely tuned people-reading skills that could be utilised to dazzle audiences of all dispositions. And like Calvin, they all had a book to sell.

'You didn't want Tony to know who I was, did you?' Calvin drawled.

'I just bumped into him. This is not something we would share outside our own branch.'

'But he asked you and you obfuscated? That's why I got us outta there.'

'I suppose I *was* obfuscating. So thanks.'

'No problem.'

Calvin allowed an uncharacteristic silence and waited.

'That's a neat party trick,' Rory finally said on cue.

'Ha ha ha ha ha ha ha … Everyone reads body-language, Rory: that unspoken ninety-three percent of face-to-face communication that Professor Albert Mehrabian discovered can reveal if someone is telling the truth. Most people don't consciously register the host of micro-expressions and unobtrusive gestures that accompany speech. That leaves them to explain their conclusions as intuition, instinct, or say, "they can just tell". However, a gifted few can perceive and comprehend the non-verbal as clearly as the verbal. The art becomes a science when you can pinpoint, record and explain every non-verbal manifestation registered by the brain's subconscious. And that's what you pay me for. I'll be giving you a detailed written report that interprets all the body-language accompanying your suspect's interview. You can replay the interview video and confirm every one of the indicators I describe. With modern one-thousand-frames per second video you'll even be able to isolate the quickest of micro-expressions on pause. Sooner or later, this will become irrefutable evidence in courtrooms.

'Of course, some people who process natural body-language skills don't know how to articulate it, but they still make damn good professional poker players or even clairvoyants. I prefer to use my talent for good. Dogs are excellent exponents of body language as well. Ha ha ha ha ha.'

Okay. Lock me in as a non-sceptic, Rory concluded to himself and said: 'That sounds like a well-practiced answer.'

'Not really, Rory. To tell you the truth, most of my work is in the corporate field. What I do lends itself to things like leadership development, executive coaching, performance management, stuff like that. That's where the real money is. I don't get as much police stuff in Australia as I did in the US. This has got my juices flowing again. Tell me about your suspect.'

Rory felt his hands untighten on the steering wheel at the prospect of a break from Calvin talking. Having already learnt that Calvin was a fairly recent Australian resident, Rory spent more than a few kilometres detailing the long history of David Dwyer and the Neilsen Scali case. Calvin was a good listener, readily throwing in enthusiastic "wows" and "incredibles" that infused Rory's account with heightened drama. His zeal ratcheted a couple of notches when Rory reached current developments: the anonymous recording, and the specific task at hand.

'That's fabulous, Rory, especially if the recording is new to him. This has the potential to become a textbook study.

"The Dwyer body-language case" will be like a precedent is in common law.'

Rory felt his hands tighten on the wheel again.

'Hang on. Let's not get ahead of the game. You need to treat your involvement as sub-judice. And who's to say how he will react and if it does tell us something.'

'Of course, Rory. I'm a professional. No need to panic.'

Rory turned to Calvin longer than he should have his eyes off the road.

'Sorry, Rory. You'll have to excuse my enthusiasm. I *do* get ahead of myself, but with good reason you'll have to agree. Interviews like the one we're about to do with David Dwyer have a habit of turning up in the public domain, especially if they are used in court. That's when the pay-off comes for me. I make a large part of my living as a public figure, so I like to maximise every high-profile thing I'm involved in. It's a natural instinct I have to hone in and latch onto that stuff. But I'll only exploit it if or when it does end up on YouTube. Rest assured, Rory.'

The sound of tyres humming on bitumen filled the car, but not for long. Dialogue and Calvin's practiced charm resumed by the time the freeway by-passed the next town of Woodend. He proved conversant and politely opinionated on anything and everything and saved the best till last. They were at the head of the queue when a red light halted Rory on the outskirts of Bendigo's CBD. Hungry Jack's stood on one side of the cross street. On the opposite corner was Bendigo's answer to Melbourne's Federation Square — an outrageously modern architectural fabrication that people either loved or hated.

'That's Bendigo Police station where we'll be interviewing Dwyer in the morning,' Rory pointed out.

'That's a police station. No way!'

It was a building never intended to be a humdrum addition to the Bendigo skyline. The architects were given carte blanche to create something noticeable on an iconic corner site safely distant from Bendigo's historic architectural heart. With no imperative to blend in, the architect cut loose with an explosive origami of angled glass and aluminium.

Rory resisted answering Yes way. 'Not bad, is it?' he said, sensing Calvin's approval.

'Not bad? It's wild, Rory. Absolutely wild! Ha ha ha ha ha. I've never seen a police station like that before. But if it was going to happen anywhere it would be in Australia, right? After all, you did come up with the Sydney Opera House. It's outrageous. I'm gonna take a picture of that …'

Calvin's astonished admiration lasted all the way to The Manse B&B. His gusto for new architecture was only exceeded by enthusiasm for old architecture. The Manse set him alight again.

'Boy, does this ever get my juices flowing, Sigrid. I used to live in a Victorian home in San Francisco. Not quite this noble but splendid in its own way … and special to me of course. You know, the gold-rush era kicked off in San Francisco, only a year or so before the phenomenon hit Australian. So there's plenty of boomtown architecture still standing there too. They do tours. You'd love it Sigrid, have you ever been?'

'I've been to America but not San Francisco.'

Sigrid, Calvin and Rory had only reached the entrance hallway, all three standing between the grand stairway and the opened double-door entrance to the parlour.

'The styles are similar. All this Edwardian and Queen Anne stuff. Not so many wrap around gardens as you have here in Bendigo, however. Of course California has the giant redwoods, so most are timber rather than brick. You should see the paint jobs, Sigrid. They call them the "Painted Ladies".'

'Excuse me. I need to see this.'

The television in the parlour had caught Rory's ear. It was the funeral of Graeme Stanley. Rory was surprised that it had made the nightly news bulletins. Stanley had managed to remain a relative unknown in the public eye, even during the gangland war when he was thought to be most active. The funeral appeared to be a small and private affair. None of Stanley's celebrity criminal clients turned up to grieve his loss and the casket was no gold-plated affair like Carl Williams'. The few males in attendance were all pall bearers. It was left to their female partners — some showing ample cleavage in their black attire — to launch into a tirade of "bleeped" swearwords directed at cameramen.

Rory stepped closer to the screen but did not recognise any of the pallbearers.

'... *was attended by a small group of family and friends,*' the newsreader confirmed.

'*A police spokesperson said that they are pursuing their inquiries but have not identified any suspects at this stage. The spokesman also said that today's arrest of former drug squad detective, David Dwyer, was not in relation to the murder of Graeme Stanley. It is understood that Graeme Stanley's body will be cremated. Nicole Tracy reporting from St Bernadette's Altona.*'

'Sorry about that. I didn't mean to bring my work home. I'll turn it off if you like.'

'The second time in a week. It's becoming a habit.' Sigrid said.

Calvin joined Rory and Sigrid in a stroll from The Manse to the Boundary Hotel for an evening meal. Only the building's missing front yard and the obligatory Carlton Draught sign distinguished the hotel from the surrounding residential neighbourhood on Hustler's Hill. For Rory it also had sentimental appeal as the first place he ate out with Sigrid.

Calvin reloaded the charm when he met Sigrid, and whenever he met anyone new, Rory was soon to learn. Sigrid held Rory's arm but was nonetheless a natural in attracting the attention of both men. Rory noticed. Calvin's easy company somehow made the episode feel like lifelong friends enjoying a breezy chance reunion. Rory realised he and Sigrid had not acquired friends to speak of and quickly moved on in his mind to savour the experience. Perhaps that's something our relationship needs, he wondered.

The pub's décor of gold-rush memorabilia brought on another enthusiastic monologue of praise from Calvin. A local remembered Rory from his upbringing in Bendigo but it was Calvin who quickly became pub favourite. A knowledgeable local was soon leading Calvin on a guided tour of each artefact and photo. Rory and Sigrid watched, and not without a smidgeon of pride despite the hint of him being a *know-all*.

Back at The Manse, nightcaps were taken in the parlour. Calvin was in full flight about work he'd done with the FBI as well as the Los Angeles and San Francisco police departments when he spotted the undeniable body language of Rory and Sigrid. He made a gracious exit.

Their impatient lovemaking was more frenzy than feeling. For Rory it evoked making-up sex — although they hadn't fought, they were nevertheless intent on putting the unsaid behind them. They soon fell apart to study the draped ceiling of Sigrid's four-poster bed.

Rory turned his head first. Sigrid turned her head and smiled back at him. Her breast glowed in the amber light of the lampshade.

'One of us should say something,' Rory whispered.

'Don't break the spell,' she told him.

'Hmm,' he half hummed, half breathed contentedly.

The afterglow lingered until Sigrid said out loud, 'I should arrange a few more murders in Bendigo.'

Rory recalled their previous edgy weekend. 'Be careful what you wish for,' he reminded her.

Sigrid rolled on her side to face him front on and brushed his face.

'Are you staying on until the weekend?'

'If only. This case is live. It'll be full-on for a while. And I need to get back for a meeting with an ex-Homicide woman doing a book on PTSD. I've already had to cancel once.'

Sigrid propped on her elbow.

'What Homicide woman … and what makes her such an authority on the subject?'

Don't break the spell indeed. How did I end up here? Rory asked himself.

'Her name's Michelle Fox-Jones and as far as PTSD goes …'

'Michelle *Fox* Jones? Is that her real name or has she turned porn star?'

Rory turned his gaze back to the four-poster canopy and laughed. 'This is not coming out right, is it?'

Sigrid was less amused. More like not amused. 'You're telling me.'

'Okay,' Rory kept his eyes on the canopy. 'That's her real name. She was diagnosed with PTSD last year and went out on sick leave. Now she's an expert with a Facebook page and a book in the pipeline.'

'Did she kill someone too?'

'No. Well not that I know about. But we haven't caught up yet. She was probably affected by grisly murders, car crashes, sieges, who knows? I haven't even looked at her Facebook page …' Rory turned his head from the four-poster canopy to face Sigrid again. 'Look, can we do this another time? I can't think of a worse post-coital conversation. Two minutes ago it was, *don't break the spell.*'

'Post-coital, is that what this is? Yeah. Okay. Sorry,' she trailed off and continued to look at him curiously with her head still propped on her palm.

'So why do you want to meet her?'

'I don't want to meet her,' he laboured. 'She asked Command if *she* could see *me* and they agreed. They want me to be their success story. I'm the one who recovered. I'm the one who came back.'

'What does she look like?'

Rory grabbed her and frustratingly nuzzled her breasts and stomach with his face. 'Grrrrrrrrrrrrrrr.'

10

'I thought we'd have the two-way mirror thing,' Calvin said to Rory.

They were seated in a meeting room at Bendigo police station with two large flat screen monitors mounted on the wall. The screens showed separate views of the same small interview room where Dwyer would be interviewed. The interview room was empty. Rory and Calvin came early so that Calvin could hear the recording prior to the interview. He didn't want to be distracted by its content once the interview was underway.

'We don't have the two-way mirror thing here. This is how we do it these days. The picture is high definition, though. Is that okay?'

Calvin rose to look closer at the screen. 'Umm … I don't think it will be as good as seeing it in the flesh. Can you go in there, sit where Dwyer will be sitting and I'll check?'

'Okay. Just hang on. I might take a moment, it's a secured area.'

A few minutes later Rory appeared on the screen and sat at the small four-seater table in the suspect-interview room.

'You should be able to hear me but I can't hear you, so I hope you're watching.'

He nevertheless paused for the answer before explaining who would be sitting where and progressively occupied each of those seats and gesticulated to the camera.

'Okay? I'm coming back now.'

Cockburn and Richard Bourke had arrived by the time Rory

came back to the meeting room.

'I was gonna say don't give up your day job, but your piss-week acting might be an improvement,' was Cockburn's greeting.

The smile cum sneer was wiped off his face in an instant. Before Cockburn or anyone else realised what was happening, Rory had him pinned to the wall with a fistful of lapel in each hand.

'You never let up do you, you stunted little piss-ant? You can't act like a half-decent cop yourself so don't start passing fucking judgement on me,' he hissed.

Cockburn was stupefied silent. Only Rory's shaking breath sounded as they froze nose to nose. Had Rory been a crim he would have been halfway to the floor with Cockburn pummelling into him hard, but the shock of such an absurd un-Rory-like outburst had struck Cockburn dumb. Bourke too; and now Rory himself.

Calvin looked on perplexed.

'Hey …' he said, to break the silence, but couldn't find more to say.

'That's enough,' Bourke said glaring at Rory. 'What the fuck do you think this is?'

He paused for a further moment, still getting his head around the situation. 'Have you forgotten what the job at hand is exactly? And you act like this in front of an invited guest?'

'It never happened,' Calvin quickly offered.

'Fucking sensitive little flower.' Cockburn said as Rory released his lapels.

'And don't you start up again,' Bourke snapped.

'Sorry … I ….' Rory's voice was still shaking.

'Save it. We're got our most-wanted in there. Probably the most wanted of our generation and we've got a job to get on with. The last thing we need right now … the very last thing … is shit like this. Get your minds on the job and show me some professionalism. Both of you … unless you want to walk through that door right now and not come back.' He threw an arm towards the meeting room door.

Rory knew it was no idle threat, at least not as far as it

concerned him. He also knew the PTSD symptom by name and by personal experience — "irrational outbursts". He thought that was something he'd left safely behind during his lengthy recovery-sabbatical, and now it shows up out of the blue as a worst-case scenario, rearing its head at work. He felt as scared as he did ashamed. He managed to nod a chastened okay to Bourke and began the breathing technique he'd been taught for just such occasions.

'Alright,' Bourke barked to let everyone know order was being restored to resume the task at hand. 'Alright,' he repeated less intensely and scanned all three faces to emphasise the point.

With due attention being paid all round, the inspector examined the floor to recall exactly where things were at before the distraction erupted. Normal-speak kicked back in as soon as Bourke lifted his head and spoke to Rory.

'Gary and I have already introduced ourselves to Calvin. He reckons the video screen will be okay. Maybe not as good as seeing the real thing, but wholly adequate for the exercise. Have I got that right, Calvin?'

Calvin noted the dominating rhetorical tone.

'That's about the strength of it, Richard. What I really need to do now is hear the tape before the interview. To be able to concentrate on David Dwyer and not be distracted by what's on the recording.'

'We were about to do that,' Rory said.

Calvin turned to Cockburn. 'What I'd like you to do, Gary, is get Dwyer in the interview room at least five minutes before you start, let me get a good look at where he's at before you spring the tape on him. Is that something you can do please?'

The request brought a smile to Cockburn's face.

'Only five minutes. My personal policy is to make 'em wait fifteen minutes minimum.'

'How was he when you arrested him?' Rory jumped in as a subject changer.

'Arrogant. No trouble, but arrogant. *This is shit. You lot are gonna come out of this looking so fucking stupid.* That sort of thing.'

'The copper looking after the cells told me he's seething,' Rory said.

Bourke took over. 'Okay, you two. That's why we're got Calvin here. Roll the tape for Calvin, Rory. I'll go and see if his lawyer is here. He's using Ramsay Braden. Braden's already been trying to shut the whole thing down.' He turned to Cockburn. 'You get them organised to have Dwyer in there at eleven-thirty.'

Cockburn nodded and left the room.

'Righto,' Calvin said, and in the process, mangled the Australianism with his Californian accent.

'I won't take notes while it's happening; that will only distract me. I'll document it later using the replay,' Calvin said.

He and Rory sat either side of the table at the end closest to the dual video screens. Calvin nevertheless had a pad and pen in front of him.

'Sure,' Rory answered.

Movement flicked onto the screen as a uniform policeman ushered Dwyer and his lawyer, Ramsay Braden, into the room. The door clunked behind them and they both looked up to the camera.

'Good morning, ladies and gentlemen,' Braden said conceitedly into the camera.

'Don't worry about that,' Calvin said to Rory. 'It's important that we see Dwyer in this pre-interview mode.'

Dwyer wore a beige jacket that bulged over a white shirt without a tie. The slimmer Braden took off his dark suit jacket and draped it on the back of his chair. He unzipped a thin leather satchel, removed a legal pad and wrote some heading details. He reached into his satchel for the morning's *Herald-Sun* newspaper, and handed it to Dwyer.

'Here, read this while they play this petty waiting and watching game. You know how it works.'

Dwyer took the paper and kept an eye on Braden for an extra moment. He no longer liked being likened to the Police.

'Boy, he's really wound up, Rory,' Calvin said, 'He's angry, that's pretty obvious, the scowl and the way he gave his lawyer the eye … but he's also scared. He's trying to hide it but see how he occasionally licks his lips; his mouth is starting to dry up. I don't know what his normal colour is but I also think he's a bit pale. And his grip on the newspaper is too tight, see? When he spoke, there was a little pulling back of the muscles around his mouth. That's a bit harder to spot but it's there. He's definitely scared.'

'That's a good thing for us, isn't it?'

'I think so, Rory, but don't get carried away yet. I can tell you, all police officers fear being in jail. I know everyone fears being in jail, but police officers … I haven't seen one who wasn't majorly affected by the prospect, no matter how confident they were in their legal case, and especially if they're innocent. They're also pretty good at trying to hide it, I have to say, but …' Calvin held his palms out in a you-can't-argue-with-the-facts gesture, 'The body-language doesn't lie, Rory.'

Cockburn opened the door and leant into the meeting room.

'Have you seen enough, Calvin?'

'Sure, Gary. Let's play ball then.'

Cockburn smiled, gave a low single thumb up, and left. Rory grimaced. *Oh fuck, he's even charmed Cockburn.*

Moments later, the backs of Bourke and Cockburn emerged onto the screens. No handshakes. Braden leant forward over his legal pad. Dwyer crossed his arms and leant into the back of the moulded plastic seat. The creak it made under his weight sounded in the meeting room where Rory and Calvin watched.

Richard Bourke placed a closed manila folder on the table. Gary did the same with the portable CD player that he carried. They sat with their backs to the cameras.

'I'm inspector Richard Bourke and this is Detective Sergeant Gary Cock …'

'I know who the fuck you are Bourke … and Cock-burn,' Dwyer spat.

Calvin noticed Cockburn's back bristle at the deliberate separate syllable sounding of his name. 'Interesting …'

'I'll start again. Gary, can you please start the equipment to record this interview.'

Bourke re-commenced reciting the formalities relating to being formally interviewed in relation to the charge of Conspiracy to Commit Murder under the Crimes Act of 1958 and unlawful disclosure of information under the Police Regulations Act of 1958. He then quickly jumped in at the deep end.

'I'm about to play an audio recording in which the accused is heard to reveal location details of the house where Clifford Neilson and Corina Scali were executed. The accused and the unknown person with whom the accused is having the conversation, both make reference to a substantial sum of money that is being exchanged for activity expected to be carried out at the said house. The address that the accused discloses on the recording is a property where the victims were being accommodated under police protection.'

'You can't just play the recording without warning. You need to provide a copy.' Braden objected.

'Well in that case, I just warned you and now I'm playing it. And here's a copy and a transcript. Okay?' Bourke retrieved a slim CD case from the manila folder and handed it to Braden. 'Can you do the honours please, Gary?'

Whirring of the spinning disc noise crept into the stillness. The impending conversation was then heralded by several seconds of ambient bush noise.

'So you came in person?'

'There. It only lasted a second. He's definitely shocked,' Calvin yelled. 'He recognised that voice.' The voice on the recording resumed after a pause.

'Against the tree, okay?'

'Here's where we think Dwyer frisks him for a wire,' Rory said.

'*Okay.*' Dwyer's voice entered the recording.

'*To answer your question, I'm not actually here in person, I'm attending a live-in training session as we speak. Witnesses from inside and outside of the Force. My presence formally recorded in the minutes.*'

At the first sound of his own voice, Dwyer let his head fall slightly forward and remained stoic as the CD continued. Rory noticed Braden propping his chin with one elbow on the table. He looked enthralled.

'*Then you'd better make sure it's your handwriting chalking up KPI's on the butchers' paper.*'

'*Are you being a smartarse?*'

'*I've come to this over-rated mosquito-ridden puddle. Are we on or not?*'

'*It's the best tadpoling spot you'll ever have the pleasure of gracing.*'

'*Not if I had a choice, Harry Butler, and I don't reckon I'd be on me pat. Fuckin' waste of money locking this place up like Pentridge. Speaking of which, did you bring it?*'

'*There's seventy-five grand.*'

'*And the rest?*'

'*Upon delivery, of course.*'

'*How?*'

'*You'll get it. Don't worry.*'

'*I mean the job. Where and when?*'

'*Nineteen Scott Street, Balwyn, two in the morning, Tuesday week. There'll be an unplanned ten-minute gap when the surveillance teams change shift. That's as long as I can manage without anyone getting suss.*'

'*Is all that written down and in the envelope?*'

'*Only the money's in the envelope.*'

Dwyer sat seemingly impassively for most of the seventeen minutes. His head remained tilted forward staring at the tabletop. When Braden coughed about a quarter way into the recording, Dwyer turned slowly and checked him out with an almost dazed look. But only for a moment. He kept his interest in the tabletop until the hitman wrong-footed him at the end of the recording.

'Just fuckin' do the thing. Okay?'

'Nineteen Bon Scott Street Balwyn, Tuesday week. Got it.'

'It's not Bon Scott Street, it's just Scott Stree ...'

The final loss of face caused his head to drop another cog downward.

The CD stopped of its own accord. Only Dwyer moved. He leant to the side of Braden's head and whispered.

'Deny it all and get me out of here.'

Braden placed his hand on Dwyer's arm, holding it there while he spoke to Bourke.

'My client has no knowledge of this recording and will not be commenting. If you like, he can listen to it at his leisure, but he doesn't expect to know anything more about it. In the meantime, can you please provide details about the recording. Why you think it is my client speaking on the recording, where and when it was recorded and by whom, and who the two people speaking on the recording are.'

Braden removed his hand from Dwyer knowing he had safely shielded him from having to speak. Knowing he would be slightly less panicked.

Bourke and Cockburn looked at each other before Cockburn answered.

'Are we all sitting in different fucking rooms listening to a different CD? We all know who *one* of the people on the CD is. And you quoting your client's response. We're sitting right here and we all know he didn't say a fucking thing.'

'And he's not going to, nor does he have to. Now, are you going to provide the details I've requested?'

'That's all you're getting for now, Mr Braden. The recording speaks for itself,' Bourke said. 'Nevertheless, we are in the process of confirming provenancial matters about the recording. We'll provide those details to you as they come to hand, but I think they're the least of your worries.'

'Well, you better have them ready for the bail hearing because this on its own is laughably inadmissible, and you know it. Come on David.'

Braden placed his unused legal pad in his satchel and rose to leave.

'Sensational!' Calvin said as Bourke and Cockburn dragged themselves back into the meeting room.

'I'm glad you think so,' Bourke said.

'No. Don't despair Richard, that was fantastic. The reality of what was captured on that recording was absolutely unknown to Dwyer until Gary hit the Play button. You might think it was a pretty impassive response … that all he gave away was a raised eyebrow or two. But let me tell you, there was plenty else going on. He was in shock. In absolute clinical shock. The instant he recognised his own voice, his mouth muscles became as rigid as iron and his blotched overweight redness paled a whole notch.

'And why wouldn't he be in shock? At the time it happened, he would have gone to great lengths to ensure nobody observed or knew about the conversation. In the unlikely event that the hitman ever told anyone about the meeting, Dwyer could deny it without fear. He has an alibi that he brags about on the recording. Now, however — more than ten years later — you throw it up at him, not as an allegation, but in Dolby Surround Sound clarity. It's not the smoking gun, it's the gun in his hand with him aiming and in the act of pulling the trigger. How can he deny it?'

Richard Bourke dropped his folder onto the table and sat down disconcertedly. 'If only you were the judge, Calvin.'

'Then you should play this video of interview to the judge. I'll show you on the replay.'

Calvin activated the interview video using a computer mouse and searched for the point where Cockburn starts the CD player.

'It's right here after those first two words. Hang on … I'll pause it.' Calvin became painstaking in finding the exact frame he was looking for. 'This could take me a moment,' he explained. 'When people have an involuntary shock moment, they usually recover quickly. Like a hand going over their open mouth. It's a natural instinct to try and hide a shock. Dwyer's recovery is even quicker because he's mindful his reaction is being scrutinised. But here it is. That split second of involuntary reaction.'

The screen was paused on an obviously fearful looking Dwyer. It was an image neither Rory, Cockburn nor Bourke had observed when it happened.

'It only lasts for a microsecond but it has everything. The upper eyelids have risen and the bottom ones have tensed. The eyes have obviously widened. His lips are stretched horizontally and you can see his eyebrows pulling together. His neck tendons have tightened too.

'This is totally involuntary, but he is mindful enough to stop it as quickly as it happened. And then the real shock begins to seep in. And this time it's more like medical shock symptoms than body-language. See this.'

Calvin moved the video forward to when Dwyer turned his head for a moment to look at Braden.

'See that look. He's dizzy or faint. He looks completely out of it, like someone who has stepped from a car crash. And that reaction is totally undisguised. But from thereon in he recovers a bit, although subtle body-language shock is still present. I'll let it play without sound and you'll see signs — like him picking at something on the back of his left hand, or chewing the inside of his cheek. He catches himself doing these things and he stops, but they creep back in. This is such a classic reaction. Even the impassiveness that he tries to pull off, it's a not an uncommon psychopathic response. You could use it in a text book.' Calvin paused to change tack. 'Of course, the way he didn't react is also significant in this case, don't you think?'

'Oh? How's that?' Richard Bourke asked.

'You can rule out any suggestion that the recording is a fake. You wouldn't get the reaction you got if it wasn't genuine. If it was fabricated or doctored in any way you'd have outrage. There was not a sniff of outrage — verbally or non-verbally.'

'True…'

'What did you think when you were in there, Richard?'

Bourke crossed his arms and took a loud beep breath through his nose. 'I honestly couldn't tell. He's such a cunning bastard that I knew he would try not to give anything away. That's why I got you here, Calvin, and you've convinced me. What about you two?'

He turned to Rory and Cockburn. Cockburn spoke first.

'I'm with you, boss. The bastard could do me at poker, but I reckon Calvin nailed it.'

'Same,' Rory said and waited for Bourke to voice perspective.

'Okay. So whether the recording is accepted as evidence or not, we can at least be certain in our own minds that it's true. If we keep building our case around the recording, then everything should fall into place. Yeah?'

It was a rhetorical "Yeah" and he pressed on.

'We need to concentrate on who the hitman is. He and FP1 are the only other links to the recording, if indeed they are different people. You come back to Melbourne and re-focus the team, Gary. Rory, you stay in Bendigo and deal with the bail hearing. Gary's been working on it with a prosecutor named Georgie Sherwood. I don't think you've met her. She'll bring you up to speed. It's a rehash of the defence you did when Dwyer was first charged, all those years ago. There's one major difference though: the recording, of course. Make that two major differences — we're also diffusing the harsh prison conditions argument. They're making special arrangements to house him down the road at Loddon Prison. Georgie Sherwood will fill you in on that too.'

Bourke turned to Calvin.

'Gary will give you a lift back to Melbourne, Calvin … and well done. I'll need you to prepare a detailed report. A very detailed report. It won't be used in court but I will need it for the DPP.'

'No problem at all Richard. It's been my pleasure, and remember — any time, any crime.'

Bourke smiled and gathered his papers as Calvin and Cockburn departed.

'It won't happen again,' Rory said as soon as they were out of earshot.

'If it does it'll be the last time,' Bourke said and he too left the room.

11

They were making their way to the fairly grand two-storey terrace that Calvin rented in Fitzgibbon Street Parkville — a leafy central suburb of Melbourne. Cockburn crawled across a couple of cross-streets until Calvin pointed ahead.

'That's it, where my black Mercedes is on the right, Gary. It's reserved parking on that side but you can pull in on the left.'

The working day had not quite ended and the residential street was dozing. Cockburn pulled the unmarked police car into the closest vacant parallel parking space. It was a few houses short of Calvin's. He buzzed his side window down to look ahead and across the street.

'Nice digs *and* car.'

He had already popped the boot so Calvin could retrieve his suitcase. Calvin answered in the throes of removing his seatbelt and alighting.

'Thanks, Gary. I've been here two years now. I really enjoy the location.'

Cockburn left the car idling. It was a no-brainer for the body-language expert that Cockburn wasn't after an offer to come in for tea or coffee. Calvin wheeled his suitcase to Cockburn's window to exchange goodbyes. He wished Cockburn well with the case and they shook hands through the car window.

Calvin had turned to cross the street and Cockburn had shifted his attention to putting the car into gear when the bomb went off. Its force threw Cockburn into uncontrollable jerkiness that resulted in the car lurching into the parked car in front of him. An alarm triggered but Cockburn wasn't hearing it. The blast had nullified his hearing. He pondered the silent movie before him in the second-and-a-half before reality registered. He could see through his own cracked windscreen that the rear window of the car in front of him had shattered into a shower of crystals sprayed across the lid of its boot. *That's too much damage for a rear-ending*, he reasoned thoughtfully until his wider vision engaged actuality.

Calvin's Mercedes had exploded. Not merely torched, but bombed. It was an all-engulfing fireball, a mere twenty metres away. Calvin had disappeared from view. Cockburn looked down to see him lying on the road beside the car. The driver side door wouldn't open. He quickly gave up on it and scrambled across the console to exit through the passenger door. He couldn't hear himself swear as he jagged his thigh on the gear lever.

Calvin had risen to his hands and knees by the time Cockburn reached him and began helping him to his feet.

'ARE YOU ALL RIGHT?' Cockburn shouted so he could hear himself.

Calvin saw his lips move and yelled back.

'WHAT?'

They gave up on communicating and Cockburn helped Calvin hobble further back along the street to escape the heat.

With life accounted for, Cockburn returned to his car and grabbed the standard issue hand-held fire extinguisher. He ducked his head when the heat hit him well short of the inferno. The extinguisher's jet could not even reach the adjacent four-wheel drive that had now caught alight. It was then that Cockburn noticed every car window and house window within close range had been blown out. He tossed the tiny extinguisher into the carnage and strode dejectedly back to Calvin, retrieving Calvin's wheelie suitcase on the way.

Calvin lifted his mobile away from his ear to shout at Cockburn. 'I'M TRYING TO PHONE IT IN BUT I DON'T KNOW IF THEY'VE ANSWERED OR IF THEY'RE HEARING ME.'

Cockburn got the gist of what Calvin mouthed and realised with alarm that he didn't have an answer. He was a trained police officer and there was no standard emergency response for this situation. If there were any sirens on the way, he wouldn't hear them. Temporary hearing loss had been spoken about at some training session or other but he couldn't remember any advice being imparted about what to do when it happened. And what if it wasn't temporary?

People were emerging from houses. Cockburn snatched Calvin's phone from his hand and ran to a young bearded guy in slippers. He thrust the phone at him and shouted. 'TALK TO THEM. TELL THEM WHAT AND WHERE.'

'No, you stay in Bendigo. The bombing is not our investigation and I don't want Georgie Sherwood doing the bail hearing on her own. Half the force is already on the case in any event.'

'There's no way Dwyer's not behind it,' Rory said to Bourke over the phone.

'And why do you think he'd be targeting Calvin Steele? Dwyer well knows that body-language interpretation is not something that could ever be raised in court. Nor is there a public scare factor in this. No one other than the police knows that Calvin played a part in nailing Dwyer, however indirectly.'

Rory gave Bourke the answer he was fishing for. 'Well that's it. It's a police scare factor.'

'Too right it is and until we know how the bomb was detonated, we can't rule out attempted murder of a police officer. What if Gary had parked a few metres closer? Between you and me, this has got Dwyer written all over it. But right now, I'm more concerned about "how" Dwyer knew.'

Rory's end of the line went quiet.

'Don't go quiet on me, Rory. I know it leaves a bad taste but you knew

this would become an internal investigation as soon as you heard about the bombing. There's only one place Dwyer could have found out about Calvin.'

'A bad taste is still a bad taste.'

'Well we're not going to sit here bellyaching about it. Before anyone else starts questioning you, tell me who had access to this knowledge.'

Quiet.

'I hope that's the sound of you thinking.'

'I *am* thinking. From memory, we only decided to engage a body-language expert the morning of the day before we interviewed Dwyer. It was a rush thing with a lot of asking around the office to see if anyone knew a credible operator. I think Gerry Denton discovered that Calvin did some work with the New South Wales force. He phoned someone in NSW to check it out and to get Calvin's contact details. We had to start by contacting his agent and it was locked in by lunchtime. Anyone sitting in our office could have gathered what was going on. That's a big enough list right there.'

Now it was Bourke's turn to mull as Rory waited.

'What about the next day?'

'I bumped into Tony Elmer from Property Crime Squad at the airport and introduced Calvin to him. I told Tony he was a consultant. He didn't question it and I don't think he'd ever heard of Calvin. Calvin's no A-list-er despite appearing on TV.'

'Hmm.'

'Some of the uniform blokes at Bendigo did recognise Calvin though. They took selfies with him. By then it would be too late for anyone to organise a bombing even if they wanted to. In fact, I don't know how the job was organised so quickly by whoever was in on it from the start. It's like the Graeme Stanley thing. That seemed to happen in no-time-flat after we got that first recording sample.'

'That's what makes it all the more worrying. Could Calvin have spoken to someone about it?' Bourke thought aloud.

'Even if he did, it wouldn't be to anyone connected to Dwyer

… or unless Calvin organised the whole thing himself. He's an unashamed self-promoter you know — only joking. But he'll be getting plenty of mileage out of this before it's over nonetheless. He's not shy of media interviews. Command will need to watch what he says.'

'Communications Branch is already onto it. The Chief Commissioner will be saying Calvin was only acting in his customary role as a specialist corporate communications expert to provide guidance in relation to interview dynamics and technique. The Chief Commissioner wants to make it clear that Calvin was not engaged for the purpose of sitting in on any interviews with any suspects or criminals.'

'That's a bit of a fudge … and it begs the next media question: So what is the line of inquiry?'

'You know the drum, Rory: We're keeping an open mind.'

'How *are* Calvin and Gary?'

'Calvin was knocked about a bit but nothing broken. I think he's all right. I know Gary is. He hasn't got all his hearing back yet but that hasn't stopped him getting straight back into the job.'

Shit. Now he's half deaf as well as half blind, Rory thought.

12

'Look at this. The cops have arrested David Dwyer for the Neilson Scali murders.'

Martha was leaning across the en-suite basin in a dark, belted skirt and black bra — her blouse and jacket were laid out on the bed. She re-focused to look beyond the mirrored reflection of her lower right eyelashes and the delicately poised mascara brush she was using. The mirror reflected Josh still in his night-time boxer shorts and threadbare, blue work singlet. He was holding an opened electronic tablet on the palm of his hand. Martha swung round and holstered the eyelash brush into its tube.

'Show me.'

She held the tablet in both hands and began reading. Josh wrapped himself around her back and watched what she read from the crook of her neck. She swiped down to the bottom of the page.

'See,' she said, and tried to look into his face, which he kept pressed against her cheek.

'It says new evidence emerged because of the reward.'

'Well, *we* know that … and it's a good thing they acknowledge it. The plan is working. Everything is on track.'

'Mmm.'

Josh let her go. She leant into the mirror again to complete the eye job. Josh propped against the door jamb and watched idly.

'They're holding him at Bendigo police station.'

'They brought him there because he lives just down the road near Castlemaine. It says that too … shit, I never knew he was that close,' Martha said.

'Not too close for you, is it?'

'More surprised, I think. At the end of the day, where he's been living is not really the issue.'

'I'm glad I didn't know. I probably would have freaked if I passed him in Bunnings or somewhere.'

'You're not going to do a number on me again, are you?'

'No. Not now he's locked up. I just think it's weird. We're more responsible than anyone for that story and we're calmly reading about it in the news like everyone else. People will pass us in the street and they'll have no idea. I mean, these days people call anything and every situation surreal, but this is truly surreal in my book. A juxtaposition of incongruities if ever I experienced one.'

'As long as they keep passing you in the street and keep having no idea that you're connected, then you've got nothing to worry about.'

'I know. Still, it makes you think, don't you think?'

Martha turned around and answered with a sceptical grin. She screwed the mascara brush into its tube, job done.

'Are you going into town today?'

'No. I've got to stay home and edit the Warburton Creek report that Sheila wrote. What about you?'

'I've got a court day. I'm first up.'

Martha arrived at Bendigo courthouse early and made her way up the M C Escher-like flights of tessellated-tile stairs to Court One. She shouldered through a prospective-jury mob on level two. On the upper level she nodded to her client's parents who waited on the wooden pew outside the courtroom. They would not see their son until he was brought into court from the cells.

Martha was surprised to see proceedings were already underway when she entered the courtroom, hugging a bundle of folders and files to her chest. Rory and Georgie Sherwood were at the prosecuting table. Ramsay Braden was standing at the defence table to address the bench. There was no accused at the defence table or in the dock; he was not required to attend. No one sat in the public gallery and no reporters were present. Proceedings had obviously begun well ahead of the normal court hours. The only faces Martha knew were the bench clerk and Magistrate, Bryce Murphy. He glanced up when the door clunked shut behind Martha.

'Ah, Miss Portillo. I'm afraid you've been shunted. We have an unscheduled bail application to deal with. I hope you don't mind. You might like to find yourself a good latte.'

Martha had a good idea what bail case was being dealt with.

'Thank you, Your Honour. I might stay and observe from the public gallery for a while. I could learn something.'

'You never know,' he smiled. 'Please continue, Mr Braden.'

Martha's instinct was immediately confirmed when Ramsay Braden referred to his client, David Dwyer.

Georgie Sherwood was soon challenging Ramsay Braden's assertions. Each response she gave began with a whimsical smile on her ever-chipper round face. A fan of thick auburn hair, almost to her shoulders, and a solid frame tottering on a good set of pins spelt all-round jolliness. Despite representing the defence, Martha quickly warmed to Georgie's peculiarly cheerful adversarial-ness. The way she treated intense legal arguments like a family discussion about who should do the dishes.

'I know Mr Dwyer is your client and I know you really want him to get bail, but don't you think you're exaggerating just a bit, Ramsay?' she smiled.

It was apparent to Martha that Georgie had already tendered a comprehensive response to David Dwyer's bail application and that Ramsay Braden needed to pull all stops out. Georgie didn't need to reinvent the wheel entirely, however, because David Dwyer had previously been charged with the same crime, notwithstanding it happened nine years earlier and bail was granted on a second appeal. The telling difference between the original arguments against bail being granted and the present situation, was the compelling new evidence provided by the recording.

All bail applications need to address the risk that the accused may interfere with witnesses. In this regard, Georgie's submission regurgitated the ludicrousness of whether that likelihood could ever be discounted when the case actually involved the murder of a witness, moreover a witness in the witness protection program. Georgie had not hesitated to cut and paste the elegant, well-constructed argument of the original case without amendment. Without realising it, she had created a forest among the trees and Braden spotted it.

'What witnesses?' Braden countered. 'The Police have landed a highly questionable anonymous recording — ten long years after the supposed fact, mind you — for which they decline to provide a smidgeon of authentication or corroboration, or anything whatsoever that will allow it to be admissible. I can only assume that Police are equally mystified by how the recording suddenly materialised from the ether. It appears to me that the Police have no idea who, if anyone, is linked to this recording. Perhaps it simply fell off the back of a truck, we just don't know. And nor do the Police, it seems. In this context I think rule one applies here, Your Honour — for a witness to be interfered with, first you need a witness. Or as Charlie Drake put it, *"If you want your boomerang to come back, well first you've got to throw it"*.'

Georgie leapt at the chance to spar.

'Charlie Drake, hey? You are showing your age, Ramsay. It is precisely because of witness concerns that the Police have been hesitant to provide further details of the recording at this stage. But I can personally assure Mr Braden that the recording did come through human channels and not by some means of teleportation or divine intervention. I can also assure the Court that the person who brought the recording to the Police is indeed fearful of the consequences of doing so and they have understandably gone to great lengths to protect their own identity. In this case more than any other, the need to honour a witness's request for anonymity cannot be overstated. The Police will be treading as carefully as Your Honour would expect them to in these circumstances.'

As much as Georgie utilised the recording to bolster the regurgitated case against Dwyer's bail, so too did Braden latch on to it to find weakness. As defence lawyer, he had the opportunity to demonstrate that the strength — and conversely, the weakness — of the evidence against his client presented "exceptional circumstances".

'I'm surprised — and in the same breath not surprised — that the Police were not more suspicious when something like this emerges out of the blue at the precise time that a million-dollar reward is offered. For less than one percent of that money, I could arrange to have a recording produced of Your Honour confessing to murdering his wife. With sound-alikes and aural equivalent of Photoshop techniques, the end product would have Your Honour convinced that you did in fact utter the confession, and that at some later date, you were struck with amnesia.

'The Crown seeks to assure us — without the support of any audio forensics, mind you — that it appears unlikely the recording has been tampered with or is in anyway a fake. But by definition, to say something is "unlikely" is admitting that the opposite is also a possibility. It's like a weather report that says Bendigo has an eighty percent chance of receiving nought to ten millimetres of rain. The truth is that there is a twenty percent certainty of receiving absolutely no rain whatsoever. On top of that, there's an eighty percent chance that also includes the prospect of no rain whatsoever. That's one hundred percent chance of receiving nothing at all. If I were a farmer, I don't think I'd be getting the seed drill out of the shed just yet.'

'Well, whether you'd make a better farmer than a lawyer and whether or not the weather has any relevance to this case, the bit you would have most trouble convincing me about Mr Braden, is the bit about my wife — I happen to be unmarried.'

'I do beg your pardon, Your Honour.'

The part of the Crown's case that Braden challenged least was the conditions in which he would be remanded in custody. As a former police officer, David Dwyer would need to be held in protective custody. Although it was nearing a decade since he served as a police officer, the State would be held negligent if it exposed him to the general prison population that might include criminals he once pursued, or their friends. First time round, Dwyer's successful bail application turned on criticism of the harsh conditions he experienced at protective unit of the Melbourne Remand Centre. This time, Inspector Richard Bourke saw to it that there were no protection beds available at the Remand Centre. The convenient unavailability of a protection bed justified the alternative arrangement Police had in mind.

Corrections Victoria was in the midst of major extension and refurbishment works at Loddon Prison at Castlemaine. The way in which those works were being staged created the opportunity to establish a temporary dedicated annex for extra protection beds.

For the Crown, the benefits were several fold. Another insurmountable weakness of the original arguments for denying bail was negated. Loddon Prison was only a few kilometres from where Dwyer lived, thereby making it difficult to argue hardship for his family. From Bourke's point of view, Dwyer would not be remanded with the mounting number of other bent cops at the Melbourne Remand Centre. There would be far less opportunity for him to establish lines of communication and influence beyond the prison. All Braden had left to argue was the expected over-lengthy period of incarceration that Dwyer would endure as a result of predictable delays in the case being heard.

Still, Braden seemed to be scoring sympathy from his Honour. Georgie and Rory leant towards each other and whispered. Should they raise the Graeme Stanley connection to put matters beyond doubt? Georgie stood.

'There is one other matter the Crown wishes to raise without notice, and it includes information that the Police wish to supress.'

His Honour asked her to proceed.

'The Police have tangible evidence that the recent murder of Graeme Stanley may be linked to this recording.'

Martha felt her body stiffen.

'A copy of an intentionally veiled communication between the Police and the recording informant, which was published innominately, was found at the crime scene. That may suggest further corruption by way of unlawful disclosure within the Police Force, although it hasn't yet been ruled out that the link might have come about otherwise. I must also add that Mr Stanley had not been identified by the Police as a suspect or a witness in the Neilson Scali case prior to his own death. However, there is a strong possibility that Mr Stanley is the person specifically referred to on the recording as "Graeme". The important thing to remember is, that despite the investigation being in its early days, a prima facie element of reprisal exists as well as a tangible link between the cases.'

Georgie sat down too quickly, making it seem like a hit and run. Ramsay Braden watched as she did so.

'Mr Braden?'

'Your Honour …' he began as he stood and held out his open palms pleadingly to the magistrate. 'It's well known that the criminal world will turn on itself at the drop of a rumour, but that's no reason my client should suddenly become default option for the Police. I remind the court that Mr Dwyer has never been convicted of a crime. Since he left the Police Force nearly a decade ago, he has developed a successful small business growing olives and producing olive oil for selected restaurants in Melbourne. A business which, I remind the Court, will be threatened if Mr Dwyer is not able to return to his property for the critical harvesting period.

'The suggestion that Mr Dwyer is somehow stalking the criminal world shows how desperate the prosecution is. It is all the more reason to allow bail. I mean, Harold Holt hasn't been found yet, do the Police want to add his kidnapping to their suspicions about my client, just for good measure? I will need much more detail if you want me to respond to the matter seriously, in the meantime I ask that it not form part of Your Honour's considerations.'

'I think you're not doing too bad yourself in the desperation stakes, Mr Braden. So let me put it this way. I intend to refuse bail at this point. However, if the accused wishes to appeal the decision at some point in the future, then I will allow that the requirement for the defence to identify new evidence, may include a lack of further evidence being provided by the Police in relation to the recording and other matters they have raised today.'

'So no further evidence shall constitute new evidence, Your Honour?'

Braden stressed the irony by holding an index finger on his chin.

'If you like, Mr Braden. And I also grant the prosecution's request for an order supressing these proceedings. Only my decision is to be made public. I hardly need to remind the few of us present in this courtroom — especially Miss Portillo, who's interest I'm sure is entirely academic — that anyone disclosing details about these proceedings will be held in contempt.'

Rory hadn't picked Georgie as a smoker. They stood by the conservatory gardens adjacent to Bendigo court as a near-empty tourist tram did battle with trucks flanking it in both directions. But a couple of diesels couldn't hide the strip of opulent nineteenth-century architectural marvels dubbed "Vienna in the Bush". Georgie gazed at the striking Shamrock Hotel and exhaled soothingly.

'How about a bite to eat and you can tell me what happened in there?' Rory interrupted her reverie.

Georgie gave him a dubious look.

'I'm sure you know exactly what went down Rory, but lunch would be nice. Do you know anywhere good? Somewhere a bit quieter.'

'As a matter of fact … I know somewhere pretty close. I'll drive you there.'

Three blocks away and they were in the converted backyard of a neighbourhood corner-shop, now an inner-city-cafe transplant called Percy and Percy.

'Nice,' Georgie said, glancing at the menu. 'How did you know about something off the beaten track like this?'

'I've been getting back to Bendigo a bit lately. Word travels pretty quickly about anywhere good.'

'Getting back to Bendigo? Did you come from here?'

'I grew up in Bendigo. This is my old 'hood.'

Georgie ignored the menu she was holding. 'And what's been bringing you back to Bendigo? Hardly a recommended career move for someone in Homicide … a female interest perhaps?'

'Perhaps. Maybe you should be the detective,' Rory smiled across the top of his menu.

The waitress arrived. 'Georgie …' Rory offered for her to order first.

'Err … the pulled-pork salad sounds good, I'll try that. And you might have to come back for desserts. I've got my eye on the hummingbird cake I saw on the counter.'

'The steak and mushroom sandwich for me, please.' Rory told the waitress and handed back the menu.

Georgie leant forward with her forearms on the table.

'I reckon you only have a matter of weeks.'

'Before they can lodge another bail application?'

'That's right. So you'd better get on your skates if you want to keep him locked up.'

Rory defaulted to his glum look. One arm propped on the table and his chin resting in the palm of his other hand.

'It wasn't a trial. I thought that such an incriminating recording would be more than enough for a bail magistrate to put paid to any suggestion of releasing him.'

'And that's why the magistrate denied bail, but Brayden planted enough seeds of doubt for the Magistrate to leave the door ajar. I did what I could, but you didn't give me much to work with. No provenance for the recording and none on the horizon as far as I can see. If you haven't got some way to verify whether the recording is ten years old or ten days old, you're going to have a major admissibility problem. A proper technical analysis wouldn't have gone astray either. I don't know if Braden was talking through his arse about it being doctored or a fake, but I'm sure Magistrate Bryce Murphy has even less idea. None of us were in a position to call his bluff. A teenage nerd might have been all you needed to dispel the suggestion, but we didn't have one.'

With her lecture complete, Georgie poured water for them both.

'We *have* got a bit to do.'

'I'd say so. What about the Parkville bombing? I know Cockburn was there. Has that got anything to do with this?'

Rory allowed a giveaway pause before he answered.

'I can't say at this stage.'

'You could if the answer was no.'

Another giveaway pause elapsed as Rory formed a cautious response.

'I can only give you the party line. No one has advised me of any link to Dwyer ...' he stated accurately, '... so we have to work with what we have to keep Dwyer locked up.'

'Then you'll need to keep picking it all apart and hope that the *where*, the *when* and the *who* for that recording is bared. But look on the bright side, Rory,' she smiled. 'Another bail hearing will mean another trip to Bendigo for you.'

'Hmm.'

13

Rory took his position at the very back of briefing area in the Homicide Branch office, leaning against the workstation screen that separated it from the open plan work area. He was early because he couldn't risk arriving late and drawing attention to himself. It was Tuesday and he was still in recovery mode from slamming into a PTSD wall on Friday night — a collision he was propelled into by the first week of "real" homicide work he'd completed since his world slewed off the tracks a lifetime ago. Not a cold case desktop exercise but an encounter with a real dead body with fresh blood.

His attempt to come to work on Monday only lasted four trams stops before he alighted to do a slow coffee-crawl back to his flat. Coffee was the only upper he allowed himself despite consuming every perilous substance available on his downward trajectory. He hoped that his distance from Cockburn was sufficient to blur the haggardness he'd seen in his shaving-face.

Inspector Richard Bourke also arrived un-customarily early. Detectives scurried to finish emails and grab a coffee. Cockburn took his place beside Bourke at the head of a table far too small to accommodate everyone. Some wheeled their office chairs over. The rest stood.

Julia with the red hair rushed a folder of photocopied documents to Cockburn. On this occasion, her hair was pulled back into a pony tail. Rory noticed she was on the better side of attractive in a younger version of Meryl Streep kind of way. He heard Bourke call her Detective Constable O'Hannagain. An Irish pedigree to match her hair. She touched Cockburn on the forearm as she made a point about the documents. Rory wondered if she was simply a touchy-feely kind of gal or … Surely not, she was out of his league. Where was Calvin when you needed him?

Bourke strained to see if anyone was still at their workstation.

'All right, let's get started. Anyone not here will have to miss out.'

The drone of background muttering came to a halt.

'As of now, and despite what I say or don't say in the media, the Graeme Stanley murder and the Neilson Scali developments are a joint investigation. I presume that everyone here has heard or read the transcript of the David Dwyer recording. What you may not know is that the recording was provided to us by an anonymous person claiming the million-dollar reward. That person has no intention of revealing their identity — even when they receive the reward, which is another story. That doesn't mean we don't try to find out who they are, but the truth is, we have bugger all to go on.

'Before we received the recording, the informant sent us a small snippet to establish their bona fides and flag an interest in the reward. To obtain the full version, we had to communicate back to them via a discreet public notice, if there is such a thing. A copy of that notice was left at the scene of Graeme Stanley's murder. That's the link to Dwyer.

'Gary and I have already interviewed David Dwyer and he's refusing to make any comment. No surprises there. Nevertheless, we believe he was aware a recording had surfaced but until we played it to him at the interview, we are certain he hadn't heard the incriminating conversation since he spoke it ten years earlier. Nor had he ever expected to. Obviously, whoever killed Graeme Stanley also knew that an audio recording had surfaced with Dwyer's voice on it.

'However, neither Dwyer nor the killer — if they are not one and the same — knew the full extent of what was said on the tape. Remember, the entire version of the recording didn't arrive in the mail until the day after Stanley was killed. It looks like whoever killed him was on a fishing expedition within the criminal world. We don't even know if Stanley was meant to be killed. They might not have intended to go beyond extracting information from him before he spoilt the party by having a heart attack.

'A copy of the public notice was undoubtedly left at the Graeme Stanley's murder scene as a message for the reward claimant … or possibly rivals. So we won't be playing that game by making the information public. We don't want to spook the claimant just yet. Nor do we want to give oxygen to another gangland war.

'My message to you all is this — don't underestimate what we're dealing with. This is an unresolved attack on the criminal justice system itself. It didn't finish for us when *Wikipedia* or *The Age* or whoever else declared the gangland killings were over. This skeleton has been hanging over our heads for a decade. Not just the heads of the people in this room, I mean the entire Force. This is our chance to place a full stop on the whole stinking episode. Let's not bugger it up.'

Bourke paused to see what effect his words were having. He took pin-dropping silence as a positive sign.

'All right. So that's our starting point for this joint investigation. We also know that bail has been denied. Anything to report from the hearing, Rory?'

Bourke squinted to see if Rory looked as bad as he appeared from a distance. Rory felt the scrutiny and pushed on.

'The downside is that the magistrate gave credence to doubts the defence threw up about the recording itself: the lack of authentication and the suggestions it could easily be a cleverly produced pastiche in response to the reward. He'll allow an appeal not too far down the track if we don't come up with anything more. Georgie reckons we've only got a matter of weeks. I'll start by getting a forensic audit and voice recognition done.'

'Well I don't want that prick back on the streets mocking us. What have you got so far from the conversation itself on recording?'

'I got Gerry to chase up the training session alibi that Dwyer brags about on the recording.'

The fact that anyone did anything for Rory was an achievement that didn't go unnoticed. Upon his return to the Force, members were not displeased that Rory was posted to the Cold Case Unit, and that the unit was accommodated on another floor of the building. Out of sight, out of favour. But some people were less successful at maintaining the rage and in any case, it's difficult to pass a grudge on to the young. The young find their own stuff to get cranky about. Rory discovered that Gerry Denton belonged to the next generation of homicide detectives. An open mind, thoughtful-looking with a buzz-cut and black rimmed glasses. Gerry stepped forward from the assembled throng to report.

'Um, Dwyer did attend a training seminar in the two weeks before Neilson and Scali were killed. It was a day-and-a-half seminar on crime-scene advances and it was conducted at Forensic Service Centre at McLeod. It ran into the night and one session was held the next morning. I retrieved an archived file from Human Resources that included an attendance list. Dwyer was on the list, of course. I couldn't track down all the attendees but those I did speak to all remembered Dwyer being there — despite it being a decade ago. Apparently he's not easy to forget.

'The downside was that none of them can recall him being absent. I had better news at the Forensic Service Centre itself. They had electronic security back then and they could retrieve the records — they don't throw away or delete anything. The bad news is that electronic security swipe-card records show Dwyer was there throughout. He couldn't have found more than forty minutes to himself. Even if that were the case, he couldn't have gone anywhere because the records show his vehicle didn't leave until the end of the course.

'Of course there's nothing to say that the taping didn't happen on another day, but if that was the case, why would Dwyer mention the training session at all?'

'Thanks, Detective Denton. I think there's a good news/bad news routine in there somewhere, but don't give up your day job for stand-up. What else did you get from the tape, Rory?'

A few patronising ha ha's punctuated groans.

'Gerry also found out that Dwyer is not an AC/DC fan. In fact, his taste in music could define him as an anti-AC/DC fan.' This one garnered some genuine laughter. Rory hastened to defend his point. 'Amusing as it sounds, this could be a critical clue. It means that someone else came up with the Bon Scott connection. A fairly committed fan I'd say ... tee-shirt wearer at the very least. It's something to keep an eye out for, especially when we go back over the Drug Squad stuff ... okay?'

Amusement subsided to murmurs of scepticism.

'Settle down,' Bourke said. 'I think Rory's right about going back over old stuff. I know we have a fresh body on our hands, but we also have ten years' worth of accumulated evidence. The identity of the other voice on the recording has to be in there somewhere. We'll get an officer to review it all. The rest of us can focus on the here and now.'

Bourke drew breath and turned to Cockburn.

'So Gary, where are we at with Graeme Stanley?'

'What?'

'GRAEME STANLEY,' he yelled. 'Are you sure you're right to be back at work? Have you heard a single word of what we're saying?'

'Yeah,' he protested. 'You might need to speak up a bit though.'

Bourke rolled his eyes. Cockburn opened his folder and glanced down.

'A bit more CCTV and a few more witnesses confirm the

times the Mercedes van came and went. Nothing more on who was driving. Inside the warehouse we have two sets of boot prints in addition to Stanley's. Tyre prints for the Mercedes. The blood is all Stanley's. A few random fibres but otherwise the scene is as clean as a whistle. The person who contacted the real estate agent was a male voice on the phone. They spun a story about coming down from Sydney. We're checking through vehicle registrations for all high-body Mercedes for any likelies. Nothing so far, except that the plates they used were stolen from a Kia sedan in Seaford. Owned by an eighteen-year-old chick named Lola.'

Cockburn left the script and changed to a more speculative tone.

'There's a certain professionalism about it, so Detective O'Hannagain has been liaising with the Anti-Gang Division. Julia was with one of the task forces before they set up the division. Julia …'

The red-headed Julia sat at the end of the table. She remained seated but straightened her posture to address the team.

'Thanks, Gary. The latest intelligence confirms what Inspector Bourke has been saying. The landscape of the Melbourne drug world has moved on. Gangs and bikies are still jockeying to fill the void left by the demise of the Tony Mokbel and Carl Williams empires. As I said at the last briefing, Graeme Stanley has a Seniors card and was pretty much living the retired life on Phillip Island. The same thing with David Dwyer. He's got a few acres where he grows olives for oil. He sells his product but it's not much more than a hobby. He has a handful of restaurant customers.

'We searched his property and came up with nothing, other than how comfortably he seems to live. Nothing extravagant but nor is he wanting. On the face of it, his computer is boring, he hardly seems to use it. It does, however, have Eraser software installed. This program writes over the residual Metadata record of deleted items that usually survive on the hard drive. The upshot is, we don't have the usual deeply buried trace of activity that took place on the computer.'

'There were no significant transactions in his known bank accounts to suggest he paid for coercive services. There was $15,000 in his safe, though. He's a punter; he says that's his kitty. And punting is probably his only amusement. If Dwyer and Stanley ever caught up with each other these days, I reckon it'd be for a game of lawn bowls.'

She didn't have the delivery to get a laugh.

'That may be so, Detective Constable O'Hannagain, but let's not forget what both men are capable of and that the ghosts of their past can easily threaten their liberty. Retirement life is a fragile concept for criminals. Neither of these two characters would hesitate to do what's necessary to protect that.

'So … I want to know who Dwyer would turn to to get a job done these days. His old contacts, his new contacts, phone and email, his phone records, which of today's players provide that sort of muscle. Some of you were on the surveillance team we had watching him when this happened. Run down every contact you observed. DID YOU HEAR THAT GARY?'

'Being done,' Cockburn answered with an affronted face.

'Good. What about the hitman stuff, Rory?'

'If you read between the lines on the recording, we're looking for a freelance from overseas. Someone with a London-ish accent. The trouble is, the world's our oyster if you think about it — someone from England, Hong Kong, Canada, the US, even New Zealand. I've submitted requests to Interpol and Scotland Yard but I'm not holding my breath. They're not sure what to tell me or whether the movements of any possibles can be traced ten years after the event. The Feds and immigration are even less helpful. I've got just as good a chance doing my own online research.'

'Do it,' Bourke said.

The room went quiet as the message began to sink in.

'Okay. If that's the full extent of where we're up to, let me deal with the elephant in the room. The Parkville bombing.' The hush seemed even quieter when Bourke said the words.

'As you know, it's not our investigation but I am being kept in the loop. At this stage they haven't established a link to the Dwyer stuff but from where I stand, no other scenarios come to mind. What's more, if a link is found, or even if one is not found, it's hard to conceive that the information chain didn't have its origins in this branch. It sickens me to tell you that but you need to know. You may be questioned by internal investigators. Heaven help us if they find someone … and heaven help that officer.'

Bourke's pause seemed to amplify a detective who was finishing a phone call in the workstation area. He hung up, grabbed the jacket from back of his chair and rushed over.

'They've found the Mercedes,' he announced.

Rory stood outside Bourke's open office door and watched the scramble to get to the scene.

'You come with me,' he heard Cockburn yell to Julia.

Bourke was back in his office and back at the computer screen.

'Where did they find the Mercedes?' he asked Rory without shifting his eyes from the screen. Rory stepped across the threshold into Bourke's office.

'Airport West. Apparently it's been abandoned in another industrial area for days.'

'Not that far from Thomastown.'

'Na.'

Bourke had become too distracted with emails to continue the conversation.

'Is Gary rooting Julia O'Hannagain?'

That averted Bourke's distraction. He looked blankly at Rory as he contemplated the question.

'Fran,' he called.

Bourke's PA, Fran, came to the door and leant around the jamb.

'What?'

'Is Gary rooting Julia?'

'I'm no judge, but …'

'Of course you're a judge. You know precisely what goes on around here. That's why I asked you.'

'Well, you didn't hear it from me …'

'But Gary's not even as tall as her,' Rory interrupted.

'Two words, Rory, Nicole Kidman,' Fran said.

'That's my point. Gary's light years from being a Keith Urban, except in height, or lack thereof.'

'All right, you two. We got the message. Makes you think though, doesn't it?'

Bourke proved his point by staring into space.

'Is that it?'

'Yeah. Thanks, Fran.'

Fran gave Rory half an eye roll that spoke a whole sentence. *He's supposed to be a detective, he runs the place for God's sake and he doesn't notice what's happening in front of his own eyes.*

Bourke waited until she was out of earshot. 'Female cop goes out with male colleague. I thought you of all people would want to leave gossip to the gossips. At least Gary's not married.'

'No, it wasn't idle curiosity, I …' *Oh shit. How did that just slip my mind. My own dumb indiscretion with Heidi. It only led to my whole life being fucked up. Fuck fuck fuck fuck.*

'… you're right. Sorry. I'll crawl back down to my cave. I'm not sure I wanted to know now that I actually know.'

'Before you slink off, have you caught up with Michelle Fox-Jones yet?'

'Almost.'

'Almost? No don't explain. Just do it. It'll be one less thing to have Command on my back about.'

14

Rory felt more comfortable meeting Michelle on neutral territory. This time the café was her choice and it was obvious that she chose carefully. Puck Specialty Coffee was not much more than a stroll into Albert Park from the St Kilda Road Police Complex, but nevertheless comfortably distant from any of the regular police coffee haunts.

At their original aborted get-together, Michelle must have sensed Rory's unease at the threateningly ordinary Four Three Four Café. Puck Specialty Coffee was the real deal. It said so in the name, twice, *specialty* and *coffee*. If you still had any doubts, the house blend listing would set your mind at ease — *60% Colombian Hula, 30% Braxil Barreiro and 10% Ethiopian Yirgacheffi.*

The place was cloistered in a lone modern shopfront below an educational furniture supplier. The neighbourhood was an otherwise uncommercial microcosm of inner Melbourne — anonymous office buildings, apartment blocks of all sizes, an old-school pub and a whole street side of original cottages and terraces.

Inside was also a good choice for the conversation about to be had. Plenty of space between tables, a quiet nook or two, and dripping with coffee-chic décor. Rory spotted Michelle through the window, already seated inside. He greeted her with, 'If I get a bad coffee here, I think it'll be a case for the Coffee Ombudsman.'

'Have you seen their Facebook page? It's full of gushing five-star reviews with an average of 4.7. Much talk about coffee greatness.'

'I'm not a Facebook person.'

'Haven't you seen mine yet? I was hoping you would get a chance to look at it before we caught up.'

Their coffees came with elaborate crema art. Michelle insisted on paying and insisted on having a treat. She opted for orange cake, Rory, the granola slice.

'Sorry, I thought I'd get it from the horse's mouth.'

'Where to start?' Michelle tasted the crema with her teaspoon as she decided how to answer her own question.

'It's probably different for you, Rory. You copped one massive dose of trauma, but this thing crept up on me for years, you know?'

'Yeah, well …' Rory shrugged. He didn't know where it was going to go.

'I never ever realised what a truckload of shit I was amassing with every brutal murder I attended. Other times, dealing with men, always men, who take that step beyond reason or consequence to avenge their own failings, usually taking it out on those they love most. Those vicious domestics and drawn-out hostage standoffs. They're getting worse, you know.

'Anyway, experiencing situations like that first hand and somehow being let down when you naively recount it in full technicolour to the court. The whole relentless amalgam becomes an ever-heavier Sword of Damocles and one day, the single horse-hair holding it above our head snaps.'

'Are you quoting from your book now?'

'I might sound melodramatic to you Rory but the weird thing is, we do it all so willingly out of a sense of duty. It never occurs to us that we are taking on too much. Even when we're ready to drop from exhaustion — physically and mentally. We have a bit of a rest, we get pissed, and front up for another dose. We don't connect what we do with the bouts of anger that come outta nowhere. Mood swings we're not even aware we're having, becoming irritable, emotionally disconnected and depressed.

Our partners are the ones who wear it but for how long? When the flashbacks and nightmares kick in, you're too scared or too fucked-up or both to confront it. We hit the piss even harder to self-medicate. Denial becomes the default option.'

The café was filling. Michelle leant across the table to try and keep her voice down, but there was no lid on the passion for her new specialist subject. Rory had no desire to argue an alternative point of view.

'I guess it happens.'

'I don't want to have a go at you, Rory, but the response you just gave me is the attitude we're up against. Do you mind if I ask if you were diagnosed with PTSD?'

'Never mentioned.' He said, proudly defensive.

'See, it's a dirty word to you and to Force Command. They're scared of getting a deluge of claims. Before I took a medical discharge, my colleagues and my managers all thought I was rorting the system on extended sick leave. Some made it clear by snubbing me, but even those who still wanted to know me would say things like, "It's only us, you don't have to put on an act". Or they want to do you a favour by getting you pissed — the universal stress reliever for coppers.

'You probably saw that when the Force was sued in court for causing PTSD, the Association declined to be involved. I tell you, Rory, the extent to which that culture is entrenched in the Force shits me. That's what this is about. I want to change that culture. Or at least put the issue out there. Get it into the spotlight.'

Rory sat with his arms crossed and didn't answer immediately. Michelle sipped her coffee.

'I do know what you mean, Michelle, and I know you have to begin somewhere …'

'Don't give me a "but" Rory, I know all the "buts". "It's always been like that. That's what police work is and it's never gonna change. A leopard can't change its spots", yadda yadda yadda.

'You don't have to *do* anything, Rory. You don't have to

come out of the PTSD closet if you don't want to. I just want to know how it is for you. You crashed in a big way, and now you're coming back in the face of a fearsome cold shoulder, albeit with some support from management. And I know there are other factors at play in your case but if you genuinely explored the root of your own state of mind, I reckon you'd be looking squarely at PTSD.'

'I know how screwed up I've been but I really don't want to look back,' he answered.

'That's okay with me. I'm not taking notes. There's no tape recorder. Why don't you tell me how you're coping now?'

He accepted there was no escape.

'Okay, but I have to warn you, I'm reluctant to explain myself. I don't know why, maybe that's a symptom too, or maybe it's just a bloke thing. But off the record, I know I was mega-traumatised by the shooting — it's a no-brainer. I had double relationship meltdowns thrown in there, Lauren *and* Heidi. Being off work, moving out of the house, my kids hating me — all thrown in for good measure. The only good side, if there's such a thing, I had no one to inflict my misery on. Then there's the alcohol, depression, Zoloft, psychotherapy. So where does the cause and effect start and end? And I don't mean that rhetorically.'

Michelle gave a head-tilt of empathy and let Rory answer his own question.

'It definitely starts and ends with the trauma. I'm trying to mend things with the kids and at least have a cordial relationship with Lauren. Finding my way back with the job is happening slowly but that's no lay-down misère either. I already know the flashbacks and the nightmares will be the hardest thing to shake off. They're abating, thank goodness, especially since I began seeing someone.' As he said it he wanted to touch wood. He knew it was only a matter of time before the nightmare reached into his time with Sigrid, and when it did, he'd be stranded in a support-free zone. 'You probably know this already, but I think I'm stuck with the nightmares whatever.'

'I admire that you have a relationship happening but don't take it for granted. Difficulty in maintaining close relationships is a big risk factor and PTSD symptoms have a habit of presenting themselves well down the track.'

The incident with Cockburn flashed into his mind.

She smiled.

'Don't think I'm smiling with any kind of smug satisfaction. I'm smiling because I think you're lucky. I was a cliché female copper, married another copper. Theoretically Alex should have understood and supported me, but it tore us apart. The hilarious thing was, Alex ended up with PTSD too, and I was too screwed up to notice and support him. You couldn't write that script, and if you did, would it be comedy or tragedy?

'You can't imagine how many "if-onlys" we both came up with, especially now that I'm doing this book. If I knew then what I know now, I reckon I could have made Alex's life as normal as he could ever hope for. Get him back to enjoying the simple things in life, have quality time together. But you're right. You can eventually move on from relationships-gone-bad, or they heal in time. PTSD is for life.'

'Fancy another cup?' Rory said.

Michelle smiled again. 'Why not?'

Rory smiled back. The hard stuff was nearly out of the way. Now they could enjoy each other's company for a bit, although one thought lingered: willing sensitivity and support for someone with PTSD, and knowledgeable … all going begging, it seemed.

'Are you with someone now, or seeing anyone?' he asked her.

'No. But I'm in a good space and I'm enjoying working on this PTSD stuff. Despite what I say, I do have plenty of supportive friends, including other coppers and ex-coppers. Funnily enough, there's also plenty of support from New South Wales. They're a bit more advanced. They have a support group, which is something I want to get involved in down here.

'I also have a publisher who's sweating on me finishing the book. They're keen to begin promoting it, which is the best bit for me. It means I can get the issue well and truly into the spotlight.'

'I'll be happy for you, as long as I don't hear about myself on any talk shows.'

'Don't worry, Rory, I don't think you're ready for anything like that either.'

'Why do you say that?'

'Well for me, the turning point came when I accepted I had PTSD and that I needed help. That acceptance didn't bring about an abrupt u-turn, mind you. It was more like a bottoming out before the graph began to creep upward. But it was a critical point nonetheless. Talking about your own case this morning, you never uttered the acronym PTSD. I think a lot more water needs to pass under your bridge. Still, it sounds like you have someone supportive to help you get there.'

Rory dropped his eyes. Michelle didn't know which nerve she'd struck.

'Let's stay in touch,' she offered as he laboured for a response. 'Why don't you think about what I've said and give me a call. Or I'll call you?'

'Yeah, I'd like that,' Rory heard himself answer.

15

'That doesn't stack up,' Inspector Rodney Ahearn said.

Inspector Ahearn was not an office person, despite his position of authority. He dressed in the SOG-style action fatigues that his fellow anti-gang division officers sometimes wore. And he sprawled over the tub chair as if it were a bean-bag. Before the Anti-Gang Division was created, Ahearn was with the Echo anti-bikie taskforce. Echo was recently merged with the Santiago taskforce, which dealt with Middle Eastern crime gangs. Although it was now one division, Ahearn was still the go-to man for bikie intelligence.

'Here it is, the owner is definitely Leon Crabtree.'

Gary Cockburn handed Ahearn a vehicle registration printout from the Queensland Department of Transport and Main Roads. Cockburn, Julia O'Hannagain and Ahearn sat in a breakout meeting space at the Anti-Gang Division offices. The area was fitted out with tub chairs around a glass coffee table. Ahearn studied the document with a frown on his sculpted face. It prompted Cockburn to reassure him.

'Same chassis number and engine number.'

Ahearn flicked the document onto the glass table.

'Hmm. Crabtree is with The Attilas motor cycle gang. They're not big players but they're serious players … or they were in Queensland until the Newman Government anti-bikie laws kicked in. Now they're jostling with a few others to fill the organised crime void created by Melbourne's gangland killings. Some contract work interrogating someone like Graeme Stanley would be right up their alley. That's if they were allowed to get away with it.'

'By other local gangs you mean?' Cockburn said.

'Exactly. From a bikie perspective, let alone any other point of view, you've got the longstanding presence of the Hells Angels and Bandidos. They've got enough shit happening between themselves without having to worry about ring-ins from up north. But apart from that, everything else is wrong.'

'Like why use their own van? And if they did use their own van, why abandon it?'

'Yep. Was it reported stolen?'

'No.'

'Any forensics?' Ahearn asked.

'Prints, DNA and fibres. But nothing we can match. They could all be pre-incident for all we know at this stage.'

'Where was it abandoned again?'

'Airport West. On the forecourt of a warehouse for lease.'

'Well I suppose you need to speak to them. Fuck knows what that will throw up. Should be interesting though.'

'How do you suggest we do that?'

'I can set it up for you. The Attilas have got premises not far from where you found the van, but you'd need a full-on raid to get in the place. I'd steer clear of that, however, until you know what you're dealing with. If we did go in there, it'd be for a good many other things we're working on, but we're not quite ready for that.

'Crabtree is an ex-Victorian and he sometimes stays with his mum in Preston when he comes to Melbourne. I'd also stay clear of his mum's place, unless you really want to kick the bull-ant nest.'

Ahearn laced his fingers and leant forward with his elbows on his knees. 'Trust me on this, Gary. We should stick to neutral ground until you find out what's really going on here.

'Why don't you leave it with me to set up a meeting with

just us three. A quiet chat to notify them that we've located an abandoned van we think belongs to them. We don't bring any anti-gang artillery. We let him bring his two-IC, or Deputy Head Hun in their lingo. Let him bring a lawyer if he wants to.'

Cockburn wasn't ready to settle the matter with a pally casual chat. He leant forward more determinedly.

'You know what we're dealing with here, don't you? This is no everyday murder, it's the next instalment in the Neilson Scali case that's been hanging over the Force for ten years. It might be the last and only real chance we get to crack this, so I don't think either of us wants to be the one to fuck it up.'

Ahearn became rigid in his pally pose. 'And how precisely do you think I'm fucking it up?'

'You're suggesting we simply have a casual chat with the Sergeant-at-Arms of a bikie gang, whose van was brazenly used in the kidnap, torture and killing of a known hitman, and ask him if he minds terribly, shedding some light on it for us?'

'Listen Gary, you're here because I know how these outfits operate. I can already tell you the Attilas did not do this. They don't lose vans, and if they do want to lose a van, they make damn sure it can't be found. At the very least they'd torch it. They don't come running to the Police when their stuff disappears. They self-insure and they do their own investigations. The fact that you've found it before they did gives you the element of surprise. You don't want to squander that by doing a full-on raid or even take him in for questioning. You do either of those things and the shutters will go up. Then you'll fuck up the chance to get some usable intelligence, which is the best you can hope for from the Attilas.'

Ahearn lightened his tone to appeal to Cockburn's sense of reasoning.

'I know it sounds too low key for you, but as I said, trust me, theirs is a complex world. This mob is not your target. They're a stepping stone.'

'On your head then,' was the most Cockburn would concede.

'You haven't said much, what do you reckon?' Ahearn said, turning to Julia. It caught her off guard.

'Oh … Yeah. A chat sounds okay.'

'Is Dermot O'Hannagain your dad?'

'Yeah.'

'I worked with him briefly in the Arms Offenders Squad. In the early days. He was good at getting results. Say g'day when you see him. He should remember me.'

'I will. He retired to Queensland, but we catch up on Skype.'

'Can you set this meeting up straight away,' Cockburn interrupted.

'Sure. Oh and one other thing. When we do meet with Crabtree, don't smile if the term Head Hun is mentioned. It doesn't go down too well.'

You're telling me, Cockburn thought. *At least it's a name they chose themselves.*

Church was the last place Cockburn expected to be meeting the sergeant-at-arms of a bikie gang. Not exactly a church, but the open space between St Mark's Christian Church and its hall-cum-Sunday-school. The bare asphalt space was entirely in character with the two 1970s dark brick creations. Describing them as creations may, however, have flattered the overly simple designs.

Importantly for the two Attilas members, a laneway ran alongside both structures to provide an exit into Degraves Street at one end and Bell Street at the other. The open meeting space was also not visible from either of those streets.

Leon Crabtree and his deputy sergeant-at-arms, or more accurately his Deputy Head Hun, strategically parked their machines facing the exits and dismounted to confront the three police leaning against their car.

Crabtree was less intimidating than Cockburn or

O'Hannagain expected. He was nonetheless big, nearing beefy with black hair slicked back into a pony tail. His face was more pudgy than hard with a Van Dyke goatee and moustache. The gold chain, ear studs and shades went without saying. Any tattoos were under cover.

Ahearn stood off the car.

'Do you need introductions?'

Crabtree stood with his fingers in his black jean pockets and looked apprehensively over each shoulder.

'You tell me. I don't know why we're here.'

'This is Detective Sergeant Cockburn and Detective O'Hannagain of the Homicide squad. They've found a van that they tell me belongs to you. Queensland registration. Would that be right?'

'Homicide?'

Crabtree checked across both shoulders again, only more hurriedly.

'That's right. The van was used in the murder of Graeme Stanley.'

'And you think we had something to do with it? Is that what this is about?'

'Do you think this is how we'd do things if we thought you were responsible?'

'Of course I fucking do. This is a perfect setup.'

Crabtree stepped into the lane to see if the entrances had been blocked off.

'There's no one else here, Leon. As a matter of fact, I *don't* think you had anything to do with Graeme Stanley, but the juries out with my two colleagues here. This is your chance to tell us about your van. Was it stolen?'

'Of course it was fucking stolen. When can we get it back?'

'Hold your horses. How come it wasn't reported stolen.'

'As-fucking-if. If it doesn't turn up or we don't turn it up, we write it off. We self-insure.'

Ahearn gave Cockburn a *I told you so* look. 'What do you reckon, Gary?'

'Where and when did it go missing,' Cockburn asked.

'A couple of weeks ago. It was stolen from the front of my mother's place at night. She doesn't like me having the bike there.'

'Uh huh,' Cockburn nodded thoughtfully and waited for more from Crabtree.

'Do you know how much those things cost and how much it costs to rent a replacement? We need to get it back.'

Cockburn swaggered closer to Crabtree.

'Didn't you hear Inspector Ahearn say this is a murder investigation? The van is evidence and you haven't told me anything about it yet. How your van happened to become involved in a murder, for example.'

Crabtree stepped into the last remaining space between himself and Cockburn.

'Ahearn will tell you who's got us in the gun, that's if it wasn't your mob trying to set us up, prick.'

'Okay, okay you two,' Ahearn said as Cockburn and Crabtree locked into some heavy-duty eyeballing.

'I can have a few educated guesses, Leon, but we need to be a bit more precise on this occasion. That's the point of this meeting. There's only us three and you two here.'

Suddenly, Crabtree spun around into a martial arts stance that startled two approaching uniformed constables.

'What the fuck?' Ahearn said.

One of the constables drew a pistol. The other simply looked frightened.

'Whoa whoa. Anti-Gang Division,' Ahearn yelled and held his badge aloft. 'It's all right constables. We're only having a conversation. What can we do for you two.'

Crabtree held his stance but looked bemused.

'We had a call from the vestry across the road. They said some bikies might be vandalising the church.'

'Sorry constables, we just bumped into our friends here and decided to stop for a chat. Tell the vestry we'll all be on our way shortly.'

'No. We're finished now.' Crabtree said. He and his deputy grabbed helmets.

'You haven't answered my question yet,' Cockburn said.

'Ahearn should know how we do things. Keep an eye out for the next drive-by.'

The constables watched and listened to the Harley racket echo between the church buildings before spilling down the laneway. They nodded to Ahearn, and wandered back down the lane.

'That went well,' Cockburn said.

'He gave you an answer. What more do you want?'

Cockburn screwed his face into a question.

'The next drive-by shooting of a rival's clubrooms. Give it twenty-four hours.'

16

'I've come to this over-rated mosquito-ridden puddle. Are we on or not?'
'It's the best tadpoling spot you'll ever have the pleasure of gracing in your lifetime.'
'Not if I had a choice, Harry Butler, and I don't reckon I'd be on me pat. Fuckin' waste of money locking this place up like Pentridge.

Rory hit Pause on his computer's media player. He had spent the past hour playing and re-playing the recording of Dwyer and the hitman.

A water supply reservoir? A sewerage treatment plant? Where else do they lock up a body of water? The botanic gardens after hours? he asked himself.

This wasn't the bit he intended to listen to when he re-opened the recording but it was a passage he was most drawn back to. He'd scoured the Melways and Google Earth for likely secured facilities with water and he was on constant vigilance wherever he drove. The answer somehow felt close. He expected it to jump out of his brain in a sudden lightbulb moment. Perhaps it was something obvious that he drove past every day.

'Fuck it,' he said aloud and reached for the mouse. He dragged the media player curser forward to another pre-determined point. He pressed Play.

'Graeme's not paying you. I am. And I don't part with money like that without seeing what I'm getting in return. But don't worry, Graeme will

be in touch if it goes pear-shaped or if it doesn't happen. He'll come to yours. I made sure his passport is current.'

Okay, Rory wondered. So he lives outside Australia and speaks with an English accent. Londoner, if anything. And was that a hint of Cockney?

So far, Interpol and the British police forces threw up precious little about possible hit men visiting Australia a decade previously. The best the Brits could offer were jibes like, 'Couldn't they find a local to do the job?'

He remembered Graeme Stanley used to be called 'Michael' because of his Michael Caine-like cockney accent. Perhaps the hitman was someone from Stanley's past. Perhaps I should try to find a British copper from Stanley's time in London. Email him a copy of the recording and see if he recognises the voice. Rory dialled Detective Gerry Denton.

'It's Rory James.'

'Oh hi, Rory. What are you up to?'

'I'm working my way through the Dwyer / hitman recording again. Can you tell me: has anyone looking into Graeme Stanley gone back to when he lived in England?'

'You mean like, before he emigrated'? Rory let Gerry answer his own question. *"Course not. Why do you want to know about back then?'*

'We might be looking for someone Stanley knew from those days.'

'I can try and track down someone over there to check their archives if you like?'

'We're gonna need a bit more than a list of previous offences. We really need to speak to a copper who dealt with him. Someone who might recognise a voice if we emailed the recording to him. Even if they've all retired in the meantime. Why don't you start with their Retired Police Association?'

'What, just ring them up?'

'Ring. *Skype.* They're retired coppers. They'll love getting their hands dirty again.'

'Yeah. Okay then.'

'And can you do me a favour and retrieve the original USB stick of the recording from evidence. I'm taking it to the Forensic Centre to get an expert analysis done.'

'I'll do that first. See you soon.'

Rory hung up and brought his attention back to the screen. He navigated to another part of the recording.

'… speaking of which, did you bring it?'
'There's seventy-five grand.'
'And the rest?'
'Upon delivery of course.'

He dragged the curser back along the recording's timeline-bar.

'… speaking of which …'

He listened to this bit again before hitting Pause and staring at the blank screen. His brain stuck on seventy-five thousand. That was only the down payment. Presuming it was half the fee, that made it one hundred and fifty thousand for a life. And more for two lives, Rory remembered. He navigated forward and quickly found what he was looking for.

'Okay, okay. Twenty more,' Dwyer's voice said.
'Forty grand … and I won't be putting that in writing either.'

That made it one hundred and ninety thousand to kill Clifford Neilson and Corina Scali. Perhaps Graeme Stanley took a cut as the middleman. A finder's fee. Suppose he took twenty-five percent, thirty percent tops. The killer still made over one hundred and thirty thousand.

To benchmark the fee, Rory retrieved an online research paper he was stunned to stumble upon when his enquiries to Interpol and the British police forces drew blanks. The British Hitman: 1974-2013 was published by Birmingham City University. *How do researchers get their hands on data like that?* he marvelled to himself again.

When he completed the pounds to dollars conversions, it seems the average cost of a hit in Britain was around $28,000. Whoever killed Neilson and Scali got top dollar, even if they had to fork out for an airfare.

The study also identified four hitman types: novices, dilettantes, journeymen, and masters. The latter seemed a certain match for the Neilson Scali hitman profile. Unfortunately, as the word "masters" implied, and its description confirmed, this category of killers were as skilled at not being nabbed as they were at carrying out the task at hand. "… the most elusive to study and the least likely to be caught" it stated. "These killers are likely to come from a military or para-military background and could be responsible for up to one hundred hits. The major reason the master killer evades justice is that they travel to an area to carry out the hit, without any local ties, leaving minimum local intelligence about the hit or the hitman". If the degree of difficulty wasn't hard enough, try adding ten years onto the investigation, Rory thought.

The abstract concluded, "It is hoped that this typology will be of use to law enforcement".

'Not,' Rory spoke out loud this time.

'Talking to yourself again. You know what they say?'

Hamish Lynott stood at Rory's office door. Rory's tea-break companion and the manager of the civilian Commercial and Electronic Branch, continued:

'You want to come downstairs for a coffee? Sounds like you need it.'

'Thanks. I will in a minute. But have a listen to this first.'

'Sure.'

Hamish sat down in the chair across the workstation from Rory. Rory switched back to the media player and began the disquieting recording from the start.

'So you came in person?'

'Is that who I think it is?' Hamish asked. Even members of the public had come to know Dwyer's distinctive voice during the years of TV news coverage of the investigation and court hearings.

'Yeah. It's David Dwyer. None of this is for your ears but I reckon you've heard enough of it when you set it up on Bourke's computer. I want to ask you a technical question.'

'About the recording?'

'Yeah. I need to confirm that it hasn't been tampered with and prove what every man and his dog knows: that it is actually Dwyer's voice. I'm about to head out to the Forensic Centre to see what they can do. Do you know about stuff like this?'

The recording was still playing and Hamish listened for another minute or so before offering an answer.

'You can stop it now. I get the picture.'

Rory clicked Pause.

'To my ear, it doesn't sound like it's been tampered with. There's no inconsistencies in the noise floor. That's the background noise. Any noticeable changes in the noise floor mean it is not a continuous recording. If that were the case, who's to say what editing may have taken place? There's one or two sound labs in the country who'll be able to sign off on that for you. The Forensic Centre should have those details. But voice recognition, that's a bit less of a science.'

'Okay then, spoil my day.'

'I'm no expert, but as I understand it, if you do want an expert opinion, you'll be relying on a trained phonetician making a call, backed up with some technical acoustic analysis. The best you can hope for is a *highly probable* or *likely* and you know how that can be torn apart in court. But that doesn't mean you can't rely on people who know Dwyer also testifying about whose voice they think it is, does it? That's your best bet I reckon. He's got a pretty distinctive voice and you wouldn't be short of reputable people who could offer an informed opinion, surely. Go for weight of numbers.'

'Not all bad then,' Rory smiled, 'What about pinning down the time and place it was recorded?'

Hamish crossed his arms and frowned.

'I know you say that in jest but you've got another problem there.'

'Shit. How can it be worse?'

'Well let me set your mind at rest about the location of the recording. It can't get any worse because there's obviously no technical way of telling where it was recorded.'

'And that's supposed to be the good news?' Rory's voice rose with incredulity.

"fraid so. The "when" is your big problem. I checked the embedded metadata on the recording when I was setting it up for Bourke. It seems that your recording is not the primary source. Although the fidelity is very good, it was nevertheless transferred to its current format about six months ago. It was probably recorded onto its current format from a microphone placed in front of a speaker. When the sound travels that few centimetres between speaker and microphone, it leaves its original embedded metadata footprint behind. More to the point, it gains another one. If you asked me when this recording was made, as a technical expert I'd have to answer, "any time between six months ago and when the tape recorder was invented".

'Unless you have someone who actually knows when it was recorded, you can't guarantee it wasn't recorded one year ago, or ten years ago.'

Rory let his head drop and shook it slowly. He lifted his gaze to Hamish and gave the wryest smile.

'How about that coffee now?'

'How about a single-malt?'

17

'So, this is the nerve-centre of the Cold Case Unit?'

Rory looked up to see Julia O'Hannagain standing in his office doorway holding some documents.

'Everyone finds their way here eventually.'

Julia's red hair was pulled back into her usual bushy pony tail. She wore a pale-blue collared shirt tucked into black slacks. The silent female appraisal of his spartan office stung. She glanced back at the grid of Commercial and Electronic Branch workstations before responding.

'No they don't.'

She even had Cockburn's bluntness — no wonder they hit it off, Rory decided.

'Well *you've* found yourself here. Any particular reason?'

Julia walked into his office and sat down. That surprised Rory.

'Gary asked me to bring you these.' She handed Rory two sheets of paper. 'They're David Dwyer's Approved Visitors List and Approved Phone List. They came from the PIU this morning. The Prisons Intelligence Unit. And Gerry said you wanted this.'

She held up a labelled clear plastic zip-lock bag holding the USB stick received from from FP1.

Julia spoke distractedly as she unapologetically scrutinised

Rory's office. She leant forward to look at paperwork on the desk, noted at which page the Melways was open, and peered at the couple of hand-written notes Rory had made on his wall calendar.

'Would you like the guided tour?' Rory asked.

'Sorry,' she said, straightening in her seat. 'It's the detective in me, I guess.'

Rory held a dubious expression, long enough to make his point and to have her break the silence.

'It's the names, dates of birth and addresses of people David Dwyer has put on his visitor and phone lists. They have to be on the list if they want to visit him, or for him to make phone calls to them.'

'I know what they are. Any surprises?'

'Na. His bookie — he's a bit of a punter. His brother, his mum, a part-timer who does work with his olive trees, and his accountant slash, "partner in crime". That's it.' She made air-quotes when she said *partner in crime*.

'You mean Bruce Taylor.'

'Yeah. Accountant. What a joke, hey? Dwyer should do himself a favour and get a proper professional.'

It was Rory's first one-on-one with Julia and everything she said seemed loaded.

'You know Bruce Taylor. A bit before your time, isn't he?'

She placed imaginary hair behind her left ear. Her actual hair was already held back tightly.

'Yeah. Way before my time. But I used to hear Dad slag off about him when Taylor got kicked out of the Force. My Dad is Dermot O'Hannagain — Inspector O'Hannagain before he retired.'

Rory consciously stopped his eyebrows from rising.

'Mmm, I remember Dermot O'Hannagain.'

He picked up the visitor list and glanced at it

'Dwyer's mum? I imagine she's a fair age. Her address is in Bundoora. Is that at a nursing home?'

'No. She's in her eighties and she still lives in the original family home. On her own. Dwyer's dad died just before this Neilson Scali stuff happened.'

Rory looked back at the list.

'Ray Samson is the bookie, right?'

'Yep.'

'Peter Dwyer, brother. That makes Angelo Neri of 20 Goroke Street Castlemaine the worker.'

'You got it.'

O'Hannagain's tone was distracted again. Her eyes fixed on the photo of Steph and Nick that Rory had pinned beside the calendar.

'Your kids?'

'Yep.'

'Uh-huh.'

Julia nodded her head in a way that told Rory she wasn't ready to leave. Rory waited.

'Anything more on the recording?' she said.

'Did Gary tell you to ask?'

'No. Just wondering. He said you were working on authenticating it. Analysing it for clues.'

Rory put the best spin he could on it.

'I've found out it hasn't been tampered with.'

'That's good.'

'Yep.'

'What about the Bon Scott reference? Did you figure out where that came from?'

Rory had given up trying to figure out how Dwyer came up with the convenient Bon Scott death-date association. More correctly, he hadn't known where to begin and thought no more about it.

'Nothing yet. Any ideas?'

'Nah. Been too busy. Nothing else then?'

Rory wondered what it was about Julia O'Hannagain that

made him so reticent. Was it because Cockburn's approach seemed to be rubbing off on her? Had he sent her on a charm offensive for intelligence? Something else?

'Not so far. How about your end? What have the Attilas got to say?'

The question startled her for a beat.

'Oh. You mean the bikie mob,' she said, betraying a momentary thought that Rory was referring to her and Cockburn as Attilas. 'They weren't involved in the Stanley thing but they know who was. We're waiting for them to show us who.'

'Show you?'

'Rod Ahearn of the Anti-Gang Division figures the Attilas were set up. He reckons they'll do a drive-by shooting within days. Whichever bikie clubrooms cop it will give us the answer.'

'I suppose it's too much to expect bikies to communicate in English.'

Rory watched Julia O'Hannagain make her way through the Commercial and Electronic Branch workstations to the lift. One or two heads turned. He picked up the approved visitor list and dialled the number that was hand written at the bottom of the page — someone's direct line at the PIU.

After many rings a male voice spat out, *Prisons Intelligence Unit*'. Somehow he managed to make it sound like one word. Rory had to clarify the answer.

'Is that the PIU?'

'Yep.'

'It's Detective Sergeant Rory James of the Homicide Squad. I wanted to speak to someone about the David Dwyer-approved visitor list.'

'What about it?'

Rory winced. What made them like this? What did they do all day? It's not like they had to mind the prisoners themselves. He pressed on.

'Am I speaking to the right person? Is this something you

handled yourself?'

'*I collected the list when I was at Loddon Prison two days ago, if that's what you mean?*'

'That is what I mean. Can you tell me who I'm talking to please?'

'*Sorry. Senior Constable Dwyer. No relation though.*'

Rory didn't know if he was more surprised to hear him say sorry or that his name was Dwyer. He hadn't told Rory his Christian name though. More teeth to pull.

'Well Senior Constable Dwyer …'

'*Steven.*'

At last. I might be talking to a human after all.

'Well Steven, you were at Loddon Prison. What did they have to say about Dwyer? David Dwyer, who I am pleased to hear is no relation.'

'*They should make it compulsory for crims to change their names. Innocent families like us cop stuff you know …*'

Rory looked to the ceiling of his office. There was something wrong about Steven Dwyer being in a unit with intelligence in its name.

'You were going to tell me what the word is about David Dwyer … Steven.'

'*Not much. They reckon he's true to type — Arrogant and resentful like all coppers are when they end up inside.*'

'Uh-huh. And how is he spending his time, did they say?'

'*Yeah. You'll like this bit. He spends his day listening to the recording you guys came up with. Playing different bits over and over. He uses ear buds, so don't ask me which bits he's interested in. He's obsessed with it, they say.*'

'That *is* interesting. Has he had any visitors or made any phone calls yet?'

'*Umm …*'

Rory heard Steven Dwyer flick through some papers.

'*… So far he's spoken to his accountant, Bruce Taylor, and Angelo Neri, his farm worker. Just taking care of business, they say. Farm business, I mean … it's a busy time for olives, apparently. I didn't mean taking care* *of business crim style.'*

'Gotcha.'

There was silence from Steven Dwyer's end.

'Any contact with his mum.'

'Nuh.'

'So that's it? Nothing else you can tell me?'

'Nuh'

He might not be related to David Dwyer but he wasn't doing a bad impression.

'Do you mind if I check in with you from time to time on this number, Steven?'

'If that's what you reckon.'

Rory looked at the phone handpiece before responding. Wasn't it the PIU's raison d'etre to provide intelligence relating to prisoners?

'I do, Steven. Thanks. See you later then.'

'Ciao.'

Click.

Rory put the handpiece in the cradle.

'Ciao?'

He looked at the authorised visitor list again and read the entry for David Dwyer's mum.

MARGARET AGNES DWYER, D.O.B. 18 MAY 1931, 42 O'CONNELL STREET BUNDOORA

'This could narrow down the search,' he said out loud and immediately lifted his head to check that Hamish Lynott was not in earshot. He seized the computer mouse and clicked his way to the Dwyer recording. He knew the exact spot to locate along the recording's timeline bar.

'I've come to this over-rated mosquito-ridden puddle. Are we on or not?'
'It's the best tadpoling spot you'll ever have the pleasure of gracing.'
'Not if I had a choice Harry Butler, and I don't reckon I'd be on me pat. Fuckin' waste of money locking this place up like Pentridge.

Tadpoling. That was strictly a childhood thing, wasn't it? No adult ever went tadpoling. Adults didn't even take kids tadpoling. It was something that kids found out for themselves. A kids-only word-of-mouth thing. Something that was automatically erased from kids' brains once they left primary school. If Dwyer was raised in Bundoora then that's the neighbourhood where he would find, *the best tadpoling spot you'll ever have the pleasure of gracing*. Let's see.

He typed 42 O'Connell Street into Google and clicked on the map option. The cropped map view did not have any blue shapes indicating bodies of water. There were plenty of green expanses close by, however. Public land most likely. At its north-west end, O'Connell Street terminated at a huge park frontage to Darebin Creek. Darebin Creek Bushland Track and Grasslands Road made their way through the parkland. There was sure to be plenty of tadpole-bearing puddles in there as well as the creek itself.

The other end of O'Connell Street ran into the six lanes of heavy traffic that was Plenty Road. On the other side of Plenty Road, the map showed another vast swathe of green. This one was labelled Agricultural Reserve and shown to be part of the La Trobe University campus. Plenty more opportunity for tadpole habitat. There could even have been more tadpoling opportunities in those days, depending on when some of these housing estates happened. How old was Dwyer?

Rory opened the on-line case file and found Dwyer's date of birth: 18 May 1956. Shared a birthday with his mum. Her birthday present Rory noted. Rory tossed the thought aside and calculated Dwyer's tadpoling years as the early and mid-nineteen sixties.

Rory zoomed out a couple of notches on the Google map. Blue patches appeared on both sides of Plenty Road, but mainly in a chain of ponds stretching across the La Trobe university campus. All well within a kilometre of O'Connell Street.

Rory stroked his chin and stared at the image.

All right. Is the place that Dwyer met the hitman in front of me on the screen? Julia O'Hannagain said Dwyer's mum lived in "the original family home". How did she know that? He would need to check it in any case, but assuming Dwyer did grow up around here, this was where he discovered tadpoling nirvana in the sixties.

A baby boomer. Baby boomers were continually banging on about their unconstrained childhoods. How they would leave home in the morning to roam the world, free of parents' fretfulness. They only came in through the back door when it was time for the evening meal. Their range would easily exceed one kilometre, even without a bike, which most kids had in that era. Darebin Creek would undoubtedly be a key attraction for pre-pubescent boys as well as all the other surrounding bushland. It was probably an era when Bundoora was still semi-rural. He could check on that later but from what he knew, La Trobe was no sandstone university. Perhaps it hadn't yet sprouted onto the pre-pubescent Dwyer landscape.

Rory leant into the screen to study the map detail.

Forensic Drive caught his eye with a double take. It jumped from the screen like your own name does in a page full of dense text. It was the address of the Victoria Police Forensic Centre in Macleod. *Of course, the suburb of Macleod adjoins Bundoora, so the Forensic Centre backs onto La Trobe University.*

Wasn't the Forensic Centre where David Dwyer attended the training course he bragged about on the recording as his alibi? Rory was pretty sure it was. The very place he was about to go to arrange for them to examine the USB stick of the recording. Machinery within Rory's brain began to whirr and drop pieces into place before his eyes. Suddenly there was no doubt that this was the neck of the woods where Dwyer met the hitman. You could take the boy out of Bundoora, but you couldn't take Bundoora out of the boy.

18

Rory left the original USB stick at the Victoria Police Forensic Centre. No new revelations there; in fact, they told him less than he had learnt from Hamish Lynott's casual evaluation. Providing the recording hadn't been tampered with, they would have no trouble obtaining an irrefutable technical report to support that analysis. They would also determine whether the recording was from the primary source and whether there was any embedded data to fix the date it was recorded.

'Do your worst,' he told them and left the complex of low, bland, flat-roofed buildings set amongst lawns, gumtrees and expansive sealed carparks. His focus was now firmly set on where it was recorded. He sat in the unmarked Police car and studied the map on his phone.

The sealed portion of Forensic Drive ended at the Centre's security gate entrance. It nevertheless continued as a dirt track for another hundred metres or so. Rory drove to an improvised car park at the end of the unmade road. About twenty car drivers had obviously discovered a shady fee and permit-free area from which they could complete their journey on foot through the band of bush that separated the Forensic Centre from the university campus. A substantial concreted pedestrian / cycling path led the way.

He followed this path on foot and the bush soon gave way

to the outer campus of large freestanding buildings set in native-treed parkland. The path had a dotted central line suggesting volumes of traffic. Perhaps in peak hour — so far he hadn't encountered a soul in either direction. Direction signage on the outer-campus ring road told him that this was the Research Park. He continued for about half a kilometre to the core of central campus buildings. The collection of seventies-brick monolithic boxes rose on the opposite bank of a moat that passed through the campus.

Rory leant on the balustrade of the pedestrian bridge and looked at the landscaped chain of water passing beneath. Judging by the modern era of the buildings, this would have been ideal undeveloped tadpoling country fifty years ago. Only one thing was lacking — it wasn't "locked up like Pentridge". Anybody could wander in here.

After being on a roll to identify the general area, Rory expected the Dwyer / hitman meeting place to jump out at him. He looked at the map and realised how large that general area was. The green bands on the map went kilometres to the east, west and north. He wasn't going to manage it all on foot.

What a cloistered existence students have, he observed as he wove his way back through the ring of massive car parks to the treed parkland perimeter of the campus. He was within sight of his car when he reached a fork in the path that had passed unnoticed on his ingoing stroll. The branch headed away from the university. Nevertheless, being so close to the Forensic Centre where Dwyer was attending a training session, it was worth a look.

The new path quickly emerged from the bush onto Terrace Way, alongside the Environment Protection Authority's vehicle testing station. The garage-like testing station faced the street's name source — a row of more than a dozen matching two-storey mid-twentieth century institution-like buildings. It resembled an ex-mental health asylum that Rory felt he should know the name of. He began running names through his mind. Larundel? Aradale? Wilsmere? Obviously not Kew Cottages, something more …

His thoughts halted at the sight of a high Cyclone-wire fence at the end of Terrace Way. As he got closer, he could see that it was no ordinary security fence. The very top had cantilevered wire-mesh overhangs of half a metre or more on both sides. Not a high bluestone wall "like Pentridge" but at least it had the look of an asylum seeker detention centre. Or it would have if it wasn't simply securing native bushland. There was no sign of anything man-made behind the wire. He headed for a sign on a locked gate where the security fence reached the roadway.

LA TROBE MELBOURNE WILDLIFE SANCTUARY. GATE 10.

A wildlife sanctuary. That's what the fence is about, keeping wildlife in, or keeping predators out. He replayed the recording in his head.

> *I've come to this over-rated mosquito-ridden puddle. Are we on or not?'*
> *'It's the best tadpoling spot you'll ever have the pleasure of gracing.'*
> *'Not if I had a choice, Harry Butler, and I don't reckon I'd be on me pat. Fuckin' waste of money locking this place up like Pentridge.*

He studied the map on his phone. There it was. A grey patch within the University grounds. Not small either. About thirty acres Rory estimated. He had been concentrating on areas shown in green. The sanctuary — the most innately green feature on the map — was shaded grey. It even had a couple of blue shapes indicating stretches of water within. — the water where Dwyer and the hitman rendezvoused? He turned back to the path he had come along. It would have taken Dwyer less than ten minutes to walk here from the Forensic Centre. Rory wouldn't be caught dead quoting John Denver … but he could still think it. *'Some days are diamonds …'*

Rory looked around, soaking in his discovery. The gate was secured with a lock that was only accessible from the other side of the wire. I wonder what security existed ten years ago? Someone will know.

'Mont Park.' He said it aloud. The name of the former psychiatric hospital came to him as he walked back past its terrace of red brick buildings. *Definitely on a roll.*

It was a couple of kilometres by road before he reached the northern side of the sanctuary along Main Drive. The sanctuary was overlooked by a new-ish upmarket housing sub-division. A signboard along the roadside alerted him before an upcoming intersection.

LA TROBE WILDLIFE SANCTUARY
ENTER VIA LA TROBE AVENUE

There was another sign at the La Trobe Avenue entrance. He parked roadside and read through the windscreen.

LA TROBE WILDLIFE SANCTUARY
• Indigenous Plant Nursery
• Bird Boxes
• Education Experiences
• Twilight Tours
• Office Hours
Sunday – Friday
10 am - 3 pm

A big blue "P" indicated parking.

The time was quarter to five. *Looks like another trip.*

The drive back gave him time to reflect on his discovery. There was every chance that Dwyer and the hitman met somewhere in the sanctuary. He might not know the precise spot but everything fitted. It was a compelling theory, but so what? He may have figured out the *where*, and even if he could prove it, he realised it was knowledge that counted for little without the *when* and the *who*. He may have been parked within a few hundred metres of where Dwyer and the hitman met, but authenticating the recording of that encounter was as distant as ever. His euphoria bubble burst as quickly as bubble-gum.

'Some days are diamonds, some days are stone'. Sometimes both on the same day.

19

'They want *me* to do it.' Richard Bourke said.

'No offence, guys…' Adrianne said to Rory and Cockburn, '…but it has to be a face that people trust absolutely. Someone people warm to instantly.' She switched her attention back to Richard Bourke. 'You've got that face Richard … *and* you know what you're talking about. Still no offence,' she added with a quick glance to Rory and Cockburn.

'Even if this person is not a criminal they still would have written police off totally, and let's be frank, you've got bugger all cards left to play on this one. You can't offer them protection. That would be like the spider inviting a fly over for dinner … telling his guests "I've changed".

'However, at some stage before they lost complete faith, they would have wondered: "Who can I go to? There must be someone you can trust in the organisation". Well let's answer that question by putting a face to it. They see your face on screen Richard and before you've opened your mouth, you're their favourite uncle, the father of the girl next door, the …'

She knew she was struggling and finished her case with a resigned, 'That's the only ounce of credibility we have to offer.'

'Okay I get it, Adrianne'

Adrianne Dahl, Assistant Director Media and Corporate Communications. Her title might include media and communications but her talk was pure marketing. She could be workshopping a proposed advertisement rather than scripting an appeal to the public about a murder. Adrianne had the glossy make-up look of a breakfast television show host off pat, along with an over-fondness for theorising the obvious.

No offence, Rory thought, *as long as we don't use your face, Adrianne.*

'I've prepared a dot point list of what you need to say,'

Adrianne dealt copies of the single page across the meeting room table to Bourke, Cockburn and Rory.

'You don't think you're going a bit early on this one?' Rory said.

Bourke jumped in to defend Adrianne and the decision to go public.

'You're the one who's telling us Dwyer's allowed to appeal his non-bail … that we're going backwards with the evidence. We started off with a red-hot recording and the more you work on it, the more useless it's becoming. When I ask a detective to follow up something I expect things to progress, or at worst, to maintain the status quo — not to go downhill.

'Unless we get some substantiation on this, Dwyer and his counsel will attack its admissibility with a Mack truck. As far as I can see, the only person who can tell us when and where this recording took place and with whom, is the person who posted it to us. Dwyer's not going to tell us and you can be sure Graeme Stanley won't be saying anything.'

Until that moment, Rory thought he was having a good day. The night before could almost have passed for "normal" in anyone's book. Buoyed by his discovery of the sanctuary, he drank to celebrate rather than medicate, despite it not being something he was ready to put on the table. Not until he could return to the sanctuary for a closer look. It might not be *the* breakthrough, but that was something to be optimistic about.

Now his flimsy equilibrium was stuck on the words: "… at worst to maintain the status quo. Not to go downhill". *Criticising my performance behind closed doors was one thing but having a go at me in front of Cockburn and Adrianne is … it's not something you expect from*

Bourke. Is he really that pissed off with me? If he is, am I really just clinging on. Fuck.

Bourke pressed on with his line of thought.

'I know you've got Gerry Denton chasing old buggers in England who might know the hitman, but even if you do end up identifying the hitman, you can be certain his first thought won't be to spill his guts and stitch himself up with a conviction.'

Struggling against glumness, Rory wasn't ready for Bourke to have the only say.

'Won't this televised statement be conceding defeat to Dwyer and his counsel?' Rory dared to question.

'No. I've thought about that and I'll be making it clear that Dwyer was arrested on the strength of what the informant has already sent us. For Dwyer and Braden Ramsay's ears, I'll make certain they know that the case against Dwyer is in the bag. Then I'll be letting our unknown informant know that by communicating with us in some way, we think they can help us identify the hitman. They more than anyone will be aware that there are two people involved in the murder of Neilson and Scali. I'll hint that the reward is not a done deal without also nailing the person who actually pulled the trigger.'

'But it is a done deal if Dwyer is pinged by the recording,' Rory said.

'Of course it's a done deal, but casting a bit of doubt might make them anxious. It could loosen things up.'

Rory nodded without conviction.

'We do know which gang killed Stanley,' Cockburn said to get in on the act.

But there was no pleasing Bourke this morning.

'Because the Attilas did a drive-by shooting on their antagonist's clubhouse? You've still got a long row to hoe there, Gary,' Bourke said. 'And when you do happen to convict them for murder, how exactly will that authenticate the Dwyer / hit man recording?'

'Okay,' Cockburn said and lifted his hands off the table to back off.

'So that brings us back to my starting point. The only person who can tell us what we want to know is the person who sent us the recording. The person who has put their hand up for the reward. We stress that they can remain anonymous and I'll leave it open to them about how they want to communicate.'

'That's why I've made these dot points, Richard. Can we run through them one by ...'

Bourke lifted his right hand to halt Adrianne. No one was immune from his contrariness.

'Thanks, and I appreciate the preparation, Adrianne. But do you mind if we do it in reverse. I'll tell you what I want to say and you tell me if I've covered everything.'

'Uh. Okay.'

'All right.' Bourke said, satisfied he had at last placated everyone in the room. He sat straighter to begin. 'I let people know that we have received information anonymously about the Neilson Scali killings that took place ten years ago. We acknowledge that the information is valuable and has resulted in David Dwyer being charged for arranging the murder. However, it is also likely that the anonymous source can help us identify the person who committed the actual killing. The person who actually pulled the trigger. The person for whom the reward of $1,000,000 dollars is offered.

'We believe the person who provided the initial information can help us reconstruct a key related event that preceded the murder. We ask that they contact us via Crime Stoppers or any anonymous means of their choosing. This person may be hesitant because they think they have no additional information to offer. However, we know that that person may not even know that they know what we want to know ... Something like that. What do you reckon?'

Adrianne remained un-customarily silent.

Cockburn remained customarily cutting, 'Are you channelling Donald Rumsfeld?'

Adrianne found voice. 'That covers most of it, Richard. Let's work on the English a bit.'

20

When Josh wasn't on a field trip, they had an unspoken weekday evening routine. Martha tended to stay late to catch up on things at the office, hoping Josh would have thought about an evening meal and have something on the go when she walked in. She always looked forward to walking in, finding out what music he had playing, and what smells emanated from the kitchen. The wine was comfortably predictable — always a cleanskin quaffing shiraz from their friend Greg Livesay. Greg was a contract winemaker for local growers who lacked the wherewithal to produce it themselves. Greg always set aside a case for himself and his friends to enjoy — always good, often very good. The TV never came on until the ABC news at seven o'clock.

She had been to the Winebank on the way home to buy something special. A Wild Duck Creek shiraz. It wasn't exactly a peace offering but things had been tenser than usual since the sanctuary recording thing began to play out. Josh seemed to be taking forever to get over the Graeme Stanley death. Nothing more had been said but a fug of unease seemed to linger. Surely resentment was not bubbling within because the scheme was of her making. *A clever scheme for which he expressed his admiration,* she justified to herself. *And hadn't they talked it through again and again?* Now that she reflected on things, *she* was always the persuader. *He*, the perennial persuade-ee.

Josh wasn't like that, she reassured herself. He would never bear a grudge, at least not out loud. Nonetheless, a top-notch wine couldn't make matters worse. If there was something simmering inside, nip it in the bud.

The music was The Bamboos, *I Got Burned*. Dinner was a production. Satay-style tuna cakes. A fresh potpourri of lemongrass, garlic, ginger, coriander, coconut, soy, lime juice and chilli sauce greeted her nostrils. The music played loud. She could sneak up on him and grab him around the waist. He kept chopping the lemongrass.

'You saw me coming!' she yelled.

'Lucky for you,' he yelled back, and held up the thirty centimetre blade in a stabbing pose.

She kissed him, released him from her hug and turned the music down to conversational level.

'I love your fish cakes; do you want me to do the salad?'

'Na, I got it covered. How was your day?'

'An office day. Nothing special. Yours?'

'Sent off a couple of applications. Had a walk in the bush. Nothing to report either.'

'What boring lives we lead. I'm gonna change. Can you pour me one of these?'

Martha produced the bottle of Wild Duck Creek wine from her bag. It wasn't the legendary opulent and equally expensive Duck Muck from the renowned Heathcote estate, but a pricy top-end choice nonetheless.

'Wow. A Wild Duck Creek. What's the occasion? Did I forget something?'

'No occasion. I just thought we deserved a treat right now.'

He looked at her with unsaid questions. In the end, he smiled and agreed.

'I guess we do.'

When Martha returned, a tomato and cucumber salad was on the bench, as was a tray of tuna patties ready to cook. Josh was on the two-seater sofa that was squeezed into the open living space. Martha's shiraz waited for her on the coffee table.

'I want to catch a bit of the news before I cook them.'

Martha sat beside him and took her glass just as the seven o'clock news theme chimed.

They sipped and chatted through suspected terrorists being arrested, a bus that rolled down an embankment and floods in Queensland. Then Richard Bourke came on to appeal to the anonymous informant about the Neilson Scali murder. They sat in statue-miming silence. It wound to an end … *Angela Fellgate reporting from the Police Media Centre, Melbourne.'*

The anonymous informant about the Neilson Scali murder reached for the remote and turned the TV off.

'I knew this would happen,' Josh said loudly. 'I just knew it. They're fucking with me now. Well that's it. I'm outta there. Fuck the reward. They've got the recording now, I'm gonna get on with my life without having to worry about that stuff ever again. If they can't convict Dwyer when it's handed to them on a plate, then that's their problem. I've done my bit.

'And that bit about the reward being for whoever actually pulled the trigger. What is that supposed to mean? Are they trying to weasel out of paying the reward? Slimy pricks. No wonder no one trusts them. I should have just sent the recording in with nothing else and left them to it.

'And don't try and change my mind this time. That's it.'

'I agree,' Martha said to calm Josh. 'I agree with you. This is no reason for us to drop our mask. There's no need at all to panic so let's just think about what it all means.'

'I'm sick of thinking about it. That's all I seem to do lately.'

It confirmed her instinct. The whole thing was preoccupying Josh's mind.

'I know. I know, Josh. You've got to stop worrying about it, though. Just let things play out. You're protected whatever happens. If they do convict Dwyer and not the hitman, then it's not our worry. In my professional opinion, I think it's a bluff that the reward is dependent on both being found guilty.

They're hoping whoever sent them the tape is ignorant of the law. They're fishing so you'll come forward and give them a description of the hitman. Or they hope you'll say something that will give away how and where the recording came about. They want to have their cake and eat it too. But like you say, that's their problem. 'I'm with you all the way, Josh. We don't do anything. We absolutely do nothing.'

'Too fucking right.'

He was still angry despite Martha's empathy but she was heartened that at least he was agreeing with her. She pushed to keep them both on the same page, and without saying it, to keep that page open.

'Absolute anonymity on our terms is our greatest protection. We said we wouldn't go any further. Let's keep it that way,' she said.

Now that he had started, Josh was intent on airing all his trepidations.

'I didn't expect the cops to play it so hard to try and out me. It feels like I'm the crim and if I breathe they'll find me. If the cops know who I am then who's to say Dwyer won't. He knew about Graeme Stanley in no time flat. Nowhere's safe from pricks like that. Look what happened to Leon Blofeld. And what about Carl Williams? They say he was going to testify against an ex-cop and he was killed in broad daylight in prison, in front of witnesses and on CCTV. Nowhere in the world would be safe. Fuck it. They can sink or swim with what we've already sent to them. We're outta there.'

Josh sat tensed on the edge of the couch. Martha put her glass down and brushed his face.

'We are so out of there Josh. Look at what I just came home to, before the news I mean. Who needs a million dollars? I can still afford to lash out on a hundred-dollar bottle of wine. From now on in, we get on with living the life we would have had if you weren't at the sanctuary on that day.'

Martha wondered, *have I just ruled out claiming the reward no matter what? Surely Josh wouldn't baulk at activating our claim if the recording did bring Dwyer down?*

21

Rory pulled into the sanctuary car park, which also served the indigenous plant nursery. It was early Sunday afternoon and there were about a dozen other cars. It appeared that most of the drivers and their passengers were browsing the rows of potted seedlings laid out before shade-houses, poly-houses and sheds. A fingerboard indicated a path to the sanctuary beyond.

'Not what I expected when you said you'd show me the sights of Melbourne,' Sigrid said.

It was the first time Rory and Sigrid had travelled together; the first time they'd been out of Bendigo together. Sigrid's guests had checked out of the B&B early and Rory suggested a Sunday drive that would stretch into Monday. It would be Sigrid's first visit to Rory's flat. It was the first time Rory would have a woman in his post-divorce home, apart from Steph.

'I'll make up for it when we go out tonight.'

He wasn't sure if it was a good idea but he knew they'd been coasting long enough and someone had to move things along. A night at his place was probably the worst romantic move he could make but he was one to get anything bad out of the way first. Like a school kid doing homework on a Friday night, although when he thought about it, he grew up with a last-thing-Sunday-night habit. He also found a potential bright side: the Sigrid / Rory magic might exorcise the nightmare spectre from his flat. *Surely that was worth the risk.*

Now he wasn't so sure. He'd spent most of the drive from Bendigo wishing they were flying to Byron Bay instead. That would be his next suggestion — if they survived this weekend. And then there was the matter of how a contentedly independent woman of means like Sigrid would view his modest existence. He'd had a cleaner in to get the place back in order but what do they say? "you can't polish a turd". They, whoever they are, also say "the best way to remove a bandaid is ..."

'Only joking,' she allayed him. 'I'm a Melbourne girl, remember. I don't need the sights. Something new is good. Where exactly are we?'

'It's a wildlife sanctuary I need to check out — behind the nursery. It's a work thing but I thought we both might find it interesting. We don't have to stay long.'

'Really. Like Healesville Sanctuary. I used to love going there as a kid.'

'I don't think it's like Healesville. That's like a zoo thing. I read that this is more about preserving animal habitat. I'm not sure there'll be too much action. More like a sanctuary in the tranquil sense.'

'I can do tranquil.'

'I *think* that's what it's like. I haven't been here before either.'

'So why on a Sunday? Don't they open through the week?'

'They are open on work days but it's a bit tricky. I want to go under the radar on this one, if you know what I mean.'

Sigrid didn't know what he meant and Rory wasn't about to elaborate: how the recording was leaked from within the Force; how Dwyer inexplicably learnt about the first instalment of the recording. The name *Graeme* was not mentioned in that first snippet but Graeme Stanley was dead before the full version arrived. Only Dwyer could have connected that original snippet with Graeme Stanley. '*...we probably still have an internal security problem,*' was all Bourke said initially. There was no "probably" about it after the bombing of Calvin Steele's car in Parkville.

It had begun with only a small circle in the know — himself, Cockburn, Bourke, the Chief Commissioner, his PA Bev, the Minister, probably the Minister's adviser too. *Big enough*, Rory thought. Now a toxic cloud hovered above the whole team. Share only what information needed to be shared, he decided.

He tried not to entertain doubts about Bourke, or even Cockburn. Did they have doubts about him? Bourke had voiced unwavering confidence in his and Cockburn's loyalty. However, Bourke's confidence in Rory's fitness to do the job was showing threatening cracks. Rory needed the sanctuary to deliver — something, anything.

'I've got no idea what you mean,' Sigrid said. 'But as long as I stay on your radar ...'

She reached for her sun hat on the back seat. It was more of a man's hat — a white straw topper with a navy band — but she couldn't have looked more womanly to Rory. She held his arm as they collected a trail map and made their way through the entrance. Rory quickly determined a route to the nearest lake. The trails were wide formed earthen paths, ideal for a Sunday afternoon stroll through native forest. No other humans were in sight. The path followed the high perimeter security fence and soon reached the main lake which had the name Main Lake. More of a swamp in Rory's opinion — black, shallow and still. Perhaps too small to even be called a lake. Maybe they should have a geological term for a small lake. *Maybe they already did*, he thought.

'It *is* tranquil here,' Sigrid said as she held his arm.

That's the point, Rory thought. This was one place you could be certain of not being observed between the hours of 3.00 pm and 10.00 am. *And look at that*, right on cue — he slapped a mosquito on his arm as he passed under a redgum by the lake. The hitman's words: "... *mosquito-ridden puddle*," resounded.

'That's the first sign of wildlife,' Sigrid said, 'And look ...' she continued a bit louder and looked down.

'Errrrr-aaahhh,' Rory uttered as he broke into a backwards

levitating Peter Garret move.

They were standing beside a lethargic looking shingle-back lizard sunning itself beside them on the path.

'Fucking hell.'

'Isn't he cute,' Sigrid said and bent to stroke the sluggish lizard despite its open mouth protest.

Meandering took them past a native canoe tree and a rusting car body which was obviously preserved as an iconic Aussie feature — a car dumped in the bush. Or perhaps left in situ as habitat.

'A Holden Belmont, I'd say. You've got to love that as much as you hate it,' Rory declared.

More intriguing was a fenced enclosure surrounding an above-ground swimming pool. Some water weeds grew in its dark water and pictures of frogs hung off the fence in a half circle around one side of the pool. Some kind of nature teaching set-up.

The first human appeared when they reached Iron Bark Hut, as it was referred to on the trail map. The structure could hardly be called a hut though; it was far too tall and spacious as well as lacking enclosed walls. The ironically rural corrugated-iron roof atop a framework of un-milled tree-size poles provided a sheltered bush function space. It was furnished with equally rustic tables and seating. A barbeque and a patina of use attested to plenty of past merriment.

An old bloke sat bent over on the end of a rough-sawn backless pew alongside an equally rough-sawn table. He clutched a handful of weeds.

'Are you alright?' Sigrid asked.

He looked up but remained hunched over. Rory realised his lack of posture had set in with age. Well into his eighties, Rory estimated when he saw the old man's face. It was a thin pale face, full of friendly creases. He took a moment to take in Sigrid and Rory before he answered.

'Yeah, just catching my breath. I've been pulling a few weeds.'

'You work here?' Sigrid asked.

'Not exactly. I used to be with the Friends of the Sanctuary volunteers before I went into the nursing home. We used to have a wonderful time on working bees. A lot of revegetation in the early days. Later on, we got into fauna surveys and other stuff. We had a great time. The other volunteers probably still do. We'd always end up here. It was usually the best part of the day. Now my daughter occasionally drops me out here for a few hours of a Sunday. When I see weeds popping up, I find I haven't lost the habit.'

'You must miss the others,' Sigrid sympathised.

'Oh, I still enjoy coming here, even on my own. It's where I grew up.'

'You grew up here? You must know how the sanctuary came about.' Rory asked.

'My oath I do. It wasn't even thought of when I was a kid. This was all part of the Mont Park lunatic asylum. They had a full-on farm set-up as well as the nuthouse. We were scared of the place but that didn't stop us exploring it.'

'Did you live anywhere near O'Connell Street?'

'O'Connell Street?' he asked himself and thought for a moment. 'Na, it must be on the west side … in Bundoora, I think. Most of that area wasn't subdivided until after the war. We were in Watsonia on the east side.'

It had been wishful thinking for Rory to image the old bloke came from anywhere near O'Connell Street, but there was still a good chance he knew more about the area and the era. 'So you were here before the war?' Rory asked and slid onto the opposite pew. Sigrid sat down beside Rory.

'My name's Rory James and this is Sigrid,' Rory said before the old bloke could answer.

'Ron. Ron Townsend' he said. 'Pleased to meet you.' He reached across the table to shake their hands. 'Yes, I was raised in this area, until the war. I came back after I got married in 1958. Mont Park still ran the farm then but it was winding down. The sanctuary started in '67, the same year as the uni.'

'So, all this area was undeveloped in the fifties and even the early sixties?' Rory pushed.

'Oh yeah. There was no university. Our kids grew up here. It was one big playground for them. For me too. I was so pleased to see this bit set aside as a sanctuary when the uni began. We weren't called greenies back then and I still don't care for the term. We were part of the Field Naturalist movement. They're still around, you know. Anyway, I took an interest in the sanctuary from day one.'

'No wonder you can't keep away, Ron,' Sigrid said and smiled.

'We had to after a while. Once they fenced it, we couldn't just wander over whenever we liked. The kids did, though. They always found a way under, over or through the original perimeter fence. The high predator-proof fence never went all the way round. It still doesn't go all the way round but they're working on it … replacing the last rough bits of old fencing. Then they'll be able to get rid of the predators. They still get foxes in here … and other predators, you know.'

'So I hear,' Rory said with conviction.

Ron and Sigrid both gave him a questioning look. The comment prompted Ron to ask, 'So what do you do for a crust, Rory?'

'I guess I'm a public servant.'

'With the environment department?'

'No. Justice.'

'Oh,' Ron said. He sounded and looked crestfallen that Rory hadn't turned out to be a fellow conservation traveller.

'What's the above-ground swimming pool used for?' Rory asked to buck Ron up.

'Ah …' Ron sprang back to life. 'That's part of the teaching set up. They get a lot of primary schools coming here on excursions. The swimming pool is like a mini wetland for critters and frogs and stuff. They teach the kids frog calls … play various frog mating calls on tape so the kids can recognise the different species and …'

'They *record* the frogs?' Rory interrupted too rudely and too loudly. Ron took Rory's excitement as genuine interest in frog calls. He pushed on, oblivious to a scowl from Sigrid.

'Indeed they do. There's at least nine species in the sanctuary. In the evenings during the breeding season, it's like the frog version of full-on pub chatter.'

'So someone actually comes out here with a recorder and a microphone to capture it on tape?'

'Yep. That's pretty much how it happens.'

'And whose job is it to do that?'

The question baffled Ron. He thought for a long moment before answering.

'I'm not sure who would have done the particular recordings they use in the sanctuary education classes. There's a lot of people who record frog calls. Froggers are like bird twitchers — always trying to capture something on tape or on camera. They're as bad as trainspotters, if you ask me. But as far as who did the actual recordings used by the sanctuary, you'd need to ask someone at the office.'

'Froggers? You're not pulling my leg are you Ron?' Sigrid said.

He laughed. 'They've got their own clubs, Sigrid. You could join them if you like.'

'I think I'll stick to the human species, Ron.'

He laughed again. 'Me too.'

'We might keep going, Ron, it's been good chatting,' Rory said, suddenly eager to move on.

'Okay then. It's been nice chatting to you both too. I hope you enjoy the rest of the sanctuary. You can learn a lot wandering around here, you know.'

'You're telling me, Ron.'

~

'That was nice, but did you have to sound so evasive. Inferring things and telling him you're a public servant with the justice department. He's an old man who's just being friendly, Rory, not some suspect you're interviewing,' Sigrid admonished.

'I suppose I was a bit guarded. I wasn't trying to bullshit him though. Something about this case, it makes me …' He had intended to say *cautious* but decided it might prolong Sigrid's reproaching. '… I dunno.'

'We're supposed to be having a day out, remember. Forget about work.'

'Okay but I want to check one thing before we leave. I'll just duck into the office. I won't be a tick.'

The pathway circuit had brought them back at the nursery. Rory left Sigrid frowning at him among the rows of potted plants.

The makeshift office cum nursery counter was manned by a bright young woman wearing khaki shorts, a sleeveless fleece and the highest-tech pair of Gortex boots he'd ever laid eyes on.

'We've been talking to one of your volunteers in the sanctuary and he was telling me about the recording you have of frog calls. He said you use them in education classes.'

'We do. Did you want to hear them?' She sounded puzzled.

'No. I was more interested in how they are recorded.'

'You mean technically. Or where we source the recordings …' She trailed off sounding even more puzzled.

'Were they recorded here in the sanctuary?'

'Oh,' she said, latching on to a question she could answer. 'Probably not. I understand the recordings came from an outside organisation. The Amphibian Research Centre or someone like that. You can go onto their Frogs of Victoria website if you want to hear any of the calls.'

Rory ignored the suggestion and asked, 'Would anyone ever record frog calls inside the sanctuary?'

'I don't think so. The only people who might have done are

some of the honours and PhD students. I understand there's been a few of those over the years. Students whose thesis investigates localised questions concerning frogs.'

'So you'd know who they were? Can you tell me their names?'

Rory had let police-speak sneak in. The cheery smile disappeared from the end of her answers.

'There'd be a few over the years, mostly before my time. You'd have to ask Professor Lamb about that.'

'Sorry. I don't want to go to that sort of trouble. I'm not as interested in the frog aspects as I am in the actual recording.' Rory's less than logical explanation only slightly eased her unease.

'You could do a search on the National Library Trove website. They have a database of most Australian theses. Maybe you should browse that for whatever it is you are interested in.'

Whatever it is you are interested in, sounded less than friendly, time to bail.

'Okay. I might do that. Thanks for your help.'

Rory started the car's engine but hesitated with his hand on the gear nob. Sigrid had her gaze well and truly locked on to him.

'What?'

'Now that's a shit-eating grin if ever I saw one.'

Sigrid's turn of phrase startled Rory.

'That's not something you say.'

'It's not every day I see such a smug, self-satisfied stupid look on someone's face. What happened in there?'

'*Some days are diamonds …*' Rory began to sing.

'Aaarrrgh … If you're gonna sing John Denver, you can drop me off here.'

Rory laughed and drove out of the sanctuary car park.

'No more work. I promise. How does St Kilda, my place, and dinner at Café Di Stasio sound?'

'I want to see your place.'

It took less than an hour to get there from Bundoora in the light Sunday afternoon traffic. Landmarks along the way triggered stories from each of them about their Melbourne lives. Rory eventually pulled up across the road from the sixties cream brick block of six flats with kitschy white-painted wrought iron balcony balustrades. He began apologising.

'The good thing about places built in the sixties is the size of the rooms. It's before they began shrinking flats to shoeboxes. I've got a balcony and there's the park over the road.' He breathed a sigh of relief that the kebab van shut up shop early on Sunday. The fact that he was on first-name terms with Aesop would not send a good message. 'The other thing going for it is: it might be the worst house in the best street but that's much better than the alternative. Oh, and a good coffee hole in Ormond Road. I'm on the upper floor … number six.'

Sigrid sank in her seat to peer up through the car windscreen.

'I do like the area but it's not going to win any architectural awards.'

'Well that's where you might be wrong. Some locals are talking about getting it heritage listed. There's not many of these left around here. They're knocking them down to build multi-storey jobs. It's like the last standing fibro shack at the beach.'

'I can see it's more than a fibro shack, Rory.'

'Don't expect too much.'

As they crossed the street on foot, Sigrid noticed the line-up of wheelie-bins along the driveway fence. It was probably not bin-night because the lids on only one pair of bins were angled upwards with overfilled rubbish. Those two had the number six roughly daubed on the side. A packed plastic bag bulging from the top of the general-waste bin had been penetrated by birds and scraps lay on the ground. The recycle bin told a different story — more than one protruding Stolichnaya bottle and a swathe of takeaway cartons. It appeared that number 6's sole occupier had more than a routine mess to clean up.

The eyesore and the moment of alarm on Sigrid's face went unnoticed by Rory as he led her to the main entrance.

When they reached the door to his flat, Rory turned the key and allowed Sigrid to cross the threshold before him. He followed, carrying her overnight bags along the short hallway to the living room. He waited as her eyes roamed.

'Spacious … and I like the polished boards. There's a richness about them that you don't get in modern houses. You're a bit spartan and Ikea-ish with the furniture though. The bookshelf on milk crates takes me back to share-house days. Can we replace that while I'm here?'

The speed at which the suggestion came out was telling.

'The actual shelf *is* from Ikea. I tossed the frame away when I lost the Allen-key.'

She tilted her head into a doubting look. Rory followed her silent inspection of the bathroom, two bedrooms and kitchen.

'It has got a certain Rory-ness to it,' she said. 'I'm glad you did the flowers. They make it feel more like a home.'

'They are good, aren't they?' Rory said, admiring the vase of deep red gladiolas that the cleaners had arranged as he had asked.

It didn't escape Sigrid's attention that he was also seeing them for the first time. Nor did the tell-tale signs of a professional cleaning job. Should she be annoyed or flattered? Should she be more concerned about the prior state of the place?

'Hmm,' she prevaricated further, then held his waist to kiss him.

'Not slumming it too much for you?'

'Well it's no Manse, but I already have one of those.'

Rory smiled an un-reassured smile. His mobile phone saved his struggle for a comeback. Sigrid released his waist and listened to Rory's side of the conversation.

'Steph. How are you?'

The sound of Steph speaking to Rory was undecipherable static to Sigrid's ears. She could nevertheless follow the path of the conversation.

'As a matter of fact, I just walked in,' Rory said next.

Sigrid imagined he'd been asked: *Are you at home?* He had answered "I" and not "we". *Hmm.*

'What? Right now?'

Steph doubtlessly said something like: *I'm in the neighbourhood, can I come round?*

'It's probably not the best time.'

Sigrid's face hardened with the realisation Rory hadn't told Steph about her.

'Yes, the place is cleaned as a matter of fact. That's not it.'

So his flat had been in a state Sigrid deduced. How bad had it been to become an issue for his daughter?

'Yes. I am as a matter of fact.'

Aha. Steph must have figured it out with: *Are you with someone?*

'No. Someone else. You haven't met.'

Sigrid already knew they hadn't met. What was new was hearing herself being referred to as "someone else". If she was "someone else", then who was someone? Her face hardened again as she tried to tune out of the rest of the conversation.

Things quickly got to the nub. She noticed Rory gradually soften his stance.

'Uh-huh.'

'I'd like to but it's probably better if I tell you when I see you.'

'Well we'll be going out later. I've booked … but …'

The bottom line was: there was no way he could refuse her coming to his flat again. He had to at least leave that door ajar.

'Yeah, that's okay. We were probably going to hang around here until we go out tonight.'

'Yeah, that'll be good.'

'See you soon, then.'

'Sigrid,' he added sheepishly before ending the call.

There was no hiding that she'd asked Rory what Sigrid's name is.

He looked up from pressing End Call on his phone. The arms that had been around his waist when the phone rang were now crossed.

'It's Steph. She's coming round. She'll be here in ten.'

'I'm sure she's very nice Rory, but you could have given me some warning.'

Her arms were still crossed.

'You heard. This is not something I planned. I haven't even told her about you yet. Anyway, it's not such a bad thing … is it?'

'Hmm.' Sigrid began and pursed her mouth. 'You might recall I've been married three times. From my experience, these things don't always go swimmingly, especially when it happens without warning.'

'Well I couldn't say no, we had a slight disagreement and now we're in a make-up phase.'

'I gathered there was something like that … oh and while you're at it — joining all these dots for me that is — if I'm the "someone else" she hasn't met, then who is the other someone she does know about?'

Rory face struck a thinking pose as he appeared to replay the conversation in his head.

'Oh. That was Michelle Fox-Jones. Steph knows about the PTSD book stuff that Michelle is keen to involve me in. Steph seemed to latch onto the idea as something that's good for me. I didn't want to dissuade her but you know … she worries about me. Anyway, I've been through this with you. Michelle's book is something I intend to steer well clear of … remember? I met up with her so she could explain what it's about, and now I'm ready to tell her no thanks.'

'You mean you'll be meeting her again.'

'I have to. But it's work stuff. Basically, it's something I was ordered to do, so I can't be too eager to dismiss the idea. I have to play the game. Anyway, why do we end up arguing about this? It's not like it's something I knew about and chased after. It's exactly the opposite in fact.'

Sigrid had pushed it far enough. She gave an unconvincing ready-to-move-on 'Hmm,' and sat down.

'You'd better tell me about your daughter then.'

There was no sigh of relief from Rory. It rankled that she referred to Steph as "his daughter" instead of as Steph.

'Steph, short for Stephanie …' he began.

The air-kisses were awkward for Steph. In Steph's world, anyone she was on cheek-kissing terms with did it properly. The clash of Steph's and Sigrid's worlds was not lost on Rory, but any hope he harboured that things could only get better, quickly vanished.

'So what are you studying, Steph?'

'Outdoor Ed.'

Had there been a way of saying so with less syllables, then Steph would have opted for it. She nevertheless knew she had to offer something.

'What do you do, Sigrid?'

'Hospitality.'

Although it broadly covered what Sigrid did, it wasn't the answer Rory expected to hear. And the way they paused before saying each other's name was chilling. It occurred to him that some women may well be from Venus, but some occupied an entirely different orbit. Perhaps that new speck of a planet they recently discovered somewhere beyond Pluto. He panicked and jumped in.

'Sigrid owns and runs a B&B in Bendigo. That's where we met. It's one of the grandest historic homes in Bendigo. Heritage listed, isn't it Sigrid?' He looked at her for help.

'Yes, Rory. It is.'

'You'd like it there,' Rory continued. 'We should get you up there for a stay. It's right near the centre of town and there's so much happening in Bendigo these days.'

Steph turned on Rory.

'What? And have you drag me around all the old haunts from when you were growing up. Most of them aren't even there anymore? I don't think so. Been there. Done that.'

She seemed triumphant to have come up with a plausible way to rebuff a stay at Sigrid's. No mind that Rory was collateral damage.

Sigrid came to Rory's rescue.

'That's right, Rory. You've forgotten what it's like to be young. Steph doesn't want to be lumbered with a couple of grown-ups carting her around to see the sights of a country town. Boring ...'

Steph turned to Sigrid, intent on not allowing her to empathise, if that's what it was. Or was she having a dig about not being a grown-up yet?

'A B&B, what qualifications do you need to run one of those?'

'Steph ...' Rory complained.

Sigrid gestured to Rory that it was okay.

'To begin with Steph, you need a lot of money. Something like The Manse, which is the name of my villa, costs at least five times what you'd pay for most decent houses in Bendigo. Even with a mortgage, you'd need an awful lot of money — which I don't have by the way — a mortgage that is.' Rory had never heard The Manse referred to as a villa, nor had Sigrid ever make a point of how much money she had.

'... but the B&B business is a people business, so you must be able to please all types. First and foremost, you have to like people to make their stay perfect. That's what it boils down to in most jobs. When you start earning a living, I think you'll even find that's the case for whatever people do in outdoor education.'

'And you know how to, "please all types"?'

It was getting ugly but Sigrid was un-fazed. It was a battle in which Steph was way out of her depth.

'I learnt my craft as an attendant on Concorde. You needed to speak French and German to deal with the elite of international travellers. Those supersonic airliners may have ceased flying but no current day service is even half as fast. Nor do they offer anywhere near the level of passenger attention.'

Speaks French and German Rory was impressed to learn for the first time.

'Why don't we sit down? Would you like a drink, Steph?' he tried.

'No thank you. I … I only wanted to make sure you're all right. I think I'll keep moving.'

She turned to glare at Sigrid, who smiled the smile of an enemy. 'Nice to have met you.'

Rory followed Steph out the door to make their goodbyes on the landing. And to have the kiss and hug that didn't happen upon her arrival.

Sigrid waited for Rory to return and close the door. 'I warned you,' she said.

'"They don't always go swimmingly" I think you said. Have you ever had one that does?' He was annoyed that "daughter meeting dad's new girlfriend" was even a thing. And he was annoyed to find himself in the unfamiliar territory of being annoyed with Sigrid.

22

The next day's making up with Steph was no easier than the strained night with Sigrid. That thaw took until their after-dinner coffees at Café Di Stasio.

With Steph he got in first and slipped out of Sigrid's earshot to phone her straight after breakfast. They both seemed wearied and resigned to getting on with a less than unenthusiastic father / daughter future. Steph blurted out things she'd weighed in her mind overnight, but not yet resolved into a perspective.

'I'm sorry. I knew you were seeing someone. But, I don't know … it's all so … in real life it's so not what I expected. But I can see how it's good for you. The flat was clean at least. I noticed that. That's a positive. And don't worry about me, I'll get used to the idea. It's just that it might take me a while.'

He could tell over the phone that she attempted a lame smile.

'No, I'm sorry, Steph. I should have filled you in earlier. And you're right that it's good for me. Heaven knows I need some light to balance …' He paused to consider how he could euphemistically describe the other half of his double life. '…some darker passing moments.' was the best he could muster.

'Oh god,' she responded to let him know how farcically understated his self-description sounded. *'I know you're trying to play it down, Dad, but that other side of you scares me too. It sounds schitzo.'*

'It really is not that bad,' he tried. 'And I'm not making excuses. I shouldn't have even gone there. I actually phoned to talk about you and me. What are you doing tonight? How does a home-cooked meal at my nice tidy flat sound? Just you and me.'

It was the most he could possibly do to make it up to her, other than somehow get un-separated and un-divorced.

'Yeah? You're not driving her back to Bendigo?'

It was going to take a while Rory noticed. She wouldn't say Sigrid's name.

'I am going to Bendigo, but I won't be staying. I have to be back in Melbourne for a four o'clock meeting. What do you say?'

Steph left a deliberate thinking-about-it silence.

'Alright then,' came her matter-of-fact reply.

It was going to take longer than he thought.

Rory called into the seafood section of the Queen Victoria market on his return trip from Bendigo. His crumbed flathead fillets and homemade tartare sauce was Steph's favourite of all the dishes he once cooked in the family home. She would expect no less. The cooking itself kept the serious conversation at bay and gave them both time to get a wine under their belts.

As usual, it was Steph who couldn't wait.

'I hated that Heidi police woman and I never even met her,' Steph announced as Rory cleared their plates.

This was it, he told himself and bought a few moments by refilling their glasses while he was on his feet.

'That's normal. That was when your mother and I were separating.' he said as he sat back down at the table.

'I know all that. But she was getting all that sympathy in the newspapers and I hated her so much I was going to go and see her in hospital.'

'You were? And say what?' Rory said with curiosity and alarm.

'I don't know. I got cold feet in the end and she would have been long out of hospital by the time I learnt about you and her. The point is though: I thought I got all of that out of my system back then … and you never ended up with her anyway, even if you and mum didn't get back together. But that's a long while ago now and I've had a lot of time to think about what it would be like when you did end up with another woman … and when mum ends up with some bloke, I suppose.' She made her afterthought sound like an even more daunting prospect. 'In my mind, I tried to be mature about it. I imagined — or hoped, I suppose — that whoever you ended up with would be someone I could like and even have an interesting rapport with. But look what happened. I acted like a sulky twelve-year-old before she had a chance to open her mouth. I hate how that just happened.'

Her gaze darted about and she lifted her glass and put it back down.

Rory reached across the table and placed a hand on one of hers to settle her attention.

'It's me who should feel guilty. I didn't warn you about Sigrid. And I've been letting you down in too many other ways. It scares me that I let things get this far out of whack. I mean it really scares me because I really should have known this could happen. One of the first things the therapist told me was that close relationships are most at risk. And yet I end up jeopardising ours in any case. I'm so sorry, Steph. I know how bad this has all been for you and I really want to make things better. I really do. You and Nick are the most precious things in my life … you always will be.'

Saying it out loud to Steph caught his breathing and he feared his eyes might well. He was nonetheless determined to hold his daughter's gaze. She sniffed to regain her own resolve and to deny Rory his moment. She wasn't finished by a long shot.

'I know that Dad but you can't cook your way out of this. It has to be more than a nice meal, saying you're sorry and making-up. I want all that too but I don't want it to fall into a cycle. I don't know much about PTSD but I know it doesn't disappear overnight — if ever. I mean, look at this place. I can see you got professional cleaners in … although you did it for her, not for me,' she hastened to add. 'And you can't tell me you'll never let the place go downhill again because of … whatever it is that happens to you. But I understand all that and as much as I don't want it to happen again, I don't want to be excluded. You're my dad and I care about you no matter what.'

This time his eyes did well and a single tear escaped. He couldn't speak.

'God, you're not supposed to cry. You're my Dad.'

Her own face struggled between trying to smile and trying harder not to crack-up too. He still had his hand on hers and he squeezed it tighter.

They held the moment until Steph sat back with a recovering, 'Look at us, will you? We're both hopeless.'

'You'll never be hopeless,' he told her. She smiled and sipped her wine.

A comfortable silence fell. A contented and comfortable silence. Nevertheless, he wondered if she wanted to know about Sigrid. Should he raise it or would that sour the mood?

'Are there any blanks you want me to fill in?'

He thought he was being tactful but she knew exactly what he was thinking.

'Let me enjoy tonight like this. Next time you can tell me everything. What she's like, how you met, whether you think we'll get on … how serious you are.'

'The last bit could be tricky.'

'You bugger. You can't leave that hanging and you know it. You said that on purpose. Well I'm not going to bite.' She threw her serviette at him with mock annoyance.

Rory was relieved. He hadn't said what he said with any purpose, it just slipped out. He genuinely didn't know how serious he was, or more worrying, how serious he wasn't. And he didn't want to talk about it, least of all with his daughter.

'Thank God,'

'That's even worse,' she said and raised a cup as if to throw that too.

23

Gerry Denton was explaining why they were sitting in a meeting room with a laptop at 9.00 o'clock in the evening.

'It's ten in the morning over there. He's old-school. He doesn't have a computer at home, so I had to wait for the local bobbies to pick him up and take him to the station.'

'So he's retired?'

'That's why it was so hard to track him down. He retired to a place called Christchurch, in Dorset. It's on the south coast. He wasn't easy to track down. Do you want to know how I found him?'

'I already know… you're a detective. That's what you do,' Rory said.

'You know how to take the wind out of someone's sails.'

'Sorry, Gerry, What's his name again?'

'Ivor Gently, Ex-Sergeant Gently.'

Rory raised an eyebrow, acknowledging the same surname as the English TV show, Inspector George Gently. Gerry looked at his watch.

'It's time. Are you ready?'

Rory gave a go-ahead gesture and Gerry clicked the green *Skype* "Call" icon. In no time, vision appeared with a female constable in uniform beside an elderly bloke in civilian clothes. They were sitting side by side at a table, as were Gerry and Rory.

'Hi there,' said the female constable. 'Can you see us?'

'Yes we can,' Gerry said. 'Are you Alicia?' he asked with far too much surprise. He had spoken to her on the phone without it occurring to him that she might be black.

'Yeeees …' she said with deliberate caution. It was her way of letting him know she knew why he was surprised. '… And this is Ivor.'

'Hello,' Ivor shouted and leant forward to peer at the vision of Gerry and Rory. 'This is my first time on Skype. It's good, isn't it?'

'It is when it works. Pleased to meet you, Ivor. I'm Detective Constable Gerry Denton and this is Detective Sergeant Rory James.'

'Hello, Rory,' Ivor and Alicia said in unison.

'I'll move aside and let you talk to Ivor. I'll be in earshot though, so let me know if you need anything.'

Alicia slid out of the picture. The screen moved as she shifted the camera to centre Ivor onto the screen. They could see that he was well into his retirement years but nevertheless buffed in a septuagenarian kind of way. His silver hair was plastered straight back from his forehead and his thin pink face glowed from a fresh shave.

'Is that better?' they heard her voice say.

'Much. Thanks Alicia.'

'I'll kick things off then,' Rory said. 'You know Graeme Stanley, Ivor?'

'I know both of them. Graeme Stanley senior and Graeme Stanley junior. Not that they were called senior or junior. The dad's been dead for quite a while so I suppose you're talking about Graeme Stanley junior.'

'I guess I am, Ivor, although Graeme Stanley junior is also dead. He was murdered a few weeks back.'

'So I hear. You're going back thirty-odd years since he lived here, though — a good few of which I've been retired — so I'm not sure whether I can tell you anything useful.'

It didn't stop him trying, though. Ivor was a talker and he'd been given the floor.

'I did check my old notebooks last night to try and jog the memory. What I can remember is: the Stanleys all lived around Hackney. I was stationed at the Hackney nick in Clapton Road for most of my career. It's not there now. The building is but the whole place has changed.

'Our main worry in those days was the dad, Graeme Stanley senior. He was a bad egg. He eventually went down for his part in knocking off the Security Express depot in Shoreditch. That put the wind up Graeme junior and his brother Brian. I reckon they would've both been in their late teens. They were already earning themselves a good kick or two up the bum from us. You could do that back then; pioneer social workers we were. Anyway, they were shaping up to follow in their dad's footsteps. When Graeme senior copped such a long stretch inside, they both decided to emigrate. We thought it would be the making of them. So did their mum Lois. Never heard much about them after that. We assumed they made something of themselves. Wishful thinking by the sound of it.'

Ivor paused.

'Wasn't it Graeme Stanley junior that did time for the armed robbery?' Rory asked.

'No. It was the dad. Graeme junior only got nicked for petty stuff. I don't think Australia would've let him in if he had a serious record, would they?'

'Well I'll be buggered,' Rory said. 'He must have put it about that he did the crime. He probably dined out on the rumour to build his own reputation. He ended up becoming one of Australia's hardest-core criminals and he's never done time … anywhere.'

'But he lived by the sword,' Ivor said. 'And it sounds like he died by the sword. I wouldn't lose sleep over it, Rory. Look on the bright side. From what I hear, his brother Brian stayed out of trouble. They didn't both follow in their dad's footsteps.'

Gerry cleared his throat.

'We were going to ask, Ivor, if Graeme would have had contact with anyone from his Hackney days,' Gerry reminded Rory. 'A ten-year-old voice-recording has come to light in relation to a murder and we reckon it could be someone from Graeme Stanley's old stomping ground. Graeme's not on the recording but a bent cop called Dwyer and someone that we don't know talk about him. Someone with what I reckon is a London accent. It's a long shot but we want to play it to you and see if it's a voice you recognise.'

'You might as well. I'm here now. I'll do what I can.'

Gerry placed a speaker near the inbuilt computer microphone and played the recording until the hitman's voice featured.

'I've come to this over-rated mosquito-ridden puddle. Are we on or not?'
'It's the best tadpoling spot you'll ever have the pleasure of gracing,'
'Not if I had a choice, Harry Butler, and I don't reckon I'd be on me pat. Fuckin' waste of money locking this place up like Pentridge. Speaking of which, did you bring it?'
'There's seventy-five grand…'

Ivor rested his chin in his hands as he listened intently. Then he thought about it intently.

'*I don't know* is the short answer. Whoever it is certainly has the Hackney accent. But it could be more than a few that I dealt with over the years. If I had to name someone, I'd say it sounded like Graeme. But that's no help, is it?'

Ivor spread his hands in a that's-all-I've-got gesture.

'Never mind, Ivor, like Gerry said, it was a long shot. And you have managed to dispel a Graeme Stanley myth. We'll just have to keep plugging away with whatever else we have. Thanks for coming in to help us.'

'Oh. My pleasure … and good luck with it, Rory. By the way, I'm not sure who Harry Butler is but Pentridge, is that your local nick?'

'Yeah. Good deduction, Ivor. It was the main Melbourne

prison until about twenty years ago. Our version of your Pentonville or Wormwood Scrubs if you like. As far as Harry Butler goes, you'd be forgiven for not knowing who he was, even if you lived here. He's a bit of a forgotten figure these days. Kinda like an early version of Steve Irwin. I presume you've heard of him over there.'

'The Crocodile Hunter?'

'Yeah, but a whole lot tamer, and big in his day from what I hear. But that's got nothing to do with what they're talking about on the recording.'

'Gotcha … I think.'

Something about Ivor's questions set off another chain of thought in Rory's head. Gerry did the signing off with Alicia before interrupting his reverie.

'How come everything is leading us backwards instead of forwards?'

It was an unintended reminder of Bourke's gripe. Indeed, Rory thought. Like a game of snakes and ladders without the ladders. Every snake he landed on took him closer to the bottom of the board. Drawing him right back to where he began his tentative return to duty.

'How come everything is leading us backwards instead of forwards?' Richard Bourke asked.

'Why does everyone keep saying that?' Rory lamented, hoping for respite.

'Because you've got abso-fucking-lutely fuck all from the recording,' Cockburn hissed. You had no trouble hearing that, Rory thought, before Cockburn kept going on about it. 'From what I hear, the evidence is getting more inadmissible by the day. And your Graeme Stanley English connection got blown out of the water. You're lucky there's some real police work being done around here.'

Rory had his mouth open to defend himself but stopped when Cockburn's last comment registered.

Bourke added an additional interruption. 'Now now, girls, we've got company,'

Rory and Cockburn turned to the door of the meeting room where the three of them sat at the end of a twenty-seat table. A dapper version of Richard Bourke stood at the doorway with a laptop and a bulging manila folder under his arm. His deeply tanned bald head melded with a brown — but nonetheless sharp — suit.

'Morning, Richard.'

'Good morning, Earl. Come in.'

Bourke rose to shake Earl Jansson's hand. He switched the laptop and file to his left arm and gripped Bourke's hand.

'This is Senior Sergeant Earl Jansson. Meet detective sergeants Rory James and Gary Cockburn.'

More handshakes and smiles ensued before Earl took his place at the table.

'Earl's with the "Sporting Integrity Unit".' Bourke said using air quotes to name the relatively new unit created by politicians in response to the latest round of sporting scandals. 'But he's not new to the game. Earl's been maintaining intelligence on sports betting since we had a real gaming-squad back in the nineties. He's been to more race meetings than either of you two have had hot dinners.'

'Someone's gotta do it,' Earl smiled.

'Well no one else is gonna get a crack at it while you're still breathing.'

Earl laughed. The easy banter betrayed a long-time friendship that neither Rory nor Cockburn asked about lest it uncork the "good old days" bottle.

'Earl's got some intelligence on Dwyer that I want both of you to hear.' He turned to Earl. 'I'll get you to paint the general picture first, Earl, because Gary has to leave shortly to pick up and question a suspect. Then you can pass on the details to Rory to start work on.'

'What suspect?' Rory asked.

'A bikie involved in the kidnap and beating of Graeme Stanley.'

Cockburn had reverted to best behaviour in the presence of Earl Jansson, but he was unable to hide his glee and smugness.

'We found out which of the longstanding Melbourne-based bikie clubs set The Attilas up for Graeme Stanley's murder. It was a matter of waiting to see who The Attilas retaliated against with a drive-by shooting of their antagonist's club house. It just so happened that the Anti-Gang Division had a phone-tap on the head honcho of who the real bikie club villains turn out to be … well they're all villains, obviously,' Cockburn corrected himself before continuing his story. 'The phone log shows that the leader of the guilty mob received a call via the Thomastown mobile phone tower at the exact time that the pathologist said Graeme Stanley carked it. We only have the metadata for the call, not a tape of the actual conversation, but we reckon the bikies "interrogating" Stanley must have panicked when he had a heart attack, and then phoned their boss. Me and Julia are about to do a reconnaissance raid with Rodney Ahearn's unit. Depending how that goes, we'll probably bring the head honcho in. Should be fun.'

'What's his name?'

'Gary can fill you in on the details later, Rory. Right now I want you both to hear what Earl has to say. Okay?'

Earl took the floor.

'Thanks, Richard. I'll start off with a bit of history because we didn't have any of this information ten years ago … back when you blokes had Dwyer in the gun the first time round. Since then we've had Judge Gordon Lewis review the integrity of the racing industry and a lot of his recommendations have been put in place, including the Office of the Racing Integrity Commissioner.

'Of course, one of the major concerns of Judge Lewis was the extent to which criminals were able to launder money through bookmakers. The embarrassing revelations he unearthed drove a lot more co-operation between racing authorities and enforcement agencies, including the Australian Crime Commission and the Australian Taxation Office. That's where we've had the biggest gains in the intelligence that I look after.'

'Including for David Dwyer,' Bourke added.

'Including for David Dwyer. In fact, as far as we know, Dwyer is in a category of his own. There's more than a few ways to skin a cat when it comes to laundering money through bookmakers. At the top of the tree are bookmakers acting in cahoots with crims. In other cases, bookmakers can get the job done by turning a blind eye. You even have some bookmakers who are genuinely unaware they're being used to launder money. For many years, we thought that Ray Samson was of the latter variety. He's always been regarded as a cleanskin.'

'Ray Samson. That's who David Dwyer uses, right?' Rory asked. 'Dwyer nominated Ray Samson on his prison phone list.'

'Yes and no, Rory. Dwyer uses other bookies when he's having a genuine punt, but he uses Samson when he does his banking. You'd better let me explain.

'Dwyer and Samson were mates in school. They both went to Preston Tech. They got into their fair share of strife back in the day, that is, until Dwyer joined the Force. Around the same time, Samson became a bookies penciller and then a bagman. People that went to school with them assumed it was a parting of the ways.

'Of course, we've been finding out that the opposite is true. At some point, they resumed their friendship, discreetly it seems, to feather each other's nests. From audits conducted by various agencies over a period of time, a pattern has emerged in regard to one of the various operating accounts used by Samson. The particular account in question appears to be dedicated to being a bank for Dwyer. Large amounts are deposited into the account in the guise of dead-set losing bets. Withdrawals are made via winnings, of course. There's nothing too conspicuous about the withdrawals except that there's no trifectas or quadies — usually place bets and sure things. Nevertheless, it's a bit hit-and-miss and it takes a bit of turnover to get the right result. But you can afford to be patient when it's all your own money. There's a few exceptions which we assume happen when a quick withdrawal is needed … but usually, there's no need for Samson to risk rigging anything. Samson then draws down his own hefty commission.

'It's taken a while to piece all this activity together but we're pretty certain that that's what's happening. Proving such collusion is a much harder nut to crack. Dwyer doesn't always place the bets himself, but we're slowly building a picture of who he does use and how they are connected to him.

'Take that job someone did on Graeme Stanley. We reckon the job cost $10,000. That's the amount of winnings paid from the account to Bruce Taylor two days beforehand. You'll probably find that Bruce Taylor is also on Dwyer's prison phone list.'

'He is. He's Dwyer's so called accountant,' Rory said. 'The $10,000 also tells us that killing Graeme Stanley was not part of the plan. Not for that price, even if it was only a down payment.'

'Well there you go,' Earl said and spread his hands as validation of everything he'd said.

'Not bad, hey?' Bourke said leaning forward on the table. 'Earl has been in the process of assembling this information in a format the Drug Squad can use to reconcile with events of the past, but he's giving us first crack at it. That's what I want you to do, Rory. Chase the $10,000 winnings paid to Bruce Taylor and find out where that went. Then see if there's any historical transactional links we can use. With a bit of luck, it'll lead you to the bikies Gary is about to visit. Which reminds me, you'd better get going.'

'Sure. See you blokes later.'

Cockburn left.

'I might head back to the office too. I'll leave you to show

Rory the details, Earl. And thanks for bringing this stuff over.'

'No worries, Richard. And do you want a tip while I'm here?'

'I know … be kind to my mother. You need some new material, Earl.'

Earl laughed, then opened his laptop to open the file of the operating account Ray Samson used exclusively for David Dwyer. He led Rory through the table of transactions and the various data they had collected in relation to each entry.

'What's this email address that pops up for some of these transactions?'

'On some occasions, Dwyer used email for bets he placed himself. I wouldn't be surprised if it's an email account that you haven't come across before. It's a webmail-based email account which means it can exist without a link to a particular PC or IP address. We didn't have his PC to check, of course, but seeing how these two blokes operate, I'd expect him to be cagey enough not to leave a trace there, even as a deleted item.'

Rory looked at the screen grimly and drew a long, loud breath in. He felt another dead-end looming.

'You're right there. His PC was as clean as a whistle.'

'Geez, don't lose heart over not locating that email account, Rory. Even if he was using a Virtual Private Network, there's more than enough bedtime reading in this file, including hard copy printouts for every bet Dwyer placed by email. The fact that Samson kept a thorough paper trail to cover his arse works in our favour. It's a win-win.'

'You wanna bet? Right now I'd settle for just one win.'

Back in his office, Rory loaded Earl Jansson's table of transactions between Ray Samson and David Dwyer on to his own computer. He decided to clear a phone call from his to-do list before opening the file and becoming engulfed by the task ahead of him. He dialled.

'*Michelle Fox-Jones speaking.*'

'Hi Michelle. It's Rory James.'

'*Hi Rory. I didn't expect you to call. I thought I'd be the one chasing you up. You haven't decided to come on board after all, have you?*'

He felt pleased to please her and to hear her voice. 'Sorry, Michelle. That's not it. But I did think about it.'

'*I'm sure you know that's the nature of the beast. It's never far from the surface. So tell me, what did you decide other than not wanting to be part of what I'm doing?*'

'Well that's it. What you're doing is not what I'm doing. I can see you're well on the way to a whole new career that you'll be very good at. Media, blogs, a book. And I can see that you're inspired. It makes you happy. I'll bet you can't wait to get stuck into it when you wake up every morning.'

'*Well you've nailed me, but you know I don't like "buts" Rory,*'

'Then I'll simply tell you that I'm also doing what I want to spend my life doing and I don't want to take on anything that will make that any more difficult than it is right now. It's a hard-enough horse to climb back on as it is.'

There was more than a beat of silence before Michelle answered.

'*You know that one-line answer from you is so loaded with stuff . . . with everything I'm trying to cut through.*'

'Perhaps. But I can only deal with my own situation and from where I sit, PTSD looks like a path for cops who don't want to be cops any longer.'

'*You know they don't have to be mutually exclusive.*'

'If only.'

'*This is a circular argument we're having. You can see that, can't you? A chicken and egg thing.*'

'I didn't think we were arguing, but I see your point.

'*Hmm.*'

'Hmm what?'

'*Are you sure you're travelling okay, Rory? I don't mind catching up again just to talk. Nothing to do with the book . . .*'

The silences between their responses were increasing as each tried to figure out what they were dancing around. If he did see her again and ended up in lengthy conversation, she would understand exactly how fraught his foray back to work had become. Did he want that kind of deep and meaningful right now? As far as her situation went, had she truly moved on from her own needy survival? Perhaps they were simply casting for an excuse to see each other again, in which case, who was doing the casting? All Rory knew was that he didn't want to decline her offer.

'Um. Perhaps I should have explained myself in person,' he said, satisfied that he was able to accept without conceding a motive.

'*Okay,*' she said slowly, sensing cautiousness. '*Let me organise something. I'll call you.*'

'All right. That would be good.'

'*I'm pleased Rory. But don't panic if you don't hear from me for a week or more. I'm about to go to Sydney to catch up with my publisher and the support group they've got up there. I'm hoping they'll point me in the direction of some affected members I can interview.*'

'No problem, Michelle. Ring me at any time.'

After hanging up, he looked at nothing in particular and replayed the conversation in his head. Earl Jansson's table of transactions eventually beckoned. He opened the file and slowly scrolled down to the most recent entry — the $10,000 paid as "winnings" to David Dwyer's accountant. He emailed those details to Gerry Denton but wasn't confident Gerry would uncover the faintest trail to follow. On the other side of the coin, Rory could see that over time, the withdrawals history reflected events with unerring accuracy. The biggest bubbles occurred at the time the hit took place on Neilson and Scali. The other withdrawal bubble happened when Dwyer purchased his hobby farm soon after he was forced to resign from the Force.

Rory stared at the screen and tapped his chin with a pen. *So what?* It's another part of the Dwyer puzzle but it's not a crime to gamble. Some people list it as their occupation. Earl Jansson has spent over a decade tracking this stuff without being able to pin anything on Ray Samson. None of that was going to change quickly, or even slowly, Rory concluded. But a hitherto unknown email account. What could that reveal?

Rory wrote down the email address on a Post It note and headed through the workstation grid to Hamish Lynott's office on the other side of the floor.

Tap tap tap.

'Got a minute?'

Hamish looked up from his screen.

'Sure, what's up Rory?'

Rory handed the Post It note to Hamish. Hamish held it up and studied it.

'Is *dwyerd21@gomail.com* who I think it is?'

'Yeah. It's a web-based email account I've just found out about. How hard is it to hack into?'

'You mean for a professional hacker to crack it … for which the answer would be, "not very hard at all". Or do you mean, how hard is it for me to get in there right here and now?'

'Umm, the latter I suppose. I kinda wanted to keep this to myself.'

'It's not impossible, but that depends on the password security. If it was set up before we all became super conscious of on-line security, you might be in with a chance. If a second verification step has since been added you're buggered — even if you're a pro. You wouldn't get in without an OPT. That's a One Time Password generated by a token or SMS-ed to his mobile phone.'

I'm so fucking sick of long shots on this case, Rory thought.

'We're talking about a bloke who has *Eraser* installed on his PC, but I do know that it's an account he's had for many years.'

'Let's have a look.'

Hamish stuck the Post It note to the frame of his computer screen and opened the Gomail sign-in page. He entered the email address and looked up to Rory.

'We can try the key-under-the pot-plant stuff for a start, date of birth or address. He's an ex-copper, right? Do you know what his rank and serial number was? That was something lazy coppers did in the early days. We had to break the habit for their Police email accounts, but who knows what bad habits they persisted with on private stuff like this?'

'Umm,' Rory said, betraying his own use of rank and serial number when email first became part of the job. 'His serial number's in the file. I'll be back in a moment.'

Rory walked back into Hamish's office with the file open to a particular page.

'Detective Senior Sergeant, D-S-S and …' he read the number. Hamish typed it in. He pressed Enter. Rory stood behind Hamish and saw the instant rejection.

'Oh well, that was the long shot. I can get Huan to have a go if you like, and turn a blind eye. I know she can crack passwords, but it'd have to be unofficial. We're the Commercial and Electronic branch. You've got your own computer gurus for this sort of thing, you know.'

'Na. I don't want you sticking your neck out. I might have to use our experts. I was hoping to keep this one close to my chest though.'

Hamish drummed his fingers on the desk and looked at the sign-in page.

'Let's try an even longer shot.'

Rory was beginning to really detest the word *long-shot*. Hamish held the Shift key down and typed D-S-S and Dwyer's serial number. The screen went white but only for a moment. An In-box summary of emails appeared.

'Fuck me.'

They both leant forward to observe the screen.

'He's not a keeper then. There's only what you see on this

page. Pretty much junk mail from vendors he uses. Only one from a real person by the look of it. Most of them have all been opened, so he must check it often enough.'

The screen went blank and Rory's mind panicked. He hadn't realised that Hamish was switching to the Sent page.

'Nothing sent, or rather, no sent items that he kept.'

'Can you go back to the Inbox and show me the item from an actual person.'

The email was shown to be from "Little I". The subject was: "Call me".

Hamish opened the email. It read:

Answer your phone or call me as soon as you get this. Something has come in that you need to know about.

Hamish watched Rory read it and think.

'Do you know what that means?'

'I might if I knew who it was from.' He didn't tell Hamish that it was dated only a day after they received the recording sample from FP1. Hamish slid the mouse.

'It doesn't look like I can help you there. I presume the surname is Little. Irene Little? Ivan Little? Ian … mean anything to you?'

'Not ringing any bells. Can you print the email for me and somehow save it on a stick? I don't want to risk it being deleted while I try and figure this out.'

'No problem. Anything else we can help you with today?' Hamish asked as he set about printing and downloading the email before he logged out of Dwyer's account.

'Well there is one other thing …'

'Oh?'

Rory retrieved his pocket notebook and flipped it open at the most recent entry.

'Can you show me how to search theses on the National Library Trove website? I had a bit of a go but got lost.'

Hamish went to the National Library of Australia site where a link to Trove's own homepage option boasted: "Discover and engage with Australian cultural collections". Theses were not listed on the array of icons for every conceivable collection — maps, newspapers, diaries, books, music … Hamish nevertheless quickly found a pathway.

'Here they are under "Books". They seem to have every university-written research thesis ever produced in Australia. Is this what you're after?'

Hamish continued tapping the keyboard as he spoke. Rory said 'Yes,' and waited … and waited.

'Look at that. I didn't know this existed. There's my own master's thesis. You can browse this every which way, by author, by date or dates, by university … Do you know what you're after or shouldn't I ask?'

'I've got a rough idea,' Rory said, politely avoiding the question of letting or not letting Hamish know what that may be. Hamish comprehended Rory's reluctance.

'Why don't I leave you to it while I pop downstairs and buy some lunch. I'll be back soon if you need a hand.'

'Thanks, mate. It shouldn't take long.'

Rory slid into Hamish's chair and considered the first search field "Keyword". He entered "Frogs" and "Calls". He thought about how he could expand upon it and added "Melbourne". Nothing else would come to mind and he moved on to the variable timeline settings for "Limit your results". The Neilson Scali murders happened ten years ago at which time the frog researcher would still have been in his or her research stage. *So nothing older than ten years.* Rory entered the date. *Give him or her a couple of years to complete the thesis, plus a generous allowance for poor performance.* Five years max, he decided. Nothing more recent than five years ago should cover it. He examined the many blank fields he had left wanting, including "Creator".

'You tell me,' he told the screen, then pressed Enter.

He was disappointed to see only four entries come up:

The re-evaluation of the microhabitat and calling behaviour of the Victorian Smooth Froglet (Geocrinia victoriana) in urban Melbourne / Joshua U Marshall

Variation in advertisement call structure of whistling frogs / Hay, Timothy D

Impacts of climate change and urban development on the spotted marsh frog (Limnodynastes tasmaniensis) in the Merri Creek corridor / Joab Wilson

Metapopulation viability of the Growling Grass Frog in Melbourne's urban growth areas / Geoffrey Heard and Michael McCarthy

He opened the first entry. It told him that the thesis was published by La Trobe University and that the study population was in and around the universities own campus at Bundoora.

One match, and on the first go. That wasn't hard. What else have we got?

Rory opened the second entry. It was from the University of Canterbury in New Zealand.

How did that get in there?

The third entry was geographically close but nonetheless separate — Merri Creek was the next creek westward from Bundoora's own Darebin Creek. The thesis was published by another Melbourne university, the School of Social Science and Planning, RMIT. *Close but no cigar.* The fourth paper, by Melbourne University researchers, also dealt with a geographically close but separate area west and north of Bundoora.

So that was it. A single match. Joshua U Marshall. Perhaps it is that simple. Rory returned to the Joshua U Marshall publication summary and printed a copy. He sat back, crossed his arms and re-read the notes on the screen. … *Geocrinia victoriana, a secretive species. Surveys of its most distinctive call were undertaken in the grounds of the university-sponsored sanctuary at Bundoora campus …* Fucking hell, he felt himself thinking. It *is* that simple. If anyone accidently recorded David Dwyer ten years ago, then it had to be Joshua U Marshall. His wishful theorising was unfolding into reality. The theory he had not dared to say out loud had just thrown up a name. It felt close enough to touch.

'What does U stand for?' he asked the computer, then typed Joshua Marshall into Google. The list began with an endless list of Joshua Marshalls on Facebook. Too many, and all without the "U" … until he opened the fourth page of Joshua Marshalls. The only Joshua Marshall with a "U" was a LinkedIn entry for the on-line professional network. As soon as the Joshua U Marshall LinkedIn page opened he knew he had the right Josh Marshall. The banner was a picture of a frog. Rory clenched his fist into a teeth-gritting internal Yes. He stared at the page in triumph, initially without even reading it. As elation settled into a self-satisfied internal pulsing, he began to study the details slowly.

Josh Marshall
Ecologist seeking new opportunities
Bendigo area, Australia / Environmental Services

Bendigo? I wasn't expecting that. Bonus.

The page listed various research survey positions Joshua held over recent years and his prime qualification of Bachelor of Biological Sciences, Zoology, Ecology, Botany, La Trobe University. Rory tried, "View Joshua's Full Profile", and was told, "Join LinkedIn to view Joshua's full profile … it's free!"

Hamish returned to the office carrying a brown paper bag and a fruit juice.

'How did you go?'

'Are you on *LinkedIn*?'

'As a matter of fact … So you did find someone of interest?'

'Not "a person of interest", more a person I'm interested in.'

Hamish smiled. 'I could log into LinkedIn for you but it won't give you anything more. Most people don't have contact details on their page. LinkedIn notifies them by email if someone logs an interest in them. You'll have to use your usual cop sources to locate him.'

'Like?'

'Here's an idea if it's not too old-school for you. The phone book. They've even got it on line these days, under White Pages.'

'Ha ha.'

Rory Googled up the White Pages and tried "Marshall, J". The screen was flooded with entries from across Australia. He refined the search to "Marshall J U". One entry appeared.

24

Rory reached the driveway to Joshua Marshall's house around eight thirty in the morning and quickly drove past. There were two vehicles at the house. Josh didn't live alone and until that moment, it was a possibility that hadn't entered Rory's head. How could that be? Now that he thought about it, it would be more unusual if Josh did live alone.

Rory's plan didn't take other people into account. Whoever Josh lived with may or may not know about the recording. If there was someone else around when he confronted Josh, and that someone was someone that Josh hadn't taken into his confidence, then he would surely clam up. There was of course the primary concern of how Josh would react to a homicide cop turning up out of the blue, let alone a cop who knew about the recording and knew Josh had sent it to the police. It wasn't fair for him to drop all that in Josh's lap in front of someone who had no idea what was going on. And what if he had the whole thing completely wrong? Until it was validated, the whole supposition was on the bizarre side of believable. If he was barking up the wrong tree, did he need someone else there to add to his own embarrassment? He definitely needed to speak to Josh alone.

In Rory's mind, he'd rehearsed his explanation for approaching Josh. To begin with, he would introduce himself as a member of the Homicide Squad. It was unavoidable and not subtle, but from much experience, he knew that the response it elicited from unsuspecting interviewees was usually telling. Despite how Josh may or may not react to his mere presence, Rory would go on to proffer, *You're probably wondering how a homicide matter could have relevance to yourself, so let me put your mind at rest from the outset. We're dealing with a cold case that happened ten years ago and we're speaking to people who, without knowing it at the time, may have been in the vicinity when the homicide was being planned. It is known that two suspects met in a particular public space and discussed the crime a day or two before it was committed. Any bystanders who happened to overhear or see that meeting — whether they were aware of it or not — would be in a position to help us with our enquiries …*

It was definitely not for other ears. He drove on.

The gravel lane came to an end within a few hundred metres of passing Josh's house. Ahead lay an un-fenced forest from which a walking or trail-bike track emerged. He navigated a three-point U-turn between tree trunks and took a slower pass past Josh's house. The established European trees and a pair of brick chimneys with corbels showed that the restored and extended weatherboard cottage was more than a world-war or two old. The detached 1960s carport housed a white Subaru Forester and a black soft-top Saab.

There were only two other residences along the lane before it entered onto the main road, which had outgrown its original classification as a lane — Tannery Lane. Rory did a U-turn in Tannery Lane and parked on the grass verge with a view back to Josh's turnoff. He was on the eastern fringe of Bendigo, only a few kilometres from the CBD.

Before he had time to contemplate his next move, the black Saab emerged. It was just beginning to pick up speed as it passed Rory, heading in the direction of Bendigo. The driver's head turned to face Rory as it passed. The mutual glimpses were full of mutual questioning recognition. *That's a face I've seen before. They seemed to recognise me too.*

The Saab driver was female. Dark shoulder length hair, thirties, too young to be from the era when Rory grew up in Bendigo. He didn't know any women currently living in town other than Sigrid. Whoever she was, she lived with Josh Marshall and it bothered Rory. It felt like she was someone he'd encountered in his work — and not that long ago. Was there a criminal element to this that he somehow missed? Did he need to re-think what has led him here? After all, he hadn't shared any of this with Bourke or Cockburn. Was he on to something more than he imagined? Should he find out who the Saab driver was before he acted? Should he find out a bit more about Josh Marshall before he barged in on a cold call?

He drummed the steering wheel with his fingers and thought about the Saab driver's face. He didn't think she was someone he had met but, *where do I know her from?*

An alarming thought entered his head. What if Josh Marshall was female? What if she was the woman who had just driven past? It's possible. Joss Stone the singer is female. Was Josh Joss Stone's shortened Christian name? Was it shortened from Joshua, or something else? There was no picture of Josh on the LinkedIn page, just the stock silhouette. And what about the middle initial "U". There were plenty of options for women, weren't there? Ursula, Unis, Uma. Only Ulysses came to mind for a bloke — surely not. And if the woman in the Saab was Josh Marshall, why did he recognise her face?

Rory drummed the steering wheel again. The clock radio told him it was ten-to-nine. *I'll give it until ten o'clock … see if the Subaru makes a move.* He switched on the car radio which was already tuned into the ABC. Presenter, Jon Faine, played Devil's advocate to a community group spokeswoman trying to stop a land-fill being established in her neighbourhood. The Devil had done a fine selection job in choosing Jon Faine as his advocate. Jon nevertheless had a fight on his hands. Trish was on a roll. 'Of course, it's a case of NIMBY, not in my back yard, you hypocrite. That's the point. Land-fills don't belong in people's back yards. They belong well away from backyards, in fact. It's a mark of first-world cities that we have landfills and sewerage works that are beyond residential areas. That's the beauty of them. I don't hear you or anyone from your neighbourhood putting up their hand to accommodate the city's rubbish, let alone your own individual rubbish. None of you seem to mind as long as it's being dumped on someone else. There's another syndrome for you. *As long as it's in someone else's backyard*, whatever the acronym is for that …' Rory smiled and ruminated about her "… that's the beauty of them" comment.

It was nearing ten o'clock. I'll just hear the news before I give this away and come up with a plan B, he thought. That was the cue for the Subaru Forester to emerge on to Tannery Lane. This time, the driver did not turn his head to look at Rory. Rory's glimpse of the driver's profile was too rapid to make out more than the hair colour — fair-ish but not blonde, under forty if he had to guess.

Rory started the car, did a U-turn and followed the Subaru into town. This is strange, he thought, tailing someone in a car, probably the first time in his police career. He hung well back until they were closer to the town centre, then he battled traffic to stay close enough to keep the Subaru in sight. The Subaru's indicator came on to park near the library in the Lyttleton Terrace. Rory double-parked and watched the driver emerge and walk in Rory's direction to the ticket machine. He still couldn't place the Saab driver but he now knew that she wasn't Josh. This was Josh, he decided.

Josh was dressed like an *ecologist seeking opportunities* if ever he'd seen one. He could have been a model for the Kathmandu catalogue — hi-tech cargo pants, hi-tech red sleeveless fleece, hi-tech hike boots. Thirty-ish, hair of some length but not long.

Rory watched Josh place the parking ticket on the car's dashboard and head across a patch of parkland between the library and the Town Hall. 'Shit. I've lost him already.' Rory said it out loud. He drove halfway around the block before he found a park. He backtracked to Josh's car on foot and observed through the windscreen that there was about forty-five minutes on the dashboard parking ticket. That gave Rory about half an hour to look around the CBD for Josh. If he hadn't found him by then, he'd come back here and hope he hadn't already left.

Rory made his way across the lawn between the library and the Town Hall and along the café strip of Bull Street. And there he was, sitting alone with a coffee at an outside table. The coffee cup was empty but he looked settled in, typing intently on his tablet. Rory went to the counter and ordered a double-shot flat white, all the while glancing outside to see that Josh was still at the table.

Josh lifted his head and gave a quick smile when Rory edged behind his chair to sit at the adjoining table. Rory sipped the coffee. Not the best brew he'd had in Bendigo, but not bad either. He looked at Josh for a moment.

I may be about to change his life forever. However, if he is responsible for making the recording, this turn of events will not be totally out of the question, no matter how unexpected. Here goes.

'I reckon if I took that empty coffee cup and checked the finger prints, it might match one we received in the post recently.'

It was total impulse. Everything Rory had been thinking of saying went out the window … and he liked what came out instead. If his theory about Josh didn't come off, nothing was lost. Josh didn't know who he was. It was just something odd a stranger said. No one would be any the wiser. There was no trail that led him here. No file notes, no conversation with colleagues, no on-line searches that could be traced to his own computer. On the other hand, if Josh did react, even slightly …

Josh did react, and not slightly.

He looked up from his tablet. Rory had turned in his seat to face Josh across the back of his chair.

'Huh?'

By the time Josh had finished making the huh sound, the reality had computed. Rory watched the blood recede from Josh's face. His eyes darted and his hands sought to grip whatever part of the table they were touching. Rory could see he was headed for the shakes or even doing a runner. He saw that every dreaded scenario Josh had imaged during the past decade had just played through his mind — like a life flashing before someone in a car crash. Was Rory a cop? Was he a bad cop? Was he one of Dwyer's mates? Were there more of them? Was …

'It's all right, Josh. I'm a policeman … an honourable one.'

Fuck. It's not enough to simply say you're a cop, Rory lamented within. It didn't bring the colour back into Josh's face but it seemed to ease his instinct to run.

'So you know.'

Rory didn't know what Josh's speaking voice sounded like, but he sensed that it was not normally as hoarse as the words that came out. Hearing those words — so you know — was also loaded with significance for Rory. He had got it right. His long, lone, unlikely line of enquiry was finally vindicated. He turned his chair to face Josh more directly.

'Not officially. That's something I need to discuss with you.'

He had to talk it down. Until this moment, Josh had enjoyed the safety of anonymity. He knew that in Josh's mind, the protective cone of daily existence had been lifted. Suddenly there was no shield of normality. He would feel exposed to the vengeful interest of those copping the consequences of his recording.

Rory's words took no effect.

'You're not in danger and I want to keep it that way,' he tried.

'You know.' This time there was resignation in Josh's voice.

'I know some things. I need to talk to you about what I do know. Not here, though. Is that okay with you?'

Josh hung his head. It was a long interval of thought before he lifted his eyes, full of defeat.

'Okay. Where and when?'

He wasn't yet out of shock but Rory was pleased to see that his brain was functioning.

'Can I come to your place? How soon does it suit you?'

'I want my lawyer there.'

'It won't be that sort of discussion and you might not want someone else to know about this just yet. Not even a lawyer.'

'She's my partner. She knows. She's the only other person in the world that knows — until now,' he added with a resentful look into Rory's eyes.

'Well now there's three of us and we need to keep it that way. So the three of us need to have a discussion.'

The woman in the Saab! That's why he recognised her. He realised she was the local lawyer who showed up at Dwyer's bail hearing. Rory remembered that she stayed on in the public gallery. No wonder. He watched Josh cogitate the logistics.

'I'll call Martha and get a time. I can ring your mobile.'

'No. Don't call me. When does she finish work?'

'About five thirty, sometimes later.'

'Why don't you ask her to finish on time today and I'll come to your place?'

'All right.'

Colour was returning to his face, along with anxiety.

'You gonna be all right?'

'Mmm,' he said with an unconvincing nod.

'I'm Detective Sergeant James by the way.'

'You know who I am,' he said as he shook Rory's hand.

'Yes, Joshua U Marshall. What does the U stand for?'

'Uriah. It's an old family name.'

Uriah. Why didn't I think of that?

'I thought it must be something unusual. I'll see you at five-thirty then, Joshua Uriah. Just a talk. It'll be all right …'

He touched Josh's shoulder as he said it and left.

~

'I remember you from court. When Dwyer was seeking bail,' were Martha's first words to Rory. Martha and Josh had come onto their front veranda to greet him. Martha was still wearing her skirt and jacket work gear.

'I recall seeing you too. I'm Detective Sergeant Rory James.'

He held his hand out to shake Martha's. Josh held back.

'Martha Portillo.'

Rory glanced around to take in the oasis of established European trees among the dry semi-bush setting. There were some newer plantings, all natives as far as he could tell.

'Thanks for meeting with me,' Rory said.

'Do we have a choice?'

'We need to talk. I want to help you if I can.'

Martha tilted her head and squinted. Was that cynicism or the low sun behind me? Rory wondered. Cynicism, he decided.

'Come in then. Can we get you a cup of tea?'

As they made their way along the front-door hallway, Rory estimated that the rear extension probably dated back to the nineteen-sixties. Joinery and furniture in the living area included some more recent additions. It all fused into a pleasing style. The Laminex table and chairs — which may have been standing in their original arrival point from the furniture store — had morphed back into vogue.

'How did you find out?' were Josh's first words. He set about making a pot of tea as Rory and Martha took a seat at the table.

'On the recording, Dwyer spoke about having an alibi set up … being at a training course. We found out that the training course was held at the Police Forensic Centre which is only a five-minute walk from the sanctuary.'

Josh paused in thought with a tea spoon of tea above the pot. 'That'd be right. He did come from that direction. The other bloke came from the other direction. The other bloke probably entered along Main Drive.' He continued spooning tea in the pot. 'But what about the sanctuary and the recording? How did you figure that out?'

'I'd been to the sanctuary. Someone I bumped into told me about frog calls. Things added up.'

'Oh.'

It was far from the full story but seemed to be enough to satisfy Josh.

'What *I* want to know is, how you managed to capture the conversation on tape and not be seen.'

Josh joined them at the table while the tea brewed. 'I was up a tree. A big redgum. I had a hammock-chair slung up there to make myself comfortable. You can spend a lot of time trying to get a good frog-call on tape. Being off the ground also eliminates the vibration you make walking around. I was pissed off when those two pricks showed up. The sanctuary was officially closed at that hour. When they lumbered in, the whole wetland went silent. Of course they never looked up. Nobody ever looks up. I had to wait it out.'

'And they came separately?'

'Yep. Dwyer arrived first. The other bloke came a minute or two later. I didn't know who Dwyer was then. I only put it together after the murders hit the papers.'

'Do you know who the other bloke was?'

'No. It wasn't anyone I've seen in the news before or since.'

'Josh hasn't done anything wrong you know,' Martha said.

'Of course not. The Police are really pleased to have the recording. It's a huge advance. There's every possibility we'll be able to put Dwyer away.'

'Every possibility?'

Martha's posture braced with indignation.

'You're a lawyer, Ms Portillo. The recording is damning and it's compelling, but you must know that it can't stand alone as evidence without serious challenge.'

'It speaks for itself and it's been handed to you on a silver platter.'

'As it stands, we have no authentication to place the recording at a particular place or time. We don't know who the other party on the recording is and there's even a possibility we could stall trying to prove it's Dwyer's voice.'

Lawyer combativeness surfaced. 'You do know all those things, especially now. You know that it took place at the sanctuary and you know that it happened when Dwyer attended a course at the Forensic Centre. You must have a date for that at least.'

'I do know all those things, but simply knowing is a long way from proving any of that if Dwyer denies it in court.'

Martha paused in want of an answer, then said in a low voice, 'I'm pleased you got the "Ms" right and call me Martha.'

Josh found an answer. 'This is why your boss went on TV, isn't it? He doesn't want me to try and identify who the other bloke was. He wants me in court to prove where and when the recording happened. That's what this is about, isn't it?'

'He's not doing it,' Martha said before Rory could answer.

'I expected you to say that.'

'Well why the fuck wouldn't we say that?' Hearing her swear caught Rory by surprise. 'This is all about what happens to people who give evidence against that prick. And the result is always the same despite what the Police try and do about it. Look at Clifford Neilson and Corina Scali — in witness protection. Look at Leon Blofeld — he copped it in jail. Once you're exposed, nowhere is safe. The whole filthy business is still being played out ten years after the event on Four Corners. Four Corners and even the fictional witness protection ones, like Hiding and Broadchurch. How far from the truth are they?

'And as soon as anything new happens, like this recording being handed in, someone else gets bumped off. You're not gonna tell me Graeme Stanley died of a heart attack, are you?'

'He did actually.'

'What?'

'Graeme Stanley did die of a heart attack. He was being beaten at the time, mind you, but the actual cause of death was a heart attack.'

A silence arrived.

'How do you have your tea?' Josh asked. He rose from the table to pour.

'Black, please. No sugar.'

Tea-doling-out-niceties ensued. Only Josh added sugar. First sips were taken and cups were replaced into saucers to cool. Rory resumed the matter at hand in a calmer tone.

'I'm not here to twist your arm.'

'You might as well, now that we're on the Police books,' Martha said.

'That's not so. This is unofficial. There's no record on file. It's all up here.' Rory tapped his temple with his forefinger.

'In your head and the heads of all your mates.'

'Not so again. This is a lead I explored on my own. At this stage, it's not something I'll be entering into the system. Not if I don't have to. I don't want the responsibility of what could happen to you … worst case scenario.'

'Fucking hell. Not even you trust the cops.' Rory still hadn't got used to Martha's swearing. '… and that doesn't alter the fact that you know. How is that meant to make us feel? We simply have to trust you, and no offence, but we don't even know you.'

'If *I* was one of the bad guys I wouldn't be sitting here having this conversation. They would have simply taken care of business.'

'That's what Martha said before you came,' Josh said.

'I hope you're not after a cut of the reward then, because we talked about writing that idea off as soon as Graeme Stanley copped it.'

Josh looked hard at Martha with the aggrieved thought of: *we didn't just talk about it, we well and truly decided about it.* Didn't we abandon all thoughts of going through with it? Rory couldn't fathom their looks. The moment passed and he gave his response.

'I'll simply be happy to see Dwyer locked up. I was on the original investigation. I've had to watch him slip through our fingers twice already, slimy bastard … incidentally, how did you plan to accept the reward?'

Martha and Josh looked at each other until one of them nodded.

'We hadn't worked that bit out yet. I've got a few vague ideas but mainly it was a bluff. As long as we established our dibs on the reward, we reckoned we could take our time. Maybe find out if the Gnomes of Zurich are still an impregnable option. Or maybe it's not possible to acquire money without leaving a trail in the computer age. I don't know …' Martha trailed off.

'I wouldn't write off the reward just yet,' Rory said.

'So where to now?' Josh asked.

'I go back to the investigation with whatever else you can tell me now. See if we can find other ways to pin down the "who" now that we know the "where" and "when". A way that doesn't require me to reveal you or your connection. What I'd like is for you to run me through what happened again. For starters, what did the other bloke look like.'

Josh sipped his tea trying to recall the mental image.

'It happened just after sunset. There was still a bit of light but not much. I mainly saw him in silhouette. I remember noticing when the shadows disappeared. The frog chorus was just beginning. He was slim but not skinny. He wore a black shirt and black pants and black shoes. Boots I think — even though it was a hot night. Dwyer was in shorts and thongs. The other bloke had black hair. A bit shorter than yours, maybe. A bit of beard growth too. I only got a brief flash of his face. He might have been early to mid-forties. Not bad looking, I think. That's about it. Oh, and an English accent … but I guess you got that from the recording.'

Rory produced a notebook from his pocket and made notes. He omitted entering a heading.

'What do you mean, you got a glimpse of his face.'

'When he lit a cigarette. The lighter illuminated his face for a good moment … and his neck. That's significant because he had a tattoo on his neck.'

'Can you describe the tattoo and where it was?'

'From where he was standing below me, it must have been on the lower right side of his neck. I think his collar would have hidden it if you were facing him at ground level, but in that moment, it was obvious from above.'

'And the design?' Rory pressed.

'I remember because it was quite original. You know when a poker player has his cards face down on the table and lifts the corner to peek at what the cards are … that's what the tattoo was. That glimpse of a thumb and the slightly upturned corners of each card. I think it was four aces, a full house, but it could have been some other combo. Something with different suits.'

Rory sipped his tea and ran the image through his memory bank. Nothing registered immediately. He could try the real database when he was back at the station. He made another note.

'One other thing. Something happens on the recording before the conversation gets going. I assumed that was Dwyer frisking the hitman. Is that right?'

Rory noticed Martha wince when he said "hitman". Up until now, it was always "the other bloke".

'That's right. It was pretty thorough, too. When Dwyer started feeling him I thought they were gay. I thought I was going to have to sit through them having sex. I didn't appreciate it at the time but sitting through them having gay sex would have been preferable to what unfolded.'

'And not recording it, thank you,' Martha added.

Rory and Josh both gave her a bemused look.

'Is that it then?' Josh said.

'Pretty much.'

'I must say we're still rather shocked … and nervous.' Martha said. 'This has happened too suddenly, you finding out about us, I mean. To be honest, the more I hear you say this is "unofficial", the dodgier it sounds. From my experience, that's not how things work with the Police. And despite what you say, I can't see us not being drawn in. So what happens in the meantime? Will we be in danger and not know it? What if we want to ask you something? Can we phone you?'

Rory drew a weary breath.

'The truth is, I really do want to keep you out of this and I think there's a good chance I can do that. I wish I could say more to convince you but to do that, I need to digest what you've confirmed to me and told me today. I won't be passing any of this on — at least not your involvement — unless I absolutely have to and I wouldn't go down that path without letting you know. I'm hoping it won't come to that and unless it does, you're are not in danger.

'On my side of the fence, however, things are never totally innocuous. So don't phone me, I'll phone you. If you absolutely have to contact me, phone The Manse B&B where I stay in Bendigo and leave a message. You don't have to leave your name; you'll be the only person to contact me there.'

The thought crossed his mind: *What if they leave a message at The Manse and Sigrid and me have stopped seeing each other? I should have thought of a better plan. Another thought followed: Why would I even imagine Sigrid and I no longer seeing each other?* The occasion of Sigrid meeting Steph for the first time may have given him a clue, had Martha not stopped the tangent of thought in its tracks.

'You mean Sigrid Dobell's?

'You know Sigrid?' Rory tried to sound un-alarmed … and un-annoyed. Fucking country towns, he thought.

'Sigrid used our practice for her conveyancing when she bought The Manse. She's lovely, we still catch up for coffee occasionally.'

*Some Women are indeed from Venus and some women are …*he figured it out … *lawyers.*

'Err, Sigrid and I are seeing each other.' It came out as sheepishly as he felt.

'Riiiiiight. She is a dark horse' He watched hitherto unease and concern drain from Martha's face. His relationship with

Sigrid did what his painstaking conversation failed to do. 'Well seeing we're all in this together and this interview didn't happen, just friends catching up with someone Josh bumped into in town today ... would you like a glass of wine before you go ... Rory?'

Wine, using his first name, chummy with Sigrid ... even Josh looked perplexed.

25

'What time do you think this is? You were going to cook.'

'I am,' Rory told Sigrid and raised the plastic grocery bags he held in each hand. 'Spaghetti bolognese.'

'Spaghetti bolognese? When you headed off this morning you said you'd be finished work by lunchtime. I was expecting a finer creation than spag bol.'

'Things didn't work out the way I thought. I'm making the sauce from scratch, though. There's plenty of red wine in my version, you know. It just means we'll eat a little late tonight,' Rory pleaded.

Sigrid laughed. 'Can you hear us? Quick, slap me out of it.'

She came over and kissed Rory — slowly.

'Would you like a drink?' he asked her.

'I'm gonna need something if I have to wait for you to cook.'

Rory lifted the groceries onto the bench and turned to kiss her again with his arms free to roam.

'I think you'd better wait, otherwise we'll be eating at midnight.'

'A fight and being sensible about having sex. I think we've got a real relationship happening here.'

'See what staying here two nights in a row does?'

They were both conscious of making extra effort after the disaster of a night in his flat. Steph's visit went badly enough but worse was to come — the first nightmare he suffered in Sigrid's company. He was beginning to wonder if the root cause of his problem was the flat itself. The nightmare was on the lesser end of the harrowing-scale but bad enough to frighten Sigrid. For Rory, the worst of it was having to calm Sigrid when he craved being comforted himself — by Sigrid or by any of the other "painkillers" he had on hand but felt compelled not to reveal. It became a long night for both of them, and an even longer drive back to Bendigo. Unnervingly, Sigrid's composure bounced back once she was on home turf. She seemed ready to resume normal transmission and never mention the episode again.

Sigrid reached high for wine glasses and low for a bottle of shiraz. She began to pour with the words, 'You won't be needing all of this in the sauce, will you?'

'No, but there's one other ingredient we need.' Rory reached into his pocket and produced two shiny leaves. 'Did you know you had a bay tree in the front garden?'

Sigrid handed the glass of wine to Rory and offered the toast, 'To spaghetti bolognese and sensible sex.'

'Hmm. Maybe we're ready to go away together. You know, I just come here, we go out or eat in, have sex and I go away again. On week days I'm at work and you're busy at weekends. What about having a getaway?'

Sigrid sipped before answering.

'Which bit don't you like, the dining with me or the having sex?'

'You know what I mean. Don't you fancy a break? When was the last time you had time off?'

Sigrid wandered over to sit at the table as Rory began unpacking his groceries onto the kitchen bench.

'I couldn't go for long. I can get Iris in to look after this place for a few days but I'd have to train someone properly to have a serious break. Where did you have in mind?'

Rory stopped what he was doing to the onion and wondered aloud. 'I don't know. I only just came up with the idea. Let me think about it.'

'Okay. Surprise me.'

'I met a friend of yours today. Martha Portillo.'

'The young lawyer? She's …' Sigrid paused, searching for the word. 'Impressive?'

'That too. Is she representing someone you're dealing with?'

'Kind of but not.'

'You should meet her partner Josh. He's a fascinating guy. Like a young David Attenborough when he gets started on his passions. I think you'd like him.'

'I did meet him. I've just come from having a wine with them both.'

Rory continued chopping and trying to look nonchalant. Sigrid placed her wine on the table and furrowed a brow.

'Is Josh in trouble?'

'No. Of course not. But they're a couple, if you talk to one you talk to the other.'

'Not if you're a policeman. What's going on?'

'Look, I can't say but neither of them have done anything wrong. I shouldn't even have mentioned that we met.'

'But you did.' A second brow furrowed.

Rory came and sat facing her at the table. 'I'll tell you what. If things work out the way I expect, we'll invite them round here and I'll cook a proper meal.'

'That's when I'll know this is a real relationship.'

26

'I'll show you mine if you show me yours,' Julia O'Hannagain said to Rory.

Gary Cockburn's office might have been empty but there was a gatekeeper to contend with. She stayed seated at the workstation she now occupied outside Cockburn's office. Rory stood before her on the official interrogatee spot. Had it been permitted, he was certain Julia would have a trapdoor and lever fitted.

'You'd be disappointed,' Rory played the game.

'I'm sure I would, but why don't you tell me what you've come up with in relation to Dwyer instead?'

She's speaking to me in cop-interviewing speak.

'Nothing my end, what about you and Gary? What happened with the bikie?'

She ignored his question. 'I didn't think you'd have anything. Been skiving up to Bendigo to be with your lady-friend, from what I hear.'

Lady-friend? Fuck. How did she know that? Has Gary got her spying on me?

'Gerry's been looking into the $10,000 paid to Ray Samson. Seeing if it made its way to the bikies.'

'… and?'

'That's why I'm here. To see Gary and Gerry. What happened with the bikie you two were gonna bring in. The one whose phone call placed him in Thomastown,' he reminded her of his earlier query.

'Oh him,' Julia said with a shake of her hair that signalled abandonment of the interrogation. 'He did it, but we don't have enough on him and the bikie cone-of–silence has come down. If he goes down for it, which I doubt he will, we won't get anything more out of him.'

'How do you know he did it?'

'He gave us an alibi to start with. Said he was home watching DVDs with his girlfriend. She vouched for him. So we asked why his phone was being used in Thomastown at the same time. His answer was: he lost his phone … someone else must've found it and used it. So Gary dials his number there and then and it starts ringing in his pocket. Dumb shit. That's when he knew he was in the shit and clammed up. We bagged his boots as evidence and had a match with prints left on the shiny concrete floor in the warehouse.'

'At least we know how it all came about.'

Rory noticed Cockburn's reflection in the glass office front behind Julia. He turned to see Cockburn and Richard Bourke arrive through the open-plan workstations.

'Has she told you?' Bourke asked Rory.

'Yeah.'

'So the bikies did the job on Graeme Stanley. Probably for the $10,000 that Bruce Taylor "withdrew" from Dwyer's account with Ray Samson. They were still using air-quotes to describe how the betting account was used as a bank. 'What have you got on the $10,000, Rory?'

'Gerry's been chasing it up. I'll call him over.'

Rory went across the floor to Gerry Denton's workstation. When they returned, Bourke, Cockburn and Julia had adjourned into Cockburn's office. Cockburn sat at his workstation. Bourke and Julia had the only two chairs. Gerry began his report without being asked.

'The bikies are under all sorts of covert monitoring by the Anti-Gang Division. Not that it helped though. As far as we can tell, the cash wasn't paid into a bikie bank account and there was no phone traffic between Taylor and the bikies … at least not from any phone in Taylor's name. Ahearn reckons you might find the cash if you raided the clubrooms. Having that kind of money lying around in bikie clubrooms wouldn't be unusual, however. He says it'd be more unusual if they had less cash on the premises. In other words, it wouldn't prove a thing. That's it.'

Everyone turned to Bourke. He steepled his fingers and thought.

'Never mind, Gerry. It's what we expected. Thanks. You and Julia can go. I want to have a word with Gary and Rory.'

Rory took Julia's seat and watched Bourke steeple his fingers again as he contemplated what he was about to say.

'I don't suppose you had a response from your TV appeal to FP1,' Rory asked.

'No. We can write that off.'

Cockburn and Rory watched him and waited. Then he was ready.

'Okay, we're getting a picture but not all of it. Where are we at with the recording, Rory?'

Rory was mindful not to put the sanctuary development on the table without forewarning Josh and Martha, and not before exhausting all of its permutations. If he ran with a half-cocked version, he could end up in deeper hot water with Bourke. He decided to keep things at ankle depth and played it straight.

'No change. We can prove the conversation has not been tampered with. We can lock that much in. The defence can introduce doubt, albeit small, about whether it's Dwyer's voice, even with our technical acoustic analysis and a phonetician making a call. We can conjecture that the recording occurred when Dwyer attended training at the Forensic Centre. We also conjecture that the very nature of the conversation places it before the murders. That's the main strength of the recording — it speaks for itself. It's not a conversation that can easily be explained away.'

'What I'm hearing is a lot of conjecturing,' Bourke said. 'No where or who the conversation was with, and nothing to corroborate or otherwise authenticate when it occurred.' he nodded in further thought. 'If that's all we can come up with, get it to the prosecutors to start looking at it.'

He turned to Cockburn.

'You haven't said much, Gary. Thoughts?'

'Me and Julia are going to have a crack at Dwyer while he's still in Loddon Prison. They've granted permission for him to appeal the non-bail decision. I know we already questioned him, but that was for the Neilson Scali murders. He hasn't been questioned about Graeme Stanley. That's my "in". A quiet chat while he's still a guest at Loddon Prison. Not a suspect interview … simply seeing if he can assist us with our enquiries.'

'Good move. But leave Julia out of it. You go with Gary, Rory. See if you can get more out of Dwyer about the recording. Didn't you tell me he's become obsessed with it?'

No I didn't, Rory answered to himself, then asked Cockburn, 'When are you seeing Dwyer?'

'Tomorrow.'

'All right. That sounds like a plan. Come and see me when you get back,' Bourke said.

Rory left Cockburn's office with Bourke. He made his way over to Gerry Denton.

'What do we have on Graeme Stanley's funeral? I saw it was on the TV news. Did we get a copy?'

'I think so. There's also some pics. Gary and Julia have already checked them out.'

'Did they say anything about it?'

'I think they thought it was the usual suspects but no actual suspects. Do you want to check it out too.'

'Yeah. Another set of eyes can't hurt. Can you email it through?'

Cockburn drove. The trip to Loddon Prison would take at least an hour.

'What's with the bag? We're not staying overnight.'

'I am. I'm staying in Bendigo and getting the train back tomorrow.'

Cockburn cast a look at Rory.

'Desperate, aren't you?'

'And you're pissed off that you've got me in the car instead of Julia O'Hannagain.'

Cockburn took his attention back to the road and ended the exchange with, 'Shit happens.'

The tone was set. Cockburn turned the radio on. Rory retrieved the Graeme Stanley file from the back seat. He began flicking through it. Muscles tightened on Cockburn's neck and he began to shoot glances at Rory. Rory relented.

'What?'

'How come you're so interested in Graeme Stanley. Your job is to slip in a few questions about the hitman recording.'

'It can't hurt to look at the bigger picture.'

'Stick to the script — leave the Graeme Stanley stuff to me.'

Rory kept reading the file.

Cockburn's head continued to swivel between Rory and the road.

'I mean it.'

'The Graeme Stanley stuff's all yours. You can ask Dwyer about it without me being there if you like, but at some point, I want ten minutes on my own with him.'

This time Cockburn took his eyes off the road for too long. Rory nodded towards a car Cockburn looked like rear-ending. He was forced to merge into the right lane without indicating. He held the wheel with both hands and took time to calm himself. A few kilometres of road-noise drone and the radio led his mind elsewhere.

'You think someone leaked about the recording?'

'We know they did. That's why we're in a car driving to Loddon Prison. That's how Graeme Stanley copped it. You nearly got blown up … REMEMBER.'

Rory yelled the last bit to remind Cockburn that his hearing still came and went. Cockburn was intent on a train of thought and ignored the jibe.

'Yeah, but. Do you wonder who did leak it?'

This time Rory looked hard at Cockburn.

'You think I did?'

The pause by Cockburn was too long. The answer was even less reassuring. 'Nah. Not really.'

'Fuck you, Gary.'

'What makes you automatically off fucking limits … Saint Rory. You can't deny it would have crossed your mind that I leaked it?'

'I know you didn't, Gary. I know that underneath it all, you're not bent.'

Cockburn savoured the compliment — for a moment.

'Underneath all what?'

'Do you really want me to start?'

'Well if you take us two out of the equation, it doesn't leave many others.'

'Exactly.'

'Do you ever wonder if …' Rory cut him off.

'Don't even go there, Gary.'

He didn't go there. Mere utterance of names would be more than enough to sully. Cockburn didn't need to be told twice, not even by Rory. The suspicion of someone immediately above them in the line of command remained buried in thought.

The thought brought them into silence for the good while it took Cockburn's mind to wander — the philosophical wander brought on by idle time spent on a road trip.

'If you had to go, the way Neilson and Scali went wouldn't be a bad option,' Cockburn said.

'Are you joking? A bullet in the back of the head. It might beat a slow death by cancer but that's about all.'

'No, that's not what I meant. I was reading the old files. In the forensic and post mortem reports it says Neilson and Scali had only just finished having sex before the gunman came in and shot them.

And Corina Scali was a hot-looking woman. Think about that.'

'Yeah, but that's not the same as dying on the actual job … doing a Billy Snedden.' Rory referred to the tabloid headline that 1970s Liberal Party leader, Sir Billy Snedden, "…died on the job" while having sex with his son's ex-girlfriend.

'Neilson had finished having a root. He'd moved on. It doesn't matter that it was only a short time afterwards. He was no longer in that rooting-thought frenzy. He was in the post-root stage of the rest of his life. He could have been plotting his next root … or what he'd be having for breakfast.'

Cockburn tilted his head thoughtfully.

'But that's the beauty of it. If someone offered you the best sex in the world as your last ever treat before facing a firing squad, it would be useless. You'd be in no state to get it up, would you? Whereas, with Clifford Neilson, he didn't know the bullet was coming and he could root himself silly. Then he goes out with a bang. Bang, bang.'

He turned to Rory with a grin and waited for Rory's reaction.

'I … But …'

'See, you can't argue with it. It's a win-win situation.'

Rory threw his hands into the air and shook his head. 'You're right about one thing. I can't argue, because I'm speechless.'

Cockburn took his eyes and smug grin back to the freeway.

'This is it,' Rory said when the Castlemaine exit from the Calder Freeway came up. The B180 off-road was soon winding through the outlying suburb of Chewton. Chewtonians would have it as a town in its own right, having survived since the gold rush with its own town hall, post office, pubs intact, as well as an impressive collection of extant miners' cottages. The elephant not mentioned in its Wikipedia room was the prison on its doorstep. The unmentioned facility accommodated a population as large as the town.

Rory and Cockburn stood by the car with its doors open as they donned their jackets in the carpark.

'It reminds me of a TAFE college,' Rory said, taking in the modern assemblage of angles, bold finishes and glass expanses. The new prison annex looked more TAFE-college-like that most TAFE colleges did.

'With bars.' Cockburn added.

'Hmm.'

'Before we go in, remind me why I should leave you alone with Dwyer.'

'He hasn't admitted to knowing anything about the recording. I want to see if he adopts the same line off the record. I reckon I can get him to at least acknowledge its existence, maybe talk a bit about it, provided there's no one else there to hear. That'll allow him to deny anything either of us say.'

'Not until I'm done then.'

'It's your show, Gary.'

They passed through the airport-like security and relieved themselves of firearms, mobile phones and wallets. A benign prison officer led them through a new breed of stainless steel barred doors that could pass as a hip corporate finish. A few more doors closed behind them with a combination of clang and electronic whirr, until they walked outside into a mass visitor area that could pass for an al-fresco McDonald's.

The paved and high-walled yard was dotted with bright coloured tables and stools. A good quarter of the entire area was a red and yellow children's playground equipped with slides and climbing apparatus and shaded by a sail-covered steel frame.

A cigarette-smoking David Dwyer was the sole occupant. He sat hunched over a yellow table for two.

The prison officer closed the gate and told Rory and Cockburn: 'I'll be here when you're ready.'

They walked over to Dwyer and took things in. No conversation was had. Drawing a third stool over to Dwyer's table was not an option; everything was cemented in place for life. Cockburn said, 'Here,' to Rory, and sat at the adjoining four-stool orange table. He summoned Dwyer over with a scowling head gesture.

'Tweedledum and Tweedle-fucking-dumber,' Dwyer said as he lumbered over at his own defiant pace. As a prisoner on remand, he was able to wear his own garb of fawn polyester trousers and a tucked-in white shirt that did everything to show off his chronic paunch.

Rory left the niceties to Cockburn and checked out the horizon. They were in a courtyard of two-storey dark grey building walls. A framed sheet of sky provided the only natural world presence.

'Settling in okay?' Cockburn said.

'Get Ramsay here if you want to ask me anything.' He squirmed on the rigid metal stool-top disc and settled with his forearms on the table. There was no power body-language to be had.

'We're not here about your case, Dwyer. We're here about a friend of yours. Graeme Stanley. Thought you might want to help us with our enquiries.' Cockburn's slight but wiry frame had no complaint with the stool. He sat erectly with his hands on his thighs and leant forward as he spoke.

Dwyer drew on his cigarette. It was the only prop he had. He exhaled towards Cockburn before speaking.

'There's your first mistake. You're assuming Stanley is someone I give a rat's arse about.'

'From what I hear from a certain bikie gang, you were not pleased that he died.'

'Like I said, I couldn't give a rat's arse one way or the other.'

'They care. I understand they're disappointed they haven't received the balance of their fee. I understand they're so disappointed that you might be safer in here. But who knows these days? Look at what happened to Carl Williams.' It was a reference to another high-profile gangland supremo, Carl Williams. He was beaten to death in 2010 at Barwon Prison when it became known that he was about to turn informant.

Dwyer gave the stare and drew on his cigarette yet again.

'You mentioned Graeme on the recording. I presume you were referring to Graeme Stanley.'

'You're doing a lot of presuming and understanding today, remember that. It's only your assumption that it's me on that recording.'

'You've got a very distinctive voice, Dwyer. I don't think there's a judge or juryman or woman in the land who'll be assuming anything else.'

'Sounds like you're the one you're trying to convince, Cockburn.'

Cockburn looked skyward to end discussion of that particular subject. He dropped his eyes to Dwyer.

'Where were you on the twentieth of last month?'

Dwyer laughed. 'Is that when he died? Give me a break.'

'Do you know where you were?'

'I would have been pruning olive trees because I haven't been to Melbourne for weeks. Ask my farmhand Angelo.'

'Okay.' Cockburn made his first note.

'Bruce Taylor. He did all right on the horses that week. Won ten grand from Ray Samson.'

Dwyer resumed his best heavy-duty stare without lifting his cigarette to his lips.

'We know how it works,' Cockburn said to underline the point he scored. 'Your mates will be going down with you before this is over, your cute little betting set-up included.'

'Is that it?'

Still no bite.

'I'm gonna get some fresh air. My colleague Detective Sergeant James has a couple more questions before we go back to the free world.'

Cockburn took his notebook and headed to the gate.

'You always did fancy being the "good cop" James.' Dwyer lit up again. 'So what's the good-cop's take on things.'

'I think you and us are in the same boat,' Rory said.

'Oh, do you now? So I scratch your back and you scratch my back. How do you figure that out, Detective?'

'For argument's sake, if we were to find out who the other person is on the David Dwyer sound-alike recording, we reckon we could take a hired killer off the streets. Make the community a safer place for me and you. If a concerned citizen was able to assist us in that regard, I'm sure that individual would be in a position to receive some sort of favoured treatment.'

Rory used the less-accusatory description, "David Dwyer sound-alike recording", to prevent Dwyer's shutters going up.

'Like the $1,000,000 reward?'

'I wouldn't go that far. But a sentence reduction might not be out of the question. As it stands, you've got nothing to hang your hat on.'

'And you're counting on me spilling my guts into the wire you're wearing.'

'There's no wire, you can check. I'm doing this because we don't want to lose the opportunity to get the hitman as well. I thought that, given your circumstances and how all this came about, you might want the same result.'

'I'm not checking you for a wire. As you might have realised, the last time I did that, they still managed to get it past me. I know that for a fact because there was no one else within a bull's roar of where I spoke to that cunt. I never kept up with technology. These days they can probably hide a microphone in your nostrils or up your arse.'

There's one admission. He did meet the hitman and he thinks the hitman somehow recorded the conversation. None too pleased about it as well.

'The offer to check me for a wire doesn't go that far,' Rory said.

'All right. So, I'll assume you're not wearing a wire, the situation is this …' Dwyer lit up another cigarette and appeared to frame his thoughts. He spoke slowly and deliberately. 'We stay with the story that I was not there when the recording was made, okay?

But I have heard the recording a couple of times since you gave me a copy, so why don't I tell you what I think this other person looks like, based solely on what I hear him say on the recording?'

'That could be helpful and appreciated,' Rory said and produced his note book and pen.

'Okay then. This is what I noticed. The two "unknown" voices on the recording mention a mutual acquaintance called Graeme. So I would speculate that one of the voices belongs to a trusted acquaintance — if not a former professional colleague — of the person called Graeme. Probably from a time when Graeme lived and plied his trade in the old dart.'

'My own speculation exactly.'

'On the recording, it sounds to me like this acquaintance of Graeme's is about your build and height, maybe even slimmer, no, more toned, I would say. He definitely speaks like a man dressed in a black shirt and black jeans. Someone with jet black hair, unshaven, perhaps heading for a beard.'

'Anything else?' Rory asked as he continued making a note that matched Josh's description.

'The English accent. Not surprising if you consider he's a mate of Stanley's.'

Another admission. The person referred to on the recording as Graeme, is Graeme Stanley. Rory didn't write it down.

'So hypothetically, a black-haired Englishman. Any tatts, scars or distinctive features?'

'Nah, Bloody poms, they all sound and look the same to me. But if you do manage to find him, you're a bloody genius.'

When Rory had Cockburn drop him off at the Castlemaine railway station, he realised he was looking forward to the half-hour train ride to Bendigo. The mammoth mid-journey tunnel made it a favourite from boyhood.

'Are you going to tell me what Dwyer said?' Cockburn asked

as Rory reached for the car door handle.

'He only spoke hypothetically. Nothing we didn't assume to be the case, though. The hitman was someone from Stanley's past in England. He suspects the hitman did the recording. He gave a useless description. Someone about my height and build with black hair. He didn't say so, but I'm sure Dwyer lost any chance of identifying him when Stanley carked it. I reckon you're right that it's a sore point between him and the bikies who stuffed that up.'

'Of course it's fucking right. That's what we're gonna do, keep picking that fucking scab.'

Rory tried to expunge the image from his mind as he collected his overnight bag from the back seat and slung the strap onto his shoulder.

At Bendigo station, he eschewed a taxi and decided to walk to The Manse through the CBD. He was still savouring the chance to rediscover landmarks of his youth. The oval's ornate grandstand conjured adolescent memories a couple of blocks before reaching the leafy residential crescent of The Manse.

The bygone residence was an entirely new Bendigo delight for Rory, one that still caused pause upon arrival. He could tell from the parked cars that there were guests, but Sigrid was not around when he went inside. He eyed the rack of tourist brochures on the hallway stand and the thought came: Maybe that's why the place never feels like home. Without being distracted by the thought, he delivered his bag to her bedroom and headed for The Manse library.

None of the book titles enticed Rory while he waited for his laptop to boot and connect to The Manse Wi-Fi. They were mostly holiday reads, apart from a pristine set of 1970s Encyclopaedia Britannica. Rory logged onto the Police intranet, checked his emails, and opened one of two from Gerry Denton — the one with the title "Funeral Footage". The footage took some time to download.

Now let's see if I saw what I thought I saw. Rory clicked the Play symbol and sat back in his chair to watch.

It began at the newsreader's desk. The screen above the female newsreader's shoulder showed an image of Graeme Stanley's coffin being shouldered through church doors. Vision soon cut to scenes of the few attendees arriving, including the couple of partners in black cleavages lashing out at cameramen. A female voiceover provided familiar commentary, '… *was attended by a small group of family and friends.*'

Rory waited for footage of the casket being shouldered out of the church. The close up only lasted for seconds before vision switched to the reporter. Pallbearing continuing in the background. *'A police spokesperson said that they are pursuing their inquiries but have not identified any suspects at this stage. The spokesman also said that today's arrest of former drug squad detective, David Dwyer, was not in relation to the murder of Graeme Stanley. It is understood …"*

He rewound and paused / played his way through the few seconds of close up video. It appeared to be filmed from a height near the footpath. The cameraman must have been on his van's rooftop platform.

The lead coffin bearer wore sun glasses and an open-necked black shirt and he kept his head forward and down. He seemed intent on not showing his face. The posture did everything to hide his face from anyone who may recognise him on the news, and everything to reveal a lower neck tattoo to a camera prying from a height.

Rory paused on the best view and zoomed in. The tattoo pixelated to a blur, but a nevertheless recognisable blur. A glimpse of a poker hand being glimpsed. A tattoo only visible from an overhead camera — or by someone up a tree.

It confirmed an image that had lodged in Rory's subconscious when he stood in The Manse with Calvin and Sigrid and watched the news item originally going to air. What his recall lacked was the tattoo owner's appearance — a face to go with the voice. Not any longer, here was the full package.

'So we have our other voice,' He said aloud and let his eyes linger on the image. The hair was black but with an added peppering of grey. The beard that Josh and Dwyer described was absent. Rory clicked on Play and let the news story play out hoping for a face shot. It never came. '… *Nicole Tracy reporting from St Bernadette's, Altona.'* Nothing better appeared.

Rory opened Gerry Denton's second email which had the subject, "Funeral pics". They were all shots taken by the Police through a long-range zoom lens, mostly in-focus face shots against a blurred background. He skipped through the photographs until he reached a focussed head and shoulders shot of the lead pallbearer. It was labelled "Brian Stanley (brother)".

He lingered on the image. An obvious family resemblance was evident, despite sunglasses. The photo was taken at eye height and slightly to the right side of front-on. As he suspected, the tattoo was now hidden by the stand-up collar of Brian Stanley's open neck shirt. The tattoo-free viewpoint was the only perspective known to David Dwyer.

Brian Stanley … he told himself, opened his pocket notebook, and flicked to the notes he had made in Cockburn's car from the Graeme Stanley file:

Graeme Stanley's younger brother. Emigrated to Australia together. Briefly worked together in Melbourne as painters and decorators before going their separate ways. Brian relocated to Perth and stayed on the straight and narrow. Flew from Western Australia to identify Graeme Stanley's body. A uniformed constable drove him from the airport to morgue. Not interviewed. Phone number. Address …

Instinct and evidence had intersected to pose a crossroads moment. Rory looked at his watch. The sun would be over the yard arm somewhere in the world. He returned to his computer with a scotch and ice, then studied the on-screen image of Brian Stanley, and thought it through.

Western Australia presented the prospect of inter-force

protocols and form-filling, as well as a further round of form-filling for travel approvals. He grimaced and turned his attention to the case. He'd need to join a lot of dots for Bourke to buy it but the story would ultimately be convincing enough. Before the dot-joining stage there was the matter of producing those actual dots and explaining why he had kept his own counsel and failed to mention any of them previously. There was nothing on file. He ran through some of those dots in his mind: Dwyer's mum's house. The wildlife sanctuary. The recording accidently made by a PhD student sitting in a tree. His meetings with Josh and Martha. The tattoo. The fingerprint.

Lay all this on the table and the guilty party would well and truly be brought into the spotlight, but not without condemning the innocent provisioner to being dragged along — a guaranteed fatal path if history was any guide. There was no doubt about the risks that such exposure entailed, the life it would almost certainly sentence Josh and Martha to. Did it have to be so? Then there was the unresolved matter of a current leak within the force.

His direction at the crossroads chose itself.

27

'Margaret River.'

'Margaret River?'

'Yeah, Margaret River. Western Australia.'

'When?'

'I need to go pretty much straight away. It's the off-season. We should be able to get a last-minute deal.'

'Need to? So our romantic getaway is another work thing?'

Sigrid crossed her arms where she stood in The Manse library doorway. The patterned white dress was just tight enough to tug at her curves. Rory had to retreat from the image he already had in his mind of them sharing a spa with a vineyard view.

'No. Not officially. I only need an hour when we're there.'

'*Not officially?* You're *kinda* dealing with Martha and Josh. We're *under the radar* at the sanctuary. Is this how it is being in a relationship with a cop? Is this why most of their marriages go pear-shaped?'

'Look ...' Rory rose from sitting at his computer and sighed loudly. 'It's not like I don't want to tell you stuff ...' He couldn't finish the sentence. Sigrid waited. 'This is like a side project. Something I really don't want to put on the table at work.'

'I didn't know policemen had side projects. It's not becoming a Post-Traumatic Stress Disorder-related thing is it?'

Huh? "A PTSD-related thing"? Right there on the tip of her tongue. It can't be her way of hinting something might be going on with Michelle ... can it? Anyway, that was simply a professional thing that came along ...

and it has run its course … just about. Has she got some way of knowing there's an attraction … how would she know if I don't know?

'What?' The word came out with a squawk of shock.

'I read that woman's web site — what the symptoms are. I know you've been there, Rory … and suffered all of them. I've lived through one of your nightmares, remember,' she added to put the matter beyond discussion. 'I also know you still cop the alienation thing at work. Is this what this is about? Are you turning into an obsessed lone wolf?'

That sounded a bit less accusative, although she did refer to Michelle as "that woman". He didn't feel out of the woods just yet.

'You looked up Michelle's web-site?'

'Yes, I did. After the nightmare thing, I want to understand. I thought I might be able to help.'

Rory tried pacing in a room too small to pace as he absorbed Sigrid's revelation. Sigrid waited until he found where to start.

'You have helped. You're one thing that has helped. You know how close to the edge I was when we met. Until the night we spent at my flat, I'd never had the nightmare when I'm with you. I've gotten beyond a lot of that stuff because of you … you and getting back to work. That's what I've been clinging on to. And that's what this particular work stuff is — just work stuff. There's a lot of mistrust around at the moment and none of it has come about because of my state of mind. It's simply how things have unfolded with this case. Well not exactly simply, but honestly, you wouldn't want to know, even if I could tell you.'

'Has it got anything to do with Martha and Josh?'

'Not if I can help it. That's precisely what I'm trying to avoid.'

'You're still fudging, Rory. Are Martha and Josh in trouble?'

Being called by name made him feel like a child being chastised.

'They have absolutely done nothing wrong and no way are they in trouble with the law. Okay?' He was talking slowly to frame an argument and to try to bring Sigrid along as he went. 'Nevertheless, through no fault of their own, by well-intentioned do-gooding in fact, there is a potential threat to them that only I'm aware of. That's why I met with Josh and Martha. They now know about it and as long as it remains strictly between the three of us, they will be safe. I know I'm still being vague, but that's the nub of why I'm not willing to share that knowledge with my colleagues. I need to resolve the case, or at least climb to the next rung, without putting any of that information on the table. And I think I can do that.'

'And that involves going to WA?' The question implied willingness to accept his justification so far. He sensed a softening.

'I can only get to that next rung by going to WA. However, if I chose to make it an official trip instead, I'd have to reveal too much, including Josh and Martha's details. Once I do that I can't undo it; it would be on the record forever. Too many people would end up knowing about it … including people I'm not sure I can trust.'

'So you're prepared to pay your own way to Perth and back to avoid Martha and Josh becoming involved in whatever it is you're not telling me?'

'Pretty much.'

'And what are the chances of you making this threat disappear forever?'

'If it plays out like I think it will, that's precisely what I think can happen.'

Sigrid's arms remained crossed but her expression unstiffened. Rory knew he'd better try and settle the matter.

'Okay, let's not even talk about Josh and Martha. In fact, I don't want you to ever mention this to Martha and Josh. We go to Margaret River for a few days. I go off to buy a newspaper, I'll only be gone for a short while but that's all the time I need to check out my hunch. And we enjoy ourselves. As far as Bourke is concerned, I'm simply on leave taking a break. I pay for the trip. This is just about you and me. Ninety-nine percent.'

Her response took a moment. It was Sigrid's turn to cogitate.

'On one condition.'

'Whatever you want,' Rory said, letting a half-smile creep into the conversation.

'I pay and I choose where we stay. I'll claim it on my tax. It'll be research. That makes it ninety-eight percent. That'll make it even. One percent each.'

Rory knew Sigrid was right. She was so right about him letting work stuff taint a romantic getaway. So why did he do it? Don't I care, he wondered? She was even right-er about his PTSD and that made it worse. There was no one left who didn't want to slap the label on him. Why did that make it easier for everyone except him to deal with it? She was right-est of all about him being a maverick. If his instinct was correct, there was absolutely no room for sharing with colleagues.

Once Rory had parked the car at Melbourne's Tullamarine Airport it was the-all-Sigrid show. She produced business-class tickets and ordered wine on the plane for them both.

'I've never flown business class. You could at least let me pay my share.' Rory said.

'My pick, my shout, you agreed. Now are you going to let it go and enjoy yourself?'

'I'll try, but I'm entering new territory.'

'Western Australia?'

'That too. I've never been, have you?'

'I've been to Broome, but never to Perth or Margaret River. It'll be an adventure for both of us. Wait till you see where we're staying.'

The mystery tour began as soon as they landed. Rory didn't even know which hire-car counter to go to. He followed Sigrid to Europcar. She did the paperwork and came away with the keys to a VW Golf Cabriolet soft-top. Her bold choice only became apparent to Rory when Sigrid clicked its doors unlocked in the carpark.

'A convertible?'

'I'm on holidays,' she said and opened the driver-side door.

As he made his way to the left-hand door, it wasn't lost on him that he had become the passenger in every sense. In his mind, he dismissed his discomfort as a clichéd male reaction to the reversal of stereotypical gender roles. This was Sigrid's natural environment and there was something unnerving to Rory about how effortlessly she inhabited it. It showed how far she'd strayed out of her comfort zone to visit his flat and meet Steph.

'Why do I get the feeling that this is going to be all five-star?' Rory said across the Cabriolet's fabric roof.

'I can afford it, and it's a tax break. I hope you're not going to whinge about any more of my choices.'

The suggestion of complaining stung. He held his hands up in surrender before patting the roof. 'Do you know how to put the top down?'

They listened to the sat-nav direct them out of the airport and into central Perth.

'We could have bypassed the CBD and gone straight onto the Kwinana Freeway, you know?'

'And miss this?'

They sat at the lights with the top down. Rory added self-conscious-ness and superfluous-ness to his increasing unease. The last thing turned heads wanted to see with a good-looking blonde woman driving a sports car, was a male passenger. He turned to Sigrid. She radiated. *Get over it*, he told himself. It might not be something he'd ever have added to a bucket-list, but as pure male fantasy, it was up there.

They reached the southern beachside town of Mandurah by lunchtime and stopped to eat. Sigrid found a café where they could park beside the al-fresco seating area and admire the Cabriolet while they dined.

'I'm seeing a side of you I didn't know. I'm not sure I can live up to the life you seem accustomed to.'

'Don't spoil this, Rory. If you can't live your fantasy on a holiday, when can you? It's supposed to be your fantasy too, remember?'

'Don't worry,' he told her. 'It's got all the elements I need for that.'

She smiled and raised her glass of local sauvignon blanc.

'To our fantasy holiday.'

Their only other stop en-route was at Busselton to check out "the longest timber-piled jetty in the Southern Hemisphere". Rory wanted to walk the full 1.8 kilometres that tapered to what looked like the horizon in the middle of the Indian Ocean. Sigrid shook the car keys at him and said, 'Our B&B awaits.'

Rory noticed that in this neck of the woods, Margaret River was one of the few towns that wasn't "up". Cowaramup, Willyabrup, Quindalup, Wonnerup, Boyanup, Dardanup, Nannup and more. When they did arrive in Margaret River, Sigrid did a slow lap of the main drag before turning westward and heading out of town.

'It's not in Margaret River itself? Is it at a winery?' Rory guessed.

'Neither. But it's not far.'

Within a few kilometres, the landscape changed to tea tree and sand.

'The beach?'

'I grew up by the sea. I can't come this close and not be by the water.'

There were glimpses of the ocean before they arrived at a broad, strikingly plain building that blocked the view. A large, tinted-glass front door and understated window slots were set in the brutalist concrete wall facing the street. It hinted at the hand of a talented architect. The true splendour of the building, however, was a climax in the making, made so by a cave-like entry with teasing glimpses of the main living area ahead.

Rory and Sigrid followed the final few steps down and stepped into that endpoint. Rory was wowed speechless. Sigrid offered a breath-taken 'Oh,' and walked slowly into the centre of the room. Her fingers covered her mouth. 'It's so much better than on the internet. I can't believe how good this is. Look …'

'I am,' said Rory.

They were drawn to the front wall of glass that had shorter windows wrapped around each side. It gave a one hundred and eighty-degree view of the Indian Ocean, edged at their feet by the Brombie, one of the best surf breaks in the world. The fringe of intervening tea tree scrub was dotted with the roofs of conventional beach houses in the hamlet of Prevelly. Their glass-fronted viewing platform seemed to hover spaceship-like atop the highest dune.

'Everything else has been a mere curtain raiser,' Rory said. 'This is abso-fucking-lutely amazing.'

'It must be. You don't usually swear. I saw pictures but I never expected it to be this impressive. It's owned by Ron Roozen. He's a local artist.'

'That's why everything's so … minimalist and luscious at the same time. I love the feel of this place. I presume he did the artwork.'

Sigrid smiled at his praise.

'You paid for this, didn't you?'

'That was the deal.'

'No. I mean you would have paid a lot to book this place.'

'Hey, you weren't gonna go there again …'

'No, that's not what I was getting at. I mean you did all this for me. I don't know what to say.'

He felt himself well up. *Fuck. Where did that come from?* he thought. Until that moment, their relationship had been defined by the absence of overly-demonstrative emotion on both their parts. Everything just happened and both of them were happy to let it just happen without question and without wanting to analyse it with each other. It was easy territory for a bloke to traverse although it put Sigrid in a different class to any other woman he'd known. And now, he was the one that cracked … and not in the way he ever imagined. Anything he questioned in his mind about their relationship usually headed in the opposite direction. How could this have happened? How would Sigrid react?

She stepped over and held his face. 'That's why.' She said.

The kiss grew too physical and they bumped into the telescope on a tripod.

'Hold that thought,' Sigrid said.

'I have been … all day.'

Sigrid smiled and left him to open the glass sliding door onto the balcony. She leant on the balustrade.

'Just look at it … and smell it. Let's walk on the beach.'

'Don't we need to get some supplies in first?'

'All taken care of. The pantry is restocked daily.'

'Drinks?'

'Pre-ordered. The only thing we need to do today is the walk on the beach. Do you think you can manage?'

Rory stood in his boxers and tee-shirt and poached an egg for breakfast. Sigrid breathed in the view. She sat at a dining chair in a short house-bathrobe and finger-combed bed-hair.

'This was such a good idea.'

'You're so right. There's a sight I'll never tire of,' he told her with unambiguous intent. 'I could spend the entire holiday right here.'

'You need to go and buy the paper first. I don't want your little job hanging over this holiday,' Sigrid said.

'I agree.'

Rory was still enjoying the novelty of driving a convertible when the sat-nav brought him to the premises signed: "Stanley's Executive Painting and Decorating. Residential and Commercial". The industrial estate carved out of forest on the southern side of Margaret River was a collection of Cyclone-wire fences and oversized sheds, some with offices appended. Stanley's zinc-alum specimen was fronted by a small two-window weatherboard office. Two cars were parked in the forecourt. The well-maintained appearance and recently repainted signage suggested the firm was travelling well. Rory halted briefly to write down the phone number and drove on.

The relatively small industrial estate seemed to have everything — cabinet makers, plumbers, engineer, diesel mechanic, even an accountant and a wine tour operator — except a phone box. Rory wasn't ready to have his long line of inquiry traceable in any way. He found one on the way back to the centre of town. His most recent encounter with a public phone must have been in the pre-mobile phone era and he had to read the instructions. He dialled and a woman answered.

'Is Brian Stanley there, please?'

'I'm sorry, Brian's out on a job. Who's calling, please?'

He didn't have a plan if Brian Stanley wasn't in the office.

'My name is Rory James. I've driven down from Perth to see Brian but the battery is dead in my mobile phone. I can't retrieve his mobile number to call him.'

'If it's about a job, I can give you his number or you could call in and see him on site.'

'You better give me the address. I don't think I've got change for another call.'

Chardonnay Avenue. Rory smiled and punched it into the sat-nav. Then he put the convertible's roof down.

Chardonnay Avenue penetrated a thick forest that reached within the town's boundary. A forest both tall and with enough undergrowth to allow only glimpses of the capacious homes within. The combination of large blocks serviced by the narrowest sealed road spoke wealth. The only anomalous presence was the cluster of tradie utes that spilled from a particular driveway, each with an obligatory, enclosed equipment-trailer hitched behind. A new mega-house was nearing completion. The painters were in, as were the flurry of other finishing trades — air conditioning, electrical, tilers, security equipment, audio visual, spa and pool guys, plumbers.

The office woman at Stanley's Executive Painting and Decorating must have phoned ahead because Rory recognised Brian Stanley standing out front. He met Rory where he parked.

'Are you Rory James?'

'Yeah, Brian Stanley?'

'How are you,' he answered and shook Rory's hand. Brian Stanley had been hands-on. His clothes were dusty and the high-vis shirt was unbuttoned far enough for the tattoo to be unhidden. He was as trimmed as he appeared carrying the coffin on television, but fitter in the flesh and perhaps even more tanned.

'It's Detective Sergeant James, from the Victorian Police.'

'What?'

Stanley placed his hands on his hips and looked at the convertible.

'That's a hire car,' Rory answered Brian Stanley's thought. 'It's about your brother.'

'Graeme? Fuck it's a famine or a feast with you blokes.' Brian Stanley was still focussing on the Cabriolet. 'I wasn't given the time of day when I flew to Melbourne to identify him. Just a car ride to the morgue and that was it. The only way I learnt what was going on was from his mates at the funeral. Now you turn up on my doorstep, on the other side of the country mind you, in that.'

He nodded towards the car.

'I needed to see you in person and I was in the neighbourhood.'

Brian Stanley cocked his head with distrust.

'Are you gonna tell me what's going on? I know you've already got Dwyer locked up for the Neilson Scali thing. Has he confessed to murdering Graeme as well?'

Brian Stanley kept his hands on his hips.

'No, that's not it,'

'Then why are you here?'

'I wanted to hear you speak.'

There was a short silence. Long enough for Rory to know that Brian Stanley understood.

'Oh yeah, why's that?' He said it flatly, as though he might know the answer.

'You know we arrested Dwyer on new evidence. A recording that turned up with an incriminating conversation between Dwyer and the hitman he hired to kill Neilson and Scali. There's no doubt that one of the voices on that tape is Dwyer's, but no one knows who the other person is that he's talking to. Not even Dwyer knows.'

'So?'

Rory settled against the Cabriolet for a longer conversation.

'The funny thing is, we've been standing here speaking for a few minutes now, and I reckon I've just heard that voice again. I might be wrong of course, but that's why we engage acoustic analysts and trained phoneticians. So things like that can be proved beyond doubt. Judges and juries like to be reassured like that.'

Brian Stanley crossed his arms and looked down. He scuffed the gravel with his camel-coloured work boots. Rory didn't expect him to be this calm.

'Did Dwyer recognise me on the news at Graeme's funeral?'

'No. I think you did a good enough job of keeping your head down there. If Dwyer knew, I think you might have had someone else call round before I got here.'

Stanley returned his attention to the ground and scuffed again. He seemed resigned.

'It's not what you think. I didn't do it, you know.' He said it with cool conviction.

'No? You meet Dwyer surreptitiously, he gives you the safe-house address for Neilsen and Scali, he pays you a small fortune, and you simply fly back here to WA. Neilson and Scali get themselves shot but that's just coincidence. Now I get it.'

Stanley shook his head and smiled wryly at the sarcasm. 'Shit, I need a drink. Come in here.' Rory became more perplexed by Stanley's assured lack of defensiveness.

He led them to the site hut in the front yard of the new house. A couple of apprentices were having a cuppa inside. They didn't appear to be Stanley's own employees.

'Piss off,' he told them with the hitman tone. So he can turn it off or on, Rory noticed. They pissed off and Rory and Stanley took over the plastic chairs. Stanley produced a bottle of scotch from a locked cabinet and poured it into a cup. He held the bottle to Rory, who gestured no.

Stanley took a good slug and rode it all the way down. He gave a shudder.

'Graeme didn't want to lose the job. The suggestion of giving his opposition a free hit on his home turf stuck in Graeme's craw. He was also passing up big money. Dwyer paid him commission to arrange for someone else to do the job but that was merely pocket money. So Graeme got me to pose as the hitman … so he could get the job for himself.

'The thing was, although Dwyer usually kept himself at arm's length from the nitty gritty, he wasn't about to part with seventy-five grand without eyeballing what he was getting in return. That meant Graeme needed someone convincing that he could trust. But that's all I did. I swore off crime when our dad went to prison. Graeme convinced me that I wouldn't be committing a crime as such, so I did it as a favour, and for the money. It was big bikkies and this business was struggling back then.'

'But Graeme had an alibi on CCTV? He was at a servo and at the Casino that night.'

'That was me too. I had time to start a beard before I met with Dwyer to get the address and the down-payment. I stayed on in Melbourne and shaved the beard off to become Graeme while he did the job. The resemblance is close enough, and we chose locations where we knew the CCTV footage would be grainy. The main worry was making sure Dwyer didn't twig when he and I met. The beard did the trick. Once we were over that hurdle, we were in the home straight.'

'So you perverted the course of justice as well as aided and abetted?'

He poured more scotch into his cup.

'Whatever, but I'm not copping murder. I've got an alibi for that. Graeme's alibi as it happens. I presume you still have that on your files.'

He drank. Rory watched. He sensed the situation was one that had played on Stanley's mind once or twice since he found out that the recording existed. Someone was bound to recognise his voice if it was ever played on the media or eventually ended up on YouTube.

'This is gonna fuck me right up, you know. This is a really good business I've built up. And I'm not bullshitting you. See that house out there,' he nodded toward the open site-hut door. 'That's top of the range around here. The owners didn't bother with other quotes. We've got a reputation as the best, and we're part of the community. There are people in town who have asked me to run for Council. I've never accepted but it tells you the level of respect I've built up.' He looked at the floor and shook his head. 'Fucking Dwyer. Why did he tape that meeting? It only put us both in the shit in the end.'

Rory leant forward in his chair. 'You reckon Dwyer taped it?'

'I know he did because I didn't. I couldn't have worn a wire if I wanted to — he frisked me like I was his new girlfriend. There was no one else within coo-ee, I know that too. We were outdoors in the open. Dwyer was the only one who could have taped us.'

So they both thought the other taped the conversation. Why disillusion either of them?

'You don't have to be in the shit,' Rory offered.

Stanley held his cup still and eyed Rory cautiously. 'Do tell.'

'On the basis of the evidence to hand, that evidence being an undisputed recorded conversation, we're looking at a double murder. If the prosecutor, for whatever reason, believes your defence and decides not to lay a murder charge, or you're found not-guilty after a long public trial, the recording still identifies you having a hand in the most long-festering crime in the State of Victoria. That's when abetting and perverting the course of justice comes in. Another drawn out long public trial right there.'

'And how does that not put me in the shit?'

'If someone with firsthand knowledge of where and when the recording took place can testify to that fact, and give evidence that Dwyer was indeed present, then the need to lay any lesser charges may become a far lower priority, or not be a priority at all.'

Stanley looked over his shoulder as if someone might be listening in.

'You want me to testify against Dwyer?'

'I know it's a dangerous business but the ground's shifting on that. He seems to be dispirited since this recording surfaced. Prison staff say he's depressed. He probably realises that whatever other business he can take care of, he can't un-record the tape. He's also about to lose the wherewithal he's always had to exercise influence and clout. His farm will go as proceeds of crime and the Gaming Squad have found where his money is stashed with a bookie mate.'

'I'm not worried about that. The cunt killed my brother.'

Rory nodded, more so at the same descriptor and depth of feeling that David Dwyer expressed for Brian Stanley.

'So you'll give evidence? You know what that means?'

'I know what you said. I testify and you don't charge me. I could also be silly enough to ask why you want my evidence when you already have the recording.'

'First of all, I said other charges *may or may not* be laid. Second of all, we can't go after Graeme because he's dead. And third of all — which is in fact *our* first of all — we want to make sure Dwyer doesn't get off. The recording could become a slippery beast in court if we don't put it beyond a bee's dick of doubt, where and when the recording was made and that it is in fact Dwyer speaking. It's more important to us that we snuff even the slightest chance of Dwyer slipping through the net on some technicality. If you do this, he might even plead guilty and you won't even need to appear in court.'

'And what if I say no? A lawyer might tell me something different.'

'That's not gonna happen, Brian. I can see you're a man who knows when he's on a good wicket. You do this and your nominated-to-stand-for-Council-world will still be waiting for you with open arms.'

Stanley sipped more slowly. The scotch was kicking in, or perhaps the catharsis of admission was having an effect.

'I've thought about this from time to time, you know. What would happen if this ever came to light? How does it play now? Do I sit and wait for the trial to come round?'

'No such luck. This all starts right here and now. You come with me to the local cop-shop and I call it in. Once that happens, other people will know and you're instantly at risk, despite what I said about Dwyer being dispirited. Word travels, notwithstanding the best intentions. You'll have to be protected until this plays out.'

Stanley laughed. 'Déjà vu … isn't this where it all started … witness protection. Witness protection for a witness to the witnesses being dis-protected.'

'Something like that. But let me assure you, that won't be lost on …'

He knew how lame he sounded saying it. Stanley laughed louder. 'Come on then. Let's get this over with.'

~

'*Where are you, Rory? I thought you were on holiday.*' Bourke said into the phone.

'I'm in Margaret River for a few days. I'll be back by the weekend.'

Rory could picture Bourke at his desk, managing by email.

'*So why the call?*'

'I bumped into Graeme Stanley's brother. He lives here.'

'*Oh yeah …*' Bourke said, instantly affecting a sceptical tone.

'It turns out he is the hitman voice talking to Dwyer on the recording.'

The silence wasn't as long as Rory expected.

'*Just like that. You go from nothing to report … nothing to report …. nothing to report … to handing me the hitman on a platter when you're taking a holiday. You fucking knew and haven't been letting on.*'

'It was a long shot. I thought I'd check it out while I was in the neighbourhood.'

'*Bullshit.*'

Rory bristled. 'Okay. I had a hunch. I gave myself an hour or so to check it out. I've done that and I'm calling it in so I can get back to my holiday. I thought you'd be pleased.'

'*Okay, okay. I am pleased. Just a bit shocked … a lot shocked actually. Tell me about it.*'

'I'm at the local cop shop with Stanley's brother. His name's Brian and he's the other voice on the recording.'

'*He's admitted it?*'

'He's admitted to being the voice but he didn't do the hit. Graeme Stanley did the job. He got his brother Brian to pose as the hitman he was supposed to be sourcing from England. Graeme Stanley didn't want someone else doing the job on his own turf … and he wanted the money.'

'*And you believe him?*'

'Yeah, it stacks up. He did of course aid and abet …he also posed as Graeme on the CCTV alibi … but he's been led to believe that those charges may not be laid if he testifies against Dwyer.'

'Led to believe by you?'

'Yeah.'

'And he's happy to give evidence in court.'

'Cooperative might be a better word, that's why I've brought him here. He's at risk as of now. If we were to lose one more witness in this case …'

Rory didn't need to say more. Bourke was silent with ramifications turning in his head.

'Did he tape the conversation in the first place. Is he FP1 and he's doing it for the reward?'

'I know he's not FP1.' It came out too fast and with too much conviction. Bourke noticed.

'Do you mind telling me how?'

The pause was telling but Rory recovered. 'Brian Stanley blames Dwyer for making the recording. Even if Brian Stanley did have a copy of the recording, he wouldn't take the risk of doing anything with it. He's got a respected business that's travelling well as far as I can tell. If the recording ended up being leaked onto You Tube, which might yet happen, someone would recognise his voice sooner or later.'

'Hmm.'

Rory watched Brian Stanley through a glass office window as he listened to Bourke thinking. He saw his chance to bail.

'I'm due back at the beach house. Can you take it from here?'

'Keep your Speedos on for a moment. We just heard from Georgie Sherwood that Ramsay Braden has won a bail appeal for Dwyer. The hearing's listed for early next week.'

Now Bourke listened to Rory thinking.

'I'll be back in Melbourne sometime Friday. I can put all this together over the weekend. I'll have things ready for us to formally re-interview Dwyer. Can you set it up for you and me to question him sometime on Monday or Tuesday?' He'll need to have Ramsay Braden there. I'll phone Georgie and give her a heads up.'

'I can do all that if you like, or I could get Gary and Julia working on things if you'd rather.'

'No.'

Rory didn't apologise or explain his being short. Let Bourke think what he may — professional jealousy, dislike of Cockburn, Rory's guarded ownership of the intelligence he unearthed, the impracticality of passing on the story — Rory didn't care. Bourke paused a beat but decided not to ask.

'Okay. Piss off then and let me speak to the head honcho there… and Rory.'

'Yeah?'

'Good work. I'll organise drinks at the Bull and Mouth. We'll celebrate properly. Friday night. Okay?'

He stood holding *The Australian* and looking at Sigrid's body, clad in two-piece bathers, taking in the sun on the sun lounge. Two glasses, one half full, and an opened bottle of local sauvignon blanc sat on the deck beside her.

'I see the sun is already over the yard arm.'

'My watch is still on Victorian time,' she said from under the hat that hid her face from the sun. '… *and* you took your time buying the paper.'

'Sorry. I had a convertible to try out. I didn't think I was gonna get a go when we were together. I also had a couple of loose ends to tie up at the local police station.'

'Was it anything to do with Martha and Josh,' the hat asked.

'Not anymore.'

Sigrid sat up and smiled at Rory.

'You missed the whales. I had a really good look through the telescope.'

'Good. What else have you got planned. I'm all yours.'

He poured himself a wine and took to the adjoining sun lounge — he fully clothed, she in her bathers. Sigrid resumed her reclining position, glass in hand.

Rory sipped and also reclined. He rolled his head to see Sigrid similarly watching him — now with a perplexed thought written on her face.

'What?' he asked.

'This is not you, is it?'

'I don't know. A convertible with the top down and a top-of-the-range beach house. I might have got there one day.'

'I don't just mean the indulgence, I mean you and me.'

He didn't answer straight away, and she waited.

'You mean you've waited until we're beginning an unbelievable getaway to have this conversation?'

'Why not? We can't avoid it forever. What's to be afraid of?'

He sat up on the edge of the lounge and leant towards her with his elbows on his knees. 'I don't know — the unknown maybe.' He made it sound obvious but explained himself nonetheless. 'Things are going along okay, aren't they? I mean we don't fight, the sex is great, and I can even handle being a kept man on this trip.'

'Just.'

'I'm getting there.'

'You failed to mention that you like me, let alone say the "L" word.'

'It's a given … surely … that's why we're together in the first place.'

'Hmm.' She pursed her mouth.

'I know that expression. Tell me what's really bothering you.'

'The role reversal is more than just me calling the shots for this trip, isn't it? You've known me long enough to know I'll never become the needy woman going on about commitment, whereas …'

'What? You're scared of me becoming too needy? Just because I got a bit emotional on you. Is that what this is about?'

'Not in a way that involves me.'

Rory didn't know what she meant but looked and felt pained

by her answer. 'You've lost me.'

Sigrid sat up to deliver her explanation.

'I think we both know that certain people would dismiss a single woman of my age, my looks, and my means as some kind of femme fatale. I don't mind because I've been known to flirt in that way when it suits me. But I can tell you that if my first husband hadn't died early, I'd still be happily married without ever having cast a roving eye. Danny was and will always be the love of my life. He's a yardstick that no one has come close to — no offence, Rory. However, that didn't mean I should stop looking. The trouble for me is that, as readily as men see things they like about me, they soon find things they don't like. I bet you're getting near that stage — notching up a thing or two to be doubtful about.'

Her self-deprecation drew a response from Rory that never stood a chance of coming out right.

'Nah, nothing really.'

'See.'

'No. I mean I'm not that unhappy the way things are.'

'"Not that unhappy". I must say I've had more ringing endorsements.'

Rory sprang from the lounge and stood at the balustrade looking at the ocean for a good moment before turning back to Sigrid.

'Now I'm afraid to open my mouth. You start up the first real conversation about us out of the blue … and without warning. No wonder I'm on the back foot. But at the risk of it coming out wrong again, let me say this: I have never underestimated what I have … what we have … and I certainly don't take it for granted. In fact, these days I probably appreciate my good fortune more than most people because I'm lumbered with a perpetual black cloud on the horizon. If I hadn't met you when I did, I reckon the black cloud would have well and truly dumped on me. I'd probably not even be a cop anymore.'

'I know, and that's a big constant to bear,' Sigrid said.

'But that's entirely my concern,' he was quick to reassure her. 'I certainly didn't bring it up as something you need to pander to. The beauty of all this is, you only have to be with me to keep all that at bay. I can take care of anything else on my own.'

'You see, I'm a distraction rather than a carer. I know that and I know I'm not about to change my spots. But if you are honest with yourself, I think you will eventually want, or need, more. Maybe sooner than you think.'

There was a lot to take in from what she said. Sigrid re-reclined and watched Rory turn to the ocean again for thought. He admitted to himself that she was right … that one or two things about her might have crossed his mind in an unsettling way — but nothing that he unduly dwelt on or considered abnormal, he persuaded himself. The PTSD stuff was harder to fathom. It was also something he didn't want to work through here and now. In the last couple of hours, he'd put a full stop on one of the State's longest running and highest profile homicides. He'd just ingested the most effective tonic imaginable for his self-worth. This precise moment should be his tipping point back to some semblance of normality. If he were to indulge himself right now, he could imagine a full-fledged return to homicide work. Why was life with Sigrid even an issue? Had the taste of a previous life suddenly caused her to re-think Rory? A more alarming question came to him.

'Are you breaking up with me?' he said.

She sensed his panic.

'No. I just thought this was a conversation you wanted to have. That's all. Now … how about we get back to our holiday? Can you top me up, please?'

She held out her empty wine glass. Rory wanted to keep holding his dumfounded look but she waggled her glass. If he thought Sigrid's cool switch back to normality was as chilling as it got, he hadn't counted on her parting shot.

'Besides,' she added. 'If anyone was going to break up with

anyone, I prefer to be the breakup-er, especially when there's another woman involved.'

Rory froze involuntarily mid pour and shook his head.

'You're not going on about Michelle Fox-Jones again, are you?'

'Me going on?'

'This discussion is getting crazier. I only had coffee with her … for work stuff at that. And I've already called her to tell her I don't want to be part of her book.' He said it with all the incredulousness he could muster.

'And you're not going to call her again?'

The plan was that she would call me, Rory remembered and heard himself answer in a calmer voice: '*I'm* not planning to do so. No.'

His own caginess was a surprise to himself. *So that's what they mean by all's fair in love and war. Right here and now it's self-preservation*, he justified to himself.

Sigrid took her own long cooling-off look at the ocean. It took a good few moments but it worked.

'They say it's going to rain, we'll have to think of something to do inside,' she finally offered.

Rory slumped back into the lounge feeling spent, but nonetheless pleased that he merely had rain to deal with. The thunder and lightning had been averted. What's more, he still had cause to celebrate. Had he been forced to concoct a dream situation for celebrating his triumph, then this would be it. And here they were, with the most of the weekend getaway still ahead of them. If she could put it behind her so coolly, he decided there was no reason why he should cut off his nose to spite his face.

'There's a Scrabble board in the cupboard,' he said.

'That sounds a bit sedentary. We might need to think of something more physical to begin with.'

They rolled their heads to give each other for the knowing smile. Rory returned his eyes to the ocean and could make out a pack of wetsuit-clad surfers bobbing patiently out back, behind the waves. Nothing rideable seemed to be happening for them but the incoming swells visible from Rory's vantage point suggested a good set would soon reach the line-up. When it did, three figures took on the first wave. Two of them were standing in no time flat. The third was less well positioned and could only take off by "dropping in" on one of the others. It forced one of the first two riders to retreat out the back of the wave. As Rory watched the remaining two surfers enjoy the longest ride, he saw clearly how things fitted together in a broader view. But the revelation was fleeting, the scene was a long way off and from where he lay, they looked like ants.

28

Inspector Richard Bourke arrived late.

The handful of Homicide staff had commandeered an alcove at the Bull and Mouth Hotel and were standing and sitting around a slow game of pool between Julia O'Hannagain and Cockburn. Bourke asked who was drinking what and headed for the bar through the dense Friday-after-work crowd to buy jugs of beer. He found Rory leaning on the bar waiting to be served for the same round of drinks. Getting a barmaid's attention at the old-school main bar wasn't easy.

'Hey, I'll get these, Rory. Can't have our detective-of-the-moment buying at his own celebration,' Bourke shouted above the din.

'It's hardly a celebration, you could fit us all in the back of a divvy van.'

It was Rory's way of telling Bourke that his achievement amounted to little among his colleagues. He had graduated from persona-non-grata to person-a-bit-grata, mainly because of the open-minded younger members of the team. Perhaps Michelle Fox-Jones was right that attitudes were changeable, he wondered.

'To be fair, a lot of the others had to attend the shooting at Kew.'

Bourke leant on the bar beside Rory and watched the bar girls' version of chaos. The only time they stood still was when they filled beer jugs from the counter-top taps. '… and Gary's here, that's a step in the right direction.'

'Only because Julia came.'

Rory waved a finger in vain as another bar girl sped past with a bunch of empty glasses-with-handles dangling from her fingers.

'That's probably good too. He's showing signs of acting like a human.'

'For now.'

Bourke turned and looked hard at Rory's profile. Rory felt the stare drill into his skull and kept his head straight ahead. 'I know Gary Cockburn is never gonna be your mate, but he did at least show up here tonight, whatever his motivation. And if that's got anything to do with his office romance, then I'd expect you of all people to cut him some slack. Neither of them is married for a start.'

The barb stung. Once again, Rory had overlooked the parallel between Cockburn and Julia and his own messy life-destroying and ultimately exposed affair with Heidi Lester. If he breathed it would sound sanctimonious. He turned to Bourke. Their noses were only inches apart as they leant cheek-by-jowl on the bar.

'Sorry. I'll keep my mouth shut.'

'You could even be happy for him. Did I tell you she's going to Perth with him on Monday to bring Brain Stanley over here from WA. They'll have a night away together in a Perth hotel.'

Rory reached for his forehead and closed his eyes.

'What?'

Rory bit his tongue and fudged. 'Nothing. I just thought of something I needed to brief him about.'

Bourke shook his head.

'This is not a PTSD thing is it? Is anything more happening with Michelle Fox … two jugs, a coke, a lemon squash and a vodka slammer.'

'Who's having the vodka? Julia?' Rory hoped to change the subject.

'Yeah. Gary might get lucky tonight. Now what's happening with Michelle Fox-Jones?'

'Nothing doing. I bailed on the book thing.' He omitted that he and Michelle spoke about catching up again nevertheless.

'Mind telling me why?'

'I told her that I think it's a path for cops who don't want to be cops any longer. This pitiful turn-up is bad enough. If I become a PTSD poster-boy on top of everything else, I wouldn't need to buy beers by the jug. I know it's not what you want to hear, but …' Rory finished the thought with an apologetic shrug.

'Don't worry about what I or anyone else thinks. You earnt yourself some clear air on this case and I think you know it. Make the most of it. Here give me a hand with these.'

So that's what redemption sounds like. One line of grudging acknowledgement shouted at a bar. He shrugged and grabbed the jugs.

Bourke and Rory arrived with the drinks just as Julia potted the eight-ball. Four of Gary's balls were left on the table.

'Next,' Julia shouted and lifted the vodka slammer from the tray Bourke was holding.

'You reckon you're good enough?' Bourke asked her.

'Get a cue and bring it on.'

Cockburn collected the jug of beer from the tray and told Bourke, 'You're about to get your arse wopped.'

He began pouring beer into Rory's glass. Rory wondered about Cockburn's beer-tempered demeanour. Maybe he was in a better place with Julia. The skin even appeared to be less tightly drawn over his skull.

'Cheers,'

'Cheers you PTSD wanker …'

Rory quickly retracted his thought.

'How did you pull the Brian Stanley thing off?'

'Something Dwyer said when I spoke to him in Loddon Prison. We were talking about the hitman having an English accent on the recording. It was a throwaway line by Dwyer but it made me think.'

'What'd he say?'

'He reckoned all those pommy bastards sounded and look the same. It nagged a bit because the English copper on Skype went on a bit about Graeme Stanley and his brother. When he heard the recording he immediately said the voice had the Hackney accent … it even sounded like Graeme Stanley to him. We expected something like that, that's why we called him, so I didn't make anything of it at first. But a "Hackney" accent? That's pretty specific.'

Cockburn laughed. 'Is that it?'

'No. The English copper also made me realise we were looking for someone who had lived in Australia for decades. A blow-in wouldn't refer to, "locked up like Pentridge" or "Harry Butler". Those are both uniquely Australian references. Our hitman had to be a long-time resident. We all should have twigged a lot earlier.'

Rory had to leave out the bit about Brian Stanley's neck tattoo. It wouldn't make sense without revealing Josh's involvement.

'Pure arse if you ask me. You'll have to start doing some proper police work sooner or later.'

The clatter of pool balls being broken brought a whoop from Julia. Bourke held his cue to the floor and shook his head as two balls went in off her break.

'I've been doing a bit of that too. I need to give you a heads-up on something before you go to WA.' Rory said to Cockburn.

'What?'

'Come outside for a smoke and I'll tell you.'

'I don't smoke … and neither do you.'

'This is definitely an outside discussion.'

'It better be,' Cockburn said and topped his glass up before following Rory. The sound faded to a muffled babble underpinned by doof-doof from music being played somewhere inside. Rory produced a folded piece of paper from his jacket pocket.

'What's that?'

'It's a copy of an email received by Dwyer.'

'How did you get that? I thought Julia came up with zip from his computer.'

'It's from a web-based email account he uses. It only exists in the cloud. The email address showed up in that betting stuff from Earl Jannson. I got someone to hack in for me.'

Cockburn was hooked. He sipped his beer.

'Who's it from and what's it about?'

'Whom and when is the pertinent question.'

'Okay Mr wise-after-the-event, whom and when?'

'The email address is, *little I ninety-nine at gomail dot com* and it was sent to Dwyer the morning after Bourke played us the first instalment of the recording. I'll read it for you.' Rory unfolded the piece of paper and read, '*Answer your phone or call me as soon as you get this. Something has come in that you need to know about.*'

Cockburn stepped aside to let two young office-worker blokes in shirts and ties pass. They were leaving through the car park.

'You reckon it's someone tipping off Dwyer when the recording first showed up?'

'I know it is.'

'So who is this Little I. Do we know anyone in the Force named Little?'

'I looked it up. There's an Ian Little at Horsham station and Ivan Little, a civilian staffer at Dandenong. I couldn't find any others. At that stage it could have been from someone who has nothing to do with the Force and the email could be referring to something else entirely.'

'But it wasn't, otherwise you wouldn't be telling me this in a pub carpark. Was it someone in the Minister's office, or the Minister? That's where I had my money.'

'Nothing to do with the Minister.'

'Then why are you dragging it out? Who was it?'

The edge had returned to Cockburn's voice. They were still standing in the carpark with beers in hand. Rory stalled before answering.

'It's Julia. I'm guessing you slept the previous night at her place or she slept at yours.'

Cockburn turned his head and looked hard at his shoulder. His lips whitened.

'You're accusing me?' He said it without looking at Rory.

'No … not of doing anything intentionally. I don't think you knew anything about it.'

'Then how do you make such a giant leap from this …' he snatched the piece of paper from Rory's hand and shook it in his face, '… to Julia and me?'

'It was something I heard Gerry Denton say. Gerry and Julia were in the same intake at the academy. The drill sergeant at the academy made the connection between Julia and her dad Dermot O'Hannagain. Dermot's mates, of whom the drill sergeant was one, knew him by the nickname Irish, so the sergeant nicknamed her Little-Irish. He'd shortened it to Little-I by the time she graduated. The nickname was only ever used by the drill sergeant, but it must have rubbed off a bit on the other students. When I wracked my brain, I remembered hearing Gerry call Julia Little-I … only once, maybe twice, but it still lurked somewhere back there.

'Julia must have fancied it as a pseudonym when she opened a Gomail account — and you can ask her why she chose to have a pseudonym. That's the format Gomail uses — surname, initial, and then a number to differentiate between people using the same surname and initial. You can get the geeks to track down the IP address on that if you don't believe me.'

Cockburn's chest heaved. 'Why would Julia have anything to do with Dwyer?' His voice had weakened in volume but gained in ferocity.

Rory straightened in a vain attempt to deflect the ire.

'It's in her blood. They're related. Dunno if you remember but the very first time Dwyer was suspended, coppers were polarised. Some gave him the benefit of the doubt because he had a good strike rate against certain dealers — courtesy of intelligence from the players he was looking after, as it turned out. Anyway, a few of the early deniers organised a fundraiser for him. It was a barbeque in someone's backyard. I forget who organised it or where it was held, but I was asked to go along and check it out. They had a fair roll-up from what I can remember … raised about five grand. Dermot O'Hannagain was definitely present. There were also a few wives in the kitchen doing salads and I ended up chatting with them. It turns out that one of the women was O'Hannagain's better half. From what I was able to pick up without even asking directly was: she's Dwyer's sister. I don't think that was ever common knowledge … neither Dwyer nor O'Hannagain put it about, but it won't take you long to confirm it. That makes Julia Dwyer's niece.'

Cockburn's jaw locked as he stared at Rory. His breathing raced.

'She's his niece, Gary. And while you're checking that out, ask her what music she was into as a kid. My money's on AC/DC cracking a mention. Apparently every generation of fifteen-year-olds throws up its own clique of Bon Scott worshippers. That's where Dwyer appropriated that little nugget from. Julia was helping him out before she was old enough to even realise it.'

Rory gave one last turn of the screw.

'And Calvin Steele? Would I be right in thinking you spoke to her when we were arranging to bring him on board? How did that work out for you?'

Cockburn turned and slammed his drink into the side of a black Lexus. Broken glass and beer dribbled down the rear door in a wide swathe.

'Fuck, fuck, fuck. You know what makes this twice as bad? Hearing it from you,' he said, jabbing a staccato finger within an inch of Rory's nose. 'You so fucking enjoyed this, didn't you? What are you going to do now? Go back inside for an extra cele-fucking-bration?'

Rory shook his head all the while that Cockburn was ranting.

'I've had enough for one night. I'll let you tell Bourke. You can keep the email.'

Rory turned to leave through the carpark. He heard Cockburn punch the rear pillar of the Lexus. Its alarm began to whoop.

'That's a CCTV camera up there,' Rory yelled.

29

Bourke and Rory took seats opposite David Dwyer and Ramsay Braden in the familiar police interview room. Dwyer sat with his arms crossed and abstained from the exchange of greetings. He was already leaving the talking to his lawyer.

Braden gave every expectation of a quick discussion. He left his jacket on and his satchel sat closed on the table top.

Rory pondered how to operate the interview recording equipment.

'I don't think any of that will be necessary Detective Sergeant James,' Braden said. 'The deal as I remember it from Magistrate Bryce Murphy, was that bail would be reconsidered in the absence of any further evidence. I'm happy for us to come to an arrangement here and now that we can present to Magistrate Gibbs at tomorrow's hearing. That way we can both save time and money.'

Bourke let Braden enjoy his self-satisfied smile before he spoke.

'I intend to let Detective Sergeant James begin recording proceedings. I'm sure you wouldn't want your client's response to the additional evidence to rely purely on our collective recollections.'

'Additional evidence. You have additional evidence?'

Braden looked at Dwyer. Dwyer sat impassively.

'Nor would we want you to accuse us of ambushing you in court, Mr Braden,' Bourke said. 'Are we ready to roll, Rory?'

Rory nodded and Bourke gave the formal preamble. As Bourke spoke, Braden extracted a legal pad from his satchel with a display of irritated weariness.

Rory kicked off the questioning.

'Mr Dwyer, during the fortnight prior to the murder of Clifford Neilson and Corina Scali, you attended a two-day seminar at the Victorian Police Forensic Centre in McLeod. The seminar dealt with crime scene forensic updates. Do you recall the occasion?'

Dwyer gave a *search-me* shrug.

'You're talking about something that may or may not have happened over ten years ago Detective Sergeant,' Braden said and proceeded to make a note on his legal pad.

'Never mind. We have records that show that was the case. Do you remember leaving the Forensic Centre premises at any time during the seminar, particularly during the evening meal recess that lasted an hour and a half?'

Dwyer shrugged again. He still hadn't spoken since Rory and Bourke entered the room.

'We have a statement from a witness who says that during the time of the training seminar recess, you met him at the nearby La Trobe Wildlife Sanctuary. The Sanctuary is a ten-minute walk from the Forensic Centre. He states that he and you had the actual conversation on the recording we played to you at the previous interview. The person who made that statement is the person you are heard talking to on the recording.' Rory paused to pose a formal question. 'Mr Dwyer, did you leave the Forensic Centre on that evening and meet someone at the La Trobe Wildlife Sanctuary?'

Had Calvin Steele been present he would point out a role reversal between Braden and Dwyer. Braden betrayed the alarm of hearing precise details for the first time. An actual time. An actual place. An actual living person. They were details that couldn't be plucked from the air. On the other hand, Dwyer remained impassively calm and kept his arms folded. Answering the question was not on his mind.

'Mr Dwyer?' Bourke pressed.

Braden sized things up.

'No comment,' Braden said. 'Can I have a moment with my client please?'

'Sure,' Bourke said with as much untroubled delight as he could muster. 'We'll just wait outside.'

Rory paused the tape and he and Bourke adjoined to stand in the corridor with their manila folders.

'Dwyer knows and he hasn't told Braden.'

'Julia's already passed it on,' Rory said.

'Mmm,' Bourke said and chewed his lip. 'It doesn't change anything, though. They might have been able to cast some doubt about whether it was Dwyer's voice on the recording. But there's no way to dismiss the evidence when we bring both voices into the court room. Especially with Brian Stanley admitting he is the other voice.'

'As long as Brian Stanley makes it into court. Before we got onto Julia, they reckon she was already sniffing around about where Brian Stanley would be housed.'

'He's in safe hands. Don't worry about that,' Bourke said.

Rory gave a questioning look.

'Him and Gary have gone fishing.'

'Is that some kind of code or euphemism?'

'No. Gary and Stanley hit it off on the flight from WA to Melbourne. I think they bonded in a Dwyer-and-his-relative-hating rant. And they're both into fishing. We sent them off with fake IDs, credit cards and new mobile phones that are permanently routed through a Melbourne land line. We can stay in touch without the system revealing their location. Only they know where they are. That's the first three weeks taken care of. And it'll give Gary time to cool down.'

'Or become even more embittered,' Rory said.

Bourke shook his head at Rory and Cockburn's continuing grudge. He glanced at his watch.

'They've had enough time.'

Bourke and Rory went back in and resumed their seats. Braden had removed his jacket and hung it on the chair-back. Rory re-activated the interview recorder.

'My client will have to check his records before answering your question. I hope you don't think that's unreasonable. As I've already pointed out, it was more than ten years ago.'

'If you like. But the evidence will be flagged at the bail appeal hearing.' Bourke said.

'And who is the person who has made the statement?' Braden asked.

'Brian Stanley.'

'And is Mr Stanley the brother of Graeme Stanley, the notorious hitman?'

'He did have a brother called Graeme, but as we know, the late Graeme Stanley has never been convicted for murder.'

'And has this Brian Stanley flagged an intention to apply for the reward being offered for the Neilson Scali murders?'

Rory jumped in to answer instead of Bourke.

'We are absolutely certain Mr Stanley was not previously aware that the recording existed. And no, he hasn't made any overtures for a reward. He has absolutely no grounds for doing so. Nor did Brian Stanley commit the murder after having the conversation with Mr Dwyer at the sanctuary. Graeme Stanley asked his brother to meet with Mr Dwyer to obtain the address and the down-payment for the hit on Neilson and Scali. Brian Stanley has a cast iron alibi for the murder itself — he took the place of the person we were led to believe was Graeme Stanley at the casino. A forensic inspection of the CCTV video has confirmed that person was in fact, Brian Stanley — not Graeme. The hit was carried out by the late Graeme Stanley.'

Braden looked to Dwyer for confirmation. Dwyer shrugged again. He had not filled Braden in on all the detail. Rory pressed the advantage.

'It's you who led us to Brian Stanley. You were the one who told me, *all those pommy bastards sound and look the same.*'

'Any other questions Mr Braden?' Bourke asked.

'Not now,' Braden sighed.

'Turn the recorder off then, Rory.'

Bourke turned his attention to Dwyer as soon as Rory switched the recorder off.

'I hope you didn't come here with your bags packed, Dwyer. You might be interested to know that your niece is re-thinking her career choice, or more correctly, it's being re-thought for her. Maybe she can look after the olive trees for you now. You might get another crop off them before the place is acquired as proceeds of crime. And if you were thinking of trying something cute with your bikie mates again, you'd better have a good credit source. We had Ray Samson's accounts frozen and his bookie's licence cancelled this morning.

'In any case, I don't think we've got anything to worry about. You're all out of mates. At least two bikie gangs for a start. Then there's Ray Samson and any pals you thought you could rely on in the Force. Julia was pretty popular. Her corruption by you hasn't gone down too well. Especially with her dad, ex-Inspector Dermot O'Hannagain and any coppers he can still get in the ear of. You can't even make new mates inside, being an ex-copper. You'd better start getting used to your own company.'

Rory watched Dwyer's face twist into unadulterated hate. Dwyer had come into the interview clinging to the belief that he was still a player. He had recovered from the emergence of the recording to contemplate his options. While he still had "ways and means", he was still in the game. He had somewhere to channel his anger, something to put his mind to, no matter how high the odds were stacked. Bourke knew this was his chance to snuff Dwyer's candle, to snatch his last "way" and his last "mean", and he had taken it.

Dwyer knew it too. His shoulders began to shake.

Braden stood and put his hand on Dwyer's shoulder. 'Don't let him get to you, David.'

Dwyer erupted from his seat to shrug Braden off.

'You can fuck off too,' he roared. His ferocity caused Braden to stagger backwards into the wall. The shock on Braden's face was enough to constrain Dwyer from further fury, but barely.

Braden snatched his satchel and jacket and left. He had intended to say nothing more but stepped back into the room to point at Dwyer and tell him, 'If you're stupid enough to go ahead with this appeal, then find yourself another lawyer.'

When Bourke and Rory followed him out, Bourke also turned back for a parting shot.

'Look on the bright side, Dwyer. You can add lawyers to the list of friends disowning you.'

30

A deal is a deal. *If things work out the way I expect, we'll invite them round here and I'll cook a proper meal.* It was a promise he didn't need to be reminded of. In Rory's mind, this would be the real celebration.

Martha and Josh brought a shiraz from their Mandurang winegrower neighbour. Rory did a lamb roast — too anxious to try anything more adventurous. Sigrid hostessed, albeit apologetically.

'My B&B guests for the weekend expected to arrive by five o'clock. I'm afraid I'll have to excuse myself for a bit when they turn up.'

Only four chairs were drawn to the twelve-seater table in The Manse dining room, but none of its traditional fine-dining tableware was spared. Candelabras, fine china, polished silverware and all manner of equipment Rory had never encountered in his culinary life — large cloche dome-lid servers, gravy boats and silver rests for the carving utensils. A refreshing French Provincial tablecloth lessened the weight of formality.

Everyone left their chairs to pile their plates from the laden serving dishes along the table's centre. Rory did laps to keep wine glasses topped up.

Rory was struck by a side of Sigrid he had not yet encountered — the comfort and ease of being among friends. Sigrid and Martha might not be lifelong buddies, yet, but they connected. When the sound of a garden frog came through the window, Josh became the entertainer.

'That's a *Limnodynastes dorsalis*,' he said to kill the room with silence. He clarified with its common name, 'A Pobblebonk! Congratulations, Sigrid. You've got your very own wetland sanctuary.'

Rory, Sigrid and Martha erupted into laughter and Josh didn't let them recover.

'He's after a female frog who'll have sex with him,' Josh told them. 'If you mimic the call and get it right, he'll answer you.'

More laughing.

'You mean I can answer him and he'll think he's about to get lucky?' Sigrid stuttered through her laughing.

'If you do it right, *you* might be the one who gets lucky. You'll get to kiss him and you never know what he'll turn into.'

'Sigrid's already got her prince,' Martha said.

'You're too kind,' Rory said and saluted Martha with his glass.

'Try it,' Josh told Sigrid. 'Like this … "Bonk".'

They all laughed. Sigrid calmed her laughter enough to try. 'Bonk.'

It came out sounding like a high-pitched "boink". Hilarity reigned.

'No. like this — bonk.'

'Boink.'

'No. You need to purse your lips more,'

This time Sigrid tried with her lips pursed watertight.

An even squeakier 'Boink' somehow emerged.

The ensuing eruption of belly laughs were only interrupted with them laughing even more at Martha's convulsive snorts. Just when there was nowhere higher to go, the frog answered, 'Bonk', and they found another notch.

The outburst was starting to wind down when the doorbell interrupted.

'My guests have arrived,' Sigrid said trying to settle all of her laughing muscles as she rose to answer the door.

Josh, Martha and Rory could hear the greetings faintly. With Sigrid gone, suddenly there was an elephant in the room.

Martha acknowledged it.

'I see you got your man, Rory. Well done.'

'Thank you. But not everything got solved.'

'Oh?'

'No. No one I know in the branch ever figured out who recorded the conversation all those years ago. Dwyer denied doing it and so did the hitman when we finally tracked him down. I guess it will always be a mystery.'

'*We* know someone in the branch who figured it out. We need to say thank you for letting us stay out of that,' Martha said.

'It was your call. I would never have gone against your wishes, however things panned out.'

'We know that now that we know you, and we really appreciate it. Especially now we can be friends.' Josh chipped in.

'Does Sigrid know anything about it?'

Rory toyed at a scrap of meat with his fork. 'No, and that's hard for me because you're her friends. But she appreciates that that's what I need to do. There's no reason why you can't tell her if you want, that's up to you. Sigrid is also a very smart woman, so don't underestimate what she might have figured out in any case.'

'Never,' Martha concurred.

'Now that we have our man, the reward will become a reality. Have you thought any more about that?'

'No, we haven't changed our minds. We don't think it's worth the risk and in any event, we never did figure out how to collect the money without being traceable. My Swiss bank account idea was a fizzer. I read that Elle Macpherson and Kerry Packer couldn't hide their money there without the tax office finding out. We're happy though. We reckon that's a pretty good default position. Happy and a lot of money might not mix.'

'I can't say I blame you, but hypothetically, there could be a third alternative.'

'Something better than happy?' Josh asked.

'Maybe. It's something I remember hearing in the dark ages

when I first joined the Force. There was a celebrated case of an anonymous person who phoned in a tip-off. They ultimately became eligible for a sizeable reward. It was in the days when all you needed to do was use a public phone box to avoid being traced. They also used a particular alias over the phone that prevented imposters taking the credit … and the money.

'In the end, they didn't risk exposing themselves by collecting the reward. They did however find a way to ensure the opportunity was not totally lost. They directed that the reward money be donated to charity.'

Martha smiled. 'Very noble. Do you remember which charity?'

'No, but I looked it up. The phone caller must have also been someone who was passionate about the environment. The money was used to purchase a pocket of Brush-tailed Rock Wallaby habitat that was about to be cleared for farming. There was still a few of the endangered specimens in the Grampians back then. It didn't save the Grampians Brush-tailed Rock Wallabies but the piece of land they acquired is now part of the national park.'

'Even noble-er,' Josh said. 'I really like the sound of the idea.'

'Yeah,' Martha said. They looked at each other with we've-got-to-do-something-like-that-too smiles.

'Yeah I thought it was a nice idea too,' Rory said. 'And then I started thinking. These days, there might be better ways to help threatened species. Something more hands-on maybe.'

'Maybe you should tell us then,' Martha said.

'Well, if I was someone capable of actively contributing to the preservation of threatened species, I might direct that any "random discretionary money" be channelled to someone like the Government's Business Victoria organisation so they could issue grants for on-ground research needed to underpin the science of threatened species. Surveys and that sort of thing.

'Of course, Business Victoria would also need to offer substantial start-up money to someone willing to establish a small eco-business dedicated to those tasks. An outfit prepared to specialise in dealing with specific threatened species and their environments — a company that would also employ a couple of indigenous youth of the area with innate knowledge of those particular environments.

'I'm sure one arm of government could work with a completely different arm of government to put something like that in place. Particularly if there was someone sympathetic within one of those organisations to drive it. Someone who could ensure only the most deserving eco-business proposal was selected.

'The publicity for such a philanthropic response would put a full-stop to the whole reward thing. The reward-recipient trail would end abruptly for any aggrieved criminals on a vengeful path.' Rory paused to see how his idea was being received. 'But I'm no environmentalist, Josh. Would something like that work — hypothetically?'

'Fuck, you amaze me, Rory. How lateral is that?'

Josh looked to Martha with his jaw hung open to indicate rapture in the concept. Rory pushed on with his hypothetical.

'Of course, someone with legal knowledge would need to document such instructions for her client, and her client would need to sign that instruction — or, as was the case in much earlier times — her client may need to "make his mark" before those instructions were dispatched.'

Martha nodded her head sagely.

Sigrid returned to find the three of them smiling and nodding at each other.

'I leave a laughing-fest and come back to a smug smiling-fest. What's going on here? What have I missed?'

'I wish I could tell you how much Rory has helped us both,' Josh said. 'You're a lucky woman.'

Rory's ringtone sounded before Sigrid could reply.

Rory retrieved the phone from his pocket and said, 'Sorry. You know, being a cop …' He stepped into the hall to answer.

They could nevertheless hear him say, 'Hello, Rory James,' along with the rest of his responses.

'Oh. Hello, how are *you?*'

He's deliberately not giving away who he's talking to, Sigrid observed from the dining room.

'No that's all right, but I'll have to call you back, I've got some friends around and we're in the middle of a meal.'

Although Martha was saying something to her, Sigrid's antenna still managed to pick up that "I've" got some friends around, not "we've" got some friends around.

'No. Don't apologise, that was the arrangement, you weren't to know. I'll call you tomorrow.'

'Yeah, me too.'

'That'd be good.'

'Okay then. Bye.'

Rory pressed End Call and kept looking at his phone thinking: *who am I going to say called?* He'd have to pass it off as some kind of work thing, which was a stretch now that he'd declined to participate in Michelle Fox-Jones' project.

He needn't have bothered creating a subterfuge. Sigrid's glare met him as soon as he stepped back in the room. The Manse had become anything but a sanctuary.

ACKNOWLEDGEMENTS

I am most grateful to Amy Doak from *Accidental Publishing*, not only for publishing *Wetland*, but for also re-packaging and re-publishing my previous novel, *A Vintage Death*, and releasing them together as companion titles; and for having such enthusiasm for the project.

Many thanks to: Jordan de Jong and Brian and Liz Steen for generously sharing their specialist knowledge; Des Lowry and Dianne Dempsey for their extensive editing; Sally Bird of *Calidris Literary Agency* for additional editing; Rosemary Sorensen, Jim Evans, Cameron King and Jennie de Jong for their valued manuscript feedback; Chris Page of TZR Reptiles and Wildlife; Karen and Ron Roozen of Roozen Residence, Margaret River; and Shay Leighton, founder of the Tough Guy Book Club. And to Mary, always.

I am an admirer of the La Trobe Wildlife Sanctuary, not least because I have jointly owned a bush sanctuary for over forty years where some of this book was inspired and written. The sinister events portrayed within the La Trobe sanctuary are of course fictitious. I also wish to pay tribute to *Under Seige*, Belinda Neil's inspiring account of her fight against post-traumatic stress disorder.

ABOUT THE AUTHOR

Colin King is a Bendigo writer, who grew up in Horsham and worked as a major-projects consultant for the Victorian state government before retiring to write. Along the way, he has played guitar in rock bands, ran marathons, led trekking parties and hand built a weekender on the Grampians fringe.

His debut novel, *A Vintage Death*, was first published in 2013. Its launch was a special event at that year's *Bendigo Writers Festival*. His second novel, *Wetland*, was published in 2018.

www.ingramcontent.com/pod-product-compliance
Lightning Source LLC
Chambersburg PA
CBHW071136180726
48291CB00007B/2200